RIVAL

THE BRIARCLIFF SOCIETY SERIES

KETLEY ALLISON

Copyright © Mitchell Tobias Publishing, 2020

Cover Design by Regina Wamba at Maeidesign
Cover Model Photography by Michelle Lancaster
www.michellelancaster.com / @lanefotograf
Cover Model, Lochie Carey

Editing by Madison Seidler

This book is a work of fiction. Names, characters, places and incidents either are products of the author's imagination or are used fictitiously. Any resemblance to actual events or locales or persons, living or dead, is entirely coincidental.

All rights reserved. Except as permitted under the U.S. Copyright Act of 1976, no part of this publication may be reproduced, distributed or transmitted in any form or by any means, or stored in a database or retrieval system, without the prior permission of the publisher.

Visit Ketley Allison's official website at www.ketleyallison.com for the latest news, book details, and other information.

BRIARCLIFF ACADEMY STUDENT PLAYLIST

Ghost - Au/Ra, Allen Walker
Taxi - EXES
Why Her Not Me - Grace Carter
Rewind - Louis Futon, Armani White
White Flag - Bishop Briggs
Undrunk - Fletcher
Better Now - Oh Wonder
you broke me first - Tate McRea
To Die For - Sam Smith
What's Good - Fenne Lily

Find the rest of the playlist on Spotify:

http://bit.ly/briarcliffsociety

1

"ou're going, Callie. That's final."

My stepfather gestures at his new wife to pass the potatoes, but he's fixated on me.

The New Wife, a.k.a. Lynda *with a Y*, lifts the platter of potato gratin before adding her opinion. "I can't understand why you would object to attending an exclusive academy for your final year of high school."

"Lynda worked hard to get you accepted, honey," Dad continues. "You should be grateful."

Pete Spencer may be my stepdad, but since I've known him longer than Lynda, I begrudgingly call him by a baby's first word. New parents pray for the day their child calls them by that name. It signifies growth, recognition, *love*.

For me, it doesn't mean much.

"Because," I say, pushing my dinner around with my fork to buy time and think of an excuse. I don't have friends to keep me here anymore. I lost them a few months ago. And the one remaining person I could count as family isn't even at this table. "Because I've grown up in the city. I've laid down roots, and I don't want to"—*leave my mom*—"leave here. Ever."

Dad lifts a forkful of Sunday night's roast to his mouth and chews. "Well, it's not like we're giving you an option. You're under my guardianship now, and I'm responsible for what's best for you."

His tone doesn't soften as he lays his claim on me. It contains nothing of his love for my mother, or what we had, or how it was taken away so brutally.

My fork lands against the china with a clatter. I glance up from my plate. "You mean *Lynda's* decided what's best, and that's whisking me away to Rhode Island, so she can start fresh with an untarnished family."

Across the table, Lynda tilts her head, her hand resting gently on the barest bump of her belly. "Callie, that's not fair."

Her tone is kind, but her hand is possessive.

"Why not? It's true," I say, blinking hard. I can't let them see me cry.

"That's not even close to accurate," Dad barks. "Apologize to Lynda. She's thinking of your future, Cal, as am I. You're better served at a school that has a direct path to the college of your choice. Your grades were excellent. Before…"

"Before what, Dad?" I sit straighter in my chair. "Go on. Say it."

His lips thin into bloodless slits while his cheeks splotch with red, like the very words are chasing the heat away from his mouth. His eyes shine under the chandelier, but it's an indeterminable glimmer. Dad could be internally raging. He could be howling. He could be wishing I'd just disappear already.

"I'm not going to ruin this dinner further by opining on your behavior this last year," he grits out. "Suffice it to say, the one hurdle stopping you from getting an education of that stature was—"

"Money," I cut in, and I make sure my sidelong glance at Lynda is noticeable. "I'm aware."

Dad shoves another bite into his mouth and falls back against his chair, his jaw muscles bulging as he chews. Although, it's not his chair, is it? Pete Spencer hit the jackpot when he attended a banquet whose attendees paid $25,000 a head to sit in the Metropolitan Museum of Art and eat canapés. Dad used his connections—he's always had those, even when he possessed empty pockets—and there he met Lynda Meyer, granddaughter of *the* Meyers line of department stores. Six months later, they were wed in a whirlwind multi-million-dollar wedding before moving into a historical monument on the Upper West Side, depositing me along with them as an afterthought.

If I ever had any doubts I was a ride-along, those are long dissipated as I sit in a ridiculous ballroom for a dining room and listen to how they're sending me away to boarding school for my senior year.

He might as well hold a trumpet while announcing I'm not his real daughter.

"Apologize, Callie," my dad says again.

I cross my arms, my appetite and my patience departing this room a long time ago.

"That's how you're going to play this?" he asks, his dark brows forming into two eclipsed moons.

"How else should I?" I ask, proud my voice isn't trembling like it wants. But my eyes emote what my voice can't. *Please tell me to stay. Confess that you love me and want to keep me. Please, Dad.*

Dad reaches a hand over the pristine white linen and perfectly aligned table settings.

My stomach lifts, as if pulled up by my heart, and I raise mine to—

Lynda clasps his hand, and they squeeze their fingers together.

"Your train departs early tomorrow morning," Dad says to me. "If this is how you'd prefer to end your dinner with us, then by all means, be my guest. I've long ago tired of your antics."

"*Antics?*" I echo shrilly. "Mom's isn't even cold in the—"

"If you're not going to eat the prime rib Sophia slaved all afternoon in the kitchen to prepare for us," Lynda says, her pale blue eyes a pair of icicles sharp enough to pierce my chest. "Then you can kindly go upstairs and spend your final evening in your room."

"That's not my room," I spit. I throw my napkin over my untouched meal despite the mild *pang* in my chest that the one person who's been nice to me in this house, Sophia, actually did slave over this food. Lynda's never lifted a chef's knife in her life. "And it isn't my bed. My home, my *life,* is on Broome and Allen Street, a place I thought you loved, too, Dad."

Dad shakes his head. "Honey, you've got to let go. This is a better life for you, don't you understand?"

"Plenty," I say, pushing to my feet.

"Wherever you're going," Dad warns, knowing full well I won't be headed upstairs, "you better be back in time for Clifton to drive you to the station. You're seventeen, Callie, and therefore my ward. You'll be attending Briarcliff Academy by this time tomorrow, do you hear me?"

A server laden with a full plate of the dessert course scuttles aside as I head to the giant oak doors and proceed into the expansive foyer.

It's all so elegant. So unfamiliar. If I'd had the chance to tell Mom about how Dad would remarry a trust-fund billionairess and we'd live in a mansion with a private grooming room for a single mini-poodle named Frans, she would've laughed her head off, then told me to finish my chow mien or she'd eat it.

Then I would've confessed to her how lonely I'd be in such empty spaces, and she would've pulled me into a hug, rubbed my back, and kissed my head, telling me there can be no loneliness when a mother loves you this much.

Tears prick, and I rub my eyes with the heels of my palms to keep them at bay.

"So help me, Callie," Dad calls down the hallway. "You will be on that train!"

As my answer, I slam the front door on a father who can't be bothered to drive me to the station after deciding to ship me off.

2

I won't admit it, but going to a new school makes me squeamish.

I clutch my duffel tighter in my lap, the rest of my luggage resting in a private section of the train a couple of cars back.

The sun hadn't even cracked open its eye when I departed Meyer House this morning. I managed dig out my mom's college tee—old, ratty and softened by wear from the trash bag Lynda filled to send to Goodwill—and paired it with my comfy jeans, worn and naturally ripped in various spots.

My phone goes off in my purse, and I pull it out. When I see who's calling, a thin smile breaks through the scowl I'd been deploying out of the train car's window. "Hey."

"Hey, kiddo," Ahmar says on the other end. "Sorry I missed you this morning. And at dinner yesterday." His voice sounds pained. "I was called away."

"It's okay. I left pretty early."

Ahmar Kazmi, my mom's former partner in the NYPD, reads me better than most. He sighs and then adds in a quiet tone, "Your momma would've wanted you to go."

I frown as I tip my head back in the seat and close my eyes. "You knew I was leaving?"

"You and I text a bunch, and I love getting your daily download, but sometimes I like to check in with the big man Pete and make sure you're treated right."

My heart twinges. The meaning of "Dad" should be given to Ahmar. I've known him since I was a toddler. He rode along with Mom and me to my first day at elementary school. Then middle school. Ahmar was there during my first break-up at twelve, and my first heartbreak at fourteen.

Ahmar was just ... there. For hugs. For sarcasm. To be taken advantage of when I wanted to win an argument against Mom.

"It's true," Ahmar says. "You can't get that kind of diploma just anywhere. Definitely not at that sham of a school you were attending here. You gotta go. Make your momma proud."

"Yeah. I'm on the train." There's little point in arguing with Ahmar, just like it wasn't worth the effort to fight with Dad and Lynda this morning. All of them stopped being able to handle me a year ago when Mom died.

This isn't the first time they've banded together in an attempt to "fix" me. I guess they get props for not surrounding me with white walls and a locked door this time.

As if sensing my inner monologue, Ahmar says, "You deserve to look forward to the future. You can turn this situation into something that can better your life. You fucking *got* this, kid. Shit..." he mutters, pulling away from the phone.

"It's okay," I say when he comes back on. "You can go." At his breathy hesitation, I add, "I'll be fine. Promise."

"You text me. Or call me. Every damn day, I don't care. I got your back."

Just like he had my mother's.

"Okay," I say. But the urge bubbles up, and I'm unable to swallow it. "Ahmar?"

"Yeah, kiddo?"

"You'll catch the guy who killed her, right?"

Static crackles between us for a few seconds. "Sweetheart," he says. "I ain't ever gonna stop."

I hold the beaten in, faded duffel bag closer to my chest as the train slows to a stop at Briarcliff Station.

My luggage Lynda packed while I was out last night follows me as I step down the train's stairs, a staffer rolling them toward me between the rows of seats. Unused to such treatment, I stutter out a thank you while lifting the suitcases onto the platform.

He lifts his attention from second suitcase as I grab it. "You a Briarcliff student?"

After a second of hesitation, I nod, lifting my the case before the train bell rings for its imminent departure. "Yeah."

"Well, shit," the guy says. "You're going to be eaten alive, young pup."

He ducks his head in just as the train's doors slide shut.

Frowning, I hitch my duffel higher on my shoulder and push forward, rolling my suitcases with one in each hand.

"Callie Ryan?"

I straighten.

"Over here," the voice says.

A man in a full suit stands at the curb. A girl stands with him in school uniform, propping up a sign with a weak wrist, while using the rest of her energy to hold her phone to her face. I squint, since the girl doesn't seem particularly helpful in angling the sign toward me, but eventually see my name scrawled in lazy cursive.

"That's me," I say as I make my way over. He busies himself lifting my luggage and carrying them over to a town car parked on the street.

The girl is wearing Briarcliff's colors of maroon, black, and white, with her plaid skirt hiked up well past her knees and shirt unbuttoned one button too low. Her long, straight hair is held back from her face with a simple black-lacquered headband, and her blazer is thrown over her arm as she gives me her profile and scrolls through her texts.

I try for polite. "Um, hi?"

Her jaw moves, but not to talk. It's to grind down on the piece of gum in her mouth. Her thumb moves across her screen at warp speed, and she's still holding up that damn sign with the help of her elbow leaning into her thin frame.

Maybe she's hearing challenged, I think as I set my own jaw. I stick my hand out. "I'm Callie."

Pop goes the bubble she's formed. "I know."

"Okay."

I decide to turn to the person who has actually acknowledged me as he approaches.

"You ready to go?" he asks.

"I think so. You're here to take me to Briarcliff Academy?"

The girl snorts, as if I've just blurted out the dumbest thing imaginable.

"I am." The man has kind eyes, softened at the edges from age. "I'm one of the school's most requested drivers, Yael."

Piper gives another snort.

Yael's proud smile falters. "If you'll come with us."

My feet don't move. I glare at the girl. "I'm gonna blame your snot nose on allergies, since you can't possibly be insulting the man who drives your ass all around town while you make out with your phone."

It's enough to get the girl to peer over her screen. "Excuse me?"

I shrug. "Or maybe you're working on your Tinder profile so you can learn about human connection. I mean, I doubt your phone works as a proper dildo." I raise my brows. "Even with the vibrate function."

Her lips peel back in disgust, but I notice Yael's subtle grin behind her as he motions to the car. The girl spins on her heel and waltzes to the passenger side door he's left open, impressively walking a straight line despite her eyes never leaving her phone's screen. The sign falls to the pavement as she steps into the vehicle with a *swish* of unimportance.

Yael follows after her, hastily picking up my discarded name and tossing it in the nearby trash can.

I don't debate whether that's a sign of things to come.

I slide in after the girl, the car's air conditioning a cool refreshment against the surprising late August heat. Gusts from the vents blow back the girl's pin-straight strands around her shoulder like her own subtle wind machine.

That same air makes my kinky brunette waves stick to my lip gloss. I pull my sunglasses from my bag and perch them on my head, scraping my hair back. This impossible doll of a human has the right idea with her headband.

Yael starts the car, and soon we're motoring off.

"What's your name?" I ask the girl.

She tongues one side of her cheek. The word "Piper" leaves her lips, and her participation surprises me enough to ask a follow-up question. "Are you a senior, too?"

She sighs. "Yes."

I purse my lips. "And you're my welcoming committee?"

She looks at me sidelong. "Lucky me."

"Awesome. Are all the new kids fortunate enough to have you be their escort?"

Piper takes a longer study of me. Her eyes are bright blue and in stark, beautiful contrast to her skin and hair.

She smiles, and it's like rays of sunshine stream into this car and rest their beams strictly on her.

With a dying star behind them.

"Oh, dear. Have I shirked my duties? Welcome to Briarcliff Academy." Piper arches a sculpted brow. "Callie, is it?"

"That's what the sign you were holding says, so yep, that's me."

Piper doesn't enjoy my wit. "Okay, *Callie*. You're coming in seventy-five percent of the way through Briarcliff's four-year attendance requirement. That type of thing happens to two types of students—charity cases and unfair connections. I assume you're—"

"The latter."

"—both," she finishes, drawing out the word.

"Look, I'm not here by choice. My ... parents ... decided it would be best to finish high school at Briarcliff. If I had it my way, I'd be back at my old school, believe me."

"Did I forget to mention there's a third type of student?" Piper smiles. "Those that are entirely ungrateful for the opportunity they've been given by getting a spot here."

Piper turns back to her phone in obvious dismissal.

I settle into my seat and stare straight ahead, Yael's unassuming form a mere shadow in my periphery as he drives us to my new place of doom.

He has the right idea in becoming a peripheral blur. It's how I survived in public school, and I guess it's a method to stay alive here, too.

"Don't despair, Callie," Piper says to me, even though she's back to texting. "The third option is what we all are. You'll fit right in." She lifts her head for a smile, which to me, resembles a silent vow of entrapment. "Promise."

3

We pass through the sleepy seaside town of Briarcliff, its coast boasting the high, jagged rocks of its name. The mix of green and stone blend its beauty into the dark blue of the Atlantic, the white crests of waves smoothing the sharp, fatal crevices below.

It's a mix of allure and destruction. I press my fingers to the car's window as we drive, utterly struck by the vision.

The picturesque Main Street gives way to a thin road with thick clusters of trees and lazy curls of fog on either side. If it weren't for the rolled-up window, I'd smell the woodsy, musky scent of peeling bark and pine needles. The lifting fog gives way to a private road, and as we draw nearer, an exquisite bronze sign peeks through the trees.

Welcome Briarcliff Academy
Home of the Wolves
resurgemus corroborari

I'd skimmed Briarcliff facts on my phone during my trip here. *Resurgemus corrobarori* is Latin for "rise with might." And the wolves are ... well ... I glance over at Piper.

We pull into a circular pavilion rimmed with expertly pruned hedges. At the center is a gray-stoned structure, two stories high and U-shaped with its wings projecting forward on each side.

I exit the car with graceful awe. The pictures I'd trolled online did *not* do this place justice.

Above the main double doors is Briarcliff's crest, carved out of stained glass, the multitude of colors set off by the early afternoon sun.

Those doors open as Piper slides out and smooths her skirt. She makes a humming sound when she notices the figure descending toward us and hastily buttons up her shirt, clips a maroon crosstie around her collar, then throws on her black blazer.

I arch a brow at her Transformer-like speed.

"Welcome to Briarcliff, Miss Ryan. I'm Headmaster Marron."

The man stops at the base of the steps, dressed in a tailored navy suit. His salt-and-pepper hair flows back in sprayed-down waves, away from his face, and shrewd gray eyes, as if the school shines through the back of his head and into his stare, regard me.

"Um ... thank you," I reply, since I can't think of anything else.

Marron's focus glides from me to Piper, but in those last seconds of study, he's catalogued all my parts, from my scuffed Converse sneakers to my unkempt, free-flowing hair.

Yet, none of his thoughts are in his expression when he fixes his cuffs and says, "Miss Harrington, thank you for your assistance today."

"It was nothing, Headmaster." Piper pastes on a wide smile. "Now that Miss Ryan's safely on school grounds, may I be excused?"

"Not just yet," Marron says. "If you'll both come with me to my office."

"But—"

"Now, Miss Harrington."

Casting a glare my way as if I'm the one responsible for Marron's decision, Piper falls into step behind him.

I turn to the car, thinking I should grab my things, but the trunk is open and empty, with Yael nowhere in sight.

I hastily catch up to Piper and Headmaster Marron at the top stair, my duffel bouncing against my thigh, and fall into step beside Piper as Marron strides into the foyer with us close behind. The floor is white marble tiles threaded with black stone.

There's a sound above, and I glance up, past the hanging chandelier and onto an indoor balcony overlooking the foyer.

Four boys stand near the wooden railing, splayed out in relaxed, yet calculated, poses. They're all in school uniform. Even from a distance, their body language exudes insolent gorgeousness, like it's *definitely* their fault they're this pretty.

Their skin is flawless. Their hair perfectly barbered. Their bodies ... *not* made for high school, and instead sculpted for some pre-ordained future.

It's the one in the middle who catches my eye, the golden sun from the large window behind him casting its rays against his thick, blond hair, run-through and textured. He's too high to see the color of his eyes, but our distance doesn't conceal the savagery of his stare.

He's not scanning the ground floor like the rest. His head follows ... me.

His fingers drum against the polished wood as we pass underneath their perch, and the prickles on the back of my neck don't stop until he's out of view.

I shiver, but it's unclear if the chills are from being at the end of someone's rope, or the sheer deep freeze of the air conditioning pumping its heart out to cool such a vast space.

We turn into a wide hallway with shining, lemon-scented

wooden cases housing trophies in glass displays, as well as the grim portraits of alumni, professors, and headmasters.

Marron continues his lithe stride, turning us down a large hallway with a domed, church-like ceiling.

A second display catches my eye, outside of Marron's office. He moves inside, but I linger, frowning at the iron crest nestled circumspectly between graduating class photos, sports team portraits, and trophies. It's not Briarcliff's, but it's familiar to me somehow.

The hammered circle with a raven at the center, spreading its wings in flight, nudges at my memories. The Latin script *altum volare in tenebris* is carved underneath. With the way my index finger hovers on the glass above it, it's like I'm *supposed* to know what it means.

"What is this?" I ask, assuming Piper is nearby.

A hand slams against the glass in front of my face. I squeal, stumbling back.

"None of your business," a low voice responds.

My hand knots against my shirt.

Luxurious bronze-colored eyes meet mine. On an average person, they'd just be brown. But I'm not ... *he's* not ... normal.

He's god-like. Beautiful.

His presence sucks all the air out of this cavernous hallway. Heat prickles along my exposed skin, my T-shirt feeling rough and uncomfortable against my nipples, a thin sports bra barely managing to keep them under wraps.

High cheekbones frame his continued, unadulterated study, a carved curvature that hugs the corners of his sharp, Cupid's bow lips.

"I, um..." I clear my throat. "What?"

He arches a blond brow, but thick, inky lashes border his unwavering stare. "I said, none of your damned business, new girl."

Blinking, I say, "I, uh…" Then, because I can think of nothing better, "You were on top."

He was the blond guy in the middle on the balcony, observing me as I stepped onto Briarcliff turf.

"Exactly how I prefer it." His eyes narrow momentarily on my face before reassuming a cold veneer. "We call it the Wolf's Den. Are you my next lamb?"

"Callie?" Piper pops her head out of Headmaster Marron's office. "Did you get lost in the five steps it took to—oh, hey, baby."

Piper peels off the doorframe to drape herself over him. She kisses him on the cheek, but his head doesn't move in her direction. His eyes don't roam to hers.

Piper asks, "What are you talking to the new girl for?"

"I'm not," he says with a lingering, hypnotic tone. "And I don't care to."

The undeserved insult, one that's been uttered in my company and out of it during the entire summer at Lynda's many societal parties, snaps me from my stupor.

"Then let me do you the honor of exiting the *public* hallway that you approached me in, and get out of your highness's way," I say.

His brow tics up again. "Do that."

My upper lip lifts in a mirroring sneer, and I whirl into Marron's office.

"Chase," I hear Piper titter, "Don't be rude."

Chase? Ugh, even the guy's name sounds douchey and unacceptable.

I take a seat across from Marron who holds court behind his desk, impatiently waiting for his charges to sit.

Piper drifts in, mentioning that Chase needed an answer to a prudent question, and Marron's face relaxes. "Chase Stone has a big year ahead of him."

Every part of my frontal lobe wants me to dismiss all factoids about Chase, and this school, but the iron raven haunts my thoughts, and I wonder why Chase used a horror-level movie introduction to scare me away from it.

"Big year for him?" I echo.

"Hardly your concern," Piper says as she crosses her legs. The pleated skirt hitches just a bit higher.

"We have the top crew in the nation," Marron supplies. He interlocks his fingers. "And Mr. Stone is both the captain and the stroke for our boys' eight."

I nod politely as if I know what he's referring to.

"Not that Miss Harrington here is to be outdone," Marron says, "She's an excellent athlete herself. Perhaps she can introduce you to the crew team once she finishes giving you a tour of the school grounds. I assume that's where Mr. Stone's headed?" he asks Piper.

Piper nods. "I plan on going to the boathouse as soon as this meeting's concluded."

She doesn't mention anything about agreeing to a tour, and I get stuck on the word *boathouse*. What other resort-like amenities will I find during my stay here?

"Ah, yes," Marron says, his expression brightening. "Onto the reason you're both in my office."

He turns to his computer, his fingers moving across the keyboard. "Calla Lily Ryan, do I have that correct?"

Piper doesn't stifle her laughter behind her hand. "That's your full name?"

I clench my jaw. "Aren't you named after a dude who leads a bunch of rats out of town?"

Piper gasps.

"Ladies," Marron warns. Then says to me, "Miss Ryan, I'd like you to apologize," Marron says. "Miss Harrington was merely voicing her intrigue over such a unique name. Weren't you, dear?"

"Of *course*," Piper simpers. She even throws in a few eyelash bats. "While we're on the topic, I also forgive Callie for suggesting I use my phone as a dildo when we first met."

Damn. She got me. And in front of the headmaster, too.

Marron coughs behind a fisted hand.

"Briarcliff students pride themselves on decorum," Marron says to me. "I'd advise against the use of such terms while on campus."

I turn to Piper and say through a toothy smile, "I whole-heartedly apologize for my attempt to stage an intervention."

Piper glares.

"Very good," Marron says, then sounds out deft strokes against his keyboard. When he's finished, he pushes back against the desk. "Because, Miss Harrington, Miss Ryan, you two will be roommates for the rest of the school year."

One beat passes.

We both exclaim, "*What?*"

4

"Headmaster, surely you're mistaken," Piper says. "Can't Callie stay with the underprivileged kids?"

I'm not even insulted. "She's right. There has to be a mix-up."

Marron responds, "Miss Ryan's family has paid the entire tuition up front, and Miss Harrington, you're the only girl left without a roommate. I must insist that you—"

"My parents *ensured* I would have a room to myself," Piper says.

"They did, but I also explained to them, if there were any enrollees, your private room was subject to change. Now, at the time," Marron continues, holding up a hand to stop whatever is coming next out of Piper's mouth, "there were no additional students meant to attend. Miss Ryan is a last-minute addition, and I do apologize, but the Meyers insisted she be given a position here. And they also *ensured* as such."

There's a different conversation going on behind Piper and Marron's eyes as they continue to politely spar. It contains a world so outside my depth, I'm closed-mouthed and confident that I'm about to share a room with this expertly disguised she-demon.

"But, Headmaster..."

"It's settled. I expect both of you to be living comfortably in the dormitory after Miss Ryan's school tour is completed. Have I made myself clear?"

Piper nods, and I follow suit.

"Wonderful." Marron stands. "I have a conference in ten minutes, so if you two will kindly busy yourselves elsewhere."

"Sure thing," I say tiredly, and throw my duffel's strap over my shoulder as I rise.

Marron smiles, and I'm surprised it's directed at me. "Miss Harrington will direct you to Thorne House. You are the recipient of a rare position in this school, Miss Ryan. I hope you enjoy your time here."

Those words have never sounded so ominous coming from such a silver wolf's lips.

Outside the headmaster's office, I ask Piper, "So, which way is—"

"I have somewhere to be," Piper clips out.

She strides down the hallway, her footsteps echoing louder the farther she retreats.

"Hey!" I call. "I'm not expecting a grand tour, but you could at least tell me to turn left or right out of this hallway!"

Piper's arm snaps out, indicating a right turn at the end of the corridor.

"Thanks bunches," I mumble, then begin my personal school tour.

I turn right, as directed, but stall halfway.

Chase waits on the opposite side, where Piper turned. She's wrapped around him again, but Chase's face—notably, his expression—lifts from her shoulder and finds me.

This boy's focus should be giving me the creepy-crawlies, but instead, it's causing the bursting-bubble kind of tingles, an effervescent buzz that ignites my blood.

Chase smiles like a skilled sorcerer cursing his victim, his grin lethal. Poisonous. Alluring.

Piper, clueless to the exchange, murmurs something in his ear. His hand dips low in response, cupping her ass through her skirt. His unblinking gaze doesn't leave mine.

I'm breathing heavier. My cheeks feel warmer. Sweat forms under my arms.

Guys like him don't exist where I'm from. I know this deep in my soul.

And so, like the skittish elk I am, I bolt in the opposite direction, and it leads me to a wood-paneled door at the end, bringing me back outside.

I burst through, blinking against the sudden brightness of the sun. I scan the lush, landscaped grounds, then sigh, hitching my bag higher on my shoulder and following the thin, paved walkway, hoping to hit something or someone that will point me in the right direction.

No students seem to be around, and no one dots the horizon. The day bursts bright and beautiful, but there isn't anyone outside to enjoy it, almost as if this small section of the world, with its old-century buildings and perfectly blossoming hedges and trees, has been enchanted into silence.

When two structures appear once I'm over a modest hill, I mutter, "This has to be right," and walk faster, my hurried footsteps the only sound. Ideally, my bags will be where I end up, too.

I get within reading distance and notice each building's placard. One states, ROSE HOUSE in bronze lettering, and the other, THORNE HOUSE.

I do a silent fist bump, glad I'm where I aimed for. Then, I glance up at the rows of windows on either side, hoping I didn't just geek out in front of the entire student body.

I pull at the double-doors leading into Thorne House, experiencing another blast of air conditioning that floats curly strands of my hair until I'm over the threshold.

There's a desk at the entrance and a girl in a basic tee and jeans chilling on the chair behind it, her feet settled on the desk's surface as she spreads out in her seat and flicks through her phone.

Great, I think. *Another one.*

"Hi," I say as I approach.

The girl looks up, her azure gaze getting wider as I come closer.

"The new girl!" she exclaims.

"Yeah," I say with a tentative smile.

The girl stands and throws out her hand. "Pleased to meet you. I'm Ivara Alling. But you can call me Ivy."

I find her smile infectious. "I'm Calla Lily Ryan, but you can call me Callie."

Ivy laughs. "Weird names unite. You and I now have a special bond because our parents were probably high when they named us. Welcome. Do you know where the powers-that-be have stored you here?"

"Uh..." I shake my head. "I haven't gotten a chance to familiarize myself with the place. My supposed Student Guide ditched the crap out of me in order to hang out with her hot boyfriend."

Ivy laughs again, and this time it encompasses the entire room. My own lips widen in response.

"I see you've met Piper Harrington and Chase Stone," she says. She tucks a strand of white-blonde hair behind her ear as she rounds the desk. "Briarcliff's benevolent rulers."

"Yeah. They're super nice."

Ivy responds with a knowing smile, then peers at my bag. "Did you get any sort of class roster or pamphlet or ... anything to help me guide you to your room?"

"If I did, Piper has it all and she's not about to give it up." I reluctantly add, "I'm her new roommate."

Ivy gasps, and it's so sudden and visceral that I laugh. "She's as bad as I think she is, isn't she?"

"Worse," Ivy whispers, but she manages to collect herself. "But that at least tells me your room number. C'mon. I'll show you."

I follow Ivy to the inlaid brass elevators. At this point, I should be used to the luxury afforded to these high school students, but who knows if I'll ever be.

Ivy steps in, and I note she's pressed the third floor—the top.

"Do you live here, too?" I ask.

"Nah. I'm what they call a 'charity case.' I live with the free rides and in a modest dorm down the road. Richardson Place."

I raise my brows. "You're here on scholarship."

"Yeah." Ivy's gaze narrows. "Is that a problem?"

I lift my hands. "Nope. I'm impressed. It must take sizable brains to get a scholarship to a school like this."

Ivy's expression softens, and she sighs as the doors open to the third floor and we step out. "You don't know the half of it. But don't fret," Ivy says, "I only had to sacrifice *two* young goats and one human baby to the ruling class in order to do it."

At my stunned silence, Ivy adds, "Too dark?"

"No," I say with a chuckle. "You're weird. I like it."

Ivy spins around and starts walking backward. One corner of her mouth lifts when she says, "I just might like you, too."

There's a sudden bounce in my step, led by this girl with fairy-light hair, dusky eyes, and a tinkling laugh. We share a smile, and I follow her, thinking I might've just made a new friend at this peculiar, intimidating new school.

5

*I*vy stops at a wooden door with a brass number plate marked 303.

"This is you," Ivy says, sweeping her arm out like a game show hostess.

Then she blinks at me. Waiting.

I roll to the balls of my feet. "I ... don't have a key."

Ivy balks. "Let me get this straight. Headmaster Marron told you to room with Piper but gave you no instruction? No key?"

"I guess he assumed Piper would do all that." I let my bag's strap slide off my shoulder. "I can wait around until she gets back, maybe in the sitting room I saw downstairs." I pause, an unwanted image of Piper wrapped around Chase—this time, he's naked—burrowing into my mind's eye. "She has to come back at some point, right?"

Ivy purses her lips. "Jury's out on that one."

I hate where my mind goes, picturing Piper doing dirty things with Chase. I also hate that I'm responding to that image with everything but disgust.

Chase is sexy, so what? He's also crude. And mean.

Ugh. *Why* do I also find that hot?

"You okay in there?" Ivy asks, tapping my temple for emphasis.

I exhale, hoping that any lingering sexual images of Chase blow out, too. "It's been a long day."

"I get it." Ivy's forehead smooths in understanding. "As a front desk clerk, I'm not supposed to do this, but you have an honest face."

Ivy pulls out a keycard, black and inlaid with a golden Briarcliff crest.

"You're letting me into a student's room without proof I'm allowed?"

Ivy laughs, the sound carrying down the hallway.

"Your face has been the talk of the school since we heard that a new kid was coming on such short notice. These people? They grow up together as soon as they're out of the womb. Attend the same daycares. Go to each other's parties. *Screw* each other. When fresh blood drips into their water, the sharks are alerted, believe me. You've been Googled, Facebooked, Instagrammed—all the things."

"Err, I'm conflicted about that."

That boulder in my gut twists its jagged edges at the thought that someone could've read about my mother.

"Like your feelings make a difference," Ivy says, poking me with her elbow. Then she stills and takes a deeper look at me. "Your skin has lost a bit of color. Are you okay? I didn't mean to offend. Me and my big mouth."

"No, no, it's fine." I try on an assuring smile. "I'm just not used to data scrapes on my life."

"I wish I could say you have nothing to worry about." But Ivy collects herself, then bounces on her toes with a grin. "Good news is, I recognize your face and have full confidence that you're rooming with Piper, since she's the only girl left without one."

Ivy presses the master keycard into the card reader above the doorknob. She doesn't knock before she swings the door open, which makes me question how often Piper is even around.

Hopefully never.

"Here you are," Ivy says, then steps aside.

I lift my bag and walk forward.

My bag drops again, this time with a heavier thud.

It's one large room with a shared bathroom and two bedrooms on either side. A twin bed sits in Piper's, just out of view. There's also a desk with attached bookshelves, a six-drawer dresser with a vanity mirror, but clothing is squished into every available space, dresses and skirts and shoes spilling out into the center room.

Despite the clutter, the rest of the space is insanely big—larger than anything I've ever lived in before my stepdad married Lynda. But that's not what's so disconcerting.

It's when I turn to what's supposed to be my room.

"Sheesh, we've been in school for a week. It looks like she's lived here for years," Ivy says behind me, eyeing supposed "shared" couch and all the clothing draped over it. She comes to a stop beside me in my bedroom doorway. "Huh. Where's all your innards?"

"I was hoping you could answer that."

My bedroom has identical furniture to Piper's—a desk, a dresser, a bed, a closet. Problem is, there aren't any drawers in the dresser or the desk, and I'm staring at an empty, wooden bed frame.

"I don't see my luggage. Or a mattress." I spin to face Ivy. Maybe I should've listened harder to Lynda about what she said I needed to pack for a rich school. "They didn't expect me to bring a mattress, did they?"

"Heck no," Ivy says, but her furrowed brow is telling me different. "I mean, no one does, unless they want their familiar six-k remote control mattress from home. Now that I think about it, there are quite a few of those..." Ivy frowns and stares up at the ceiling.

"Ivy, stay with me here," I say. "I'm not the kind of kid who brings their own bed to school."

"Then I dunno what to tell you, dude. Your half should be outfitted."

And there's my *aha* moment. "Piper."

Ivy's realization follows suit. "She must've stolen everything."

"But how? I just saw her, and the walk took me fifteen minutes."

Ivy grows serious. "Don't underestimate the power of Piper and her minions. She got on her phone the minute your back was turned. Her younger sister waltzed into Thorne House just before you, with some of her friends. I assumed it was to steal the coffee from the cart offered to seniors." Ivy grimaces. "Guess I was wrong."

I spin in a circle. "Piper got people to remove my *shelves*? Seriously?"

"You ain't seen nothing yet," Ivy mutters, but before I can comment, she pulls her phone out and starts typing. "I'll find it for you, don't worry."

I nod and pace around the room, my bag swinging at my side. I park it on the wooden slats of my bed frame.

"Look on the bright side," Ivy says. "Because you're on the top floor, you get the highest ceilings."

I look up at the wooden beams, with two hanging light fixtures, and blink back tears.

Piper's brief spurt of immaturity is nothing. I should be used to the feelings of an outsider by now.

I say to Ivy, lowering my chin once I've willed the tears away, "I think I'll wait in the sitting room downstairs until my luggage gets here."

"Good idea."

"Yeah, assuming Piper hasn't redirected it to the trash or something."

"Probably a—oh, crikey." Ivy breathes out. "That might be where it is."

I ask after a resigned sigh, "Where's the school dump?"

Ivy answers, but I'm wandering and don't catch it. A shimmer on the kitchenette's counter draws my attention. A black envelope rests there, embossed in gold and torn open. An unfolded letter sits near it, also matte black. It's so at odds with the messy rainbow of colors of Piper that I'm drawn to it, my arm lifting of its own accord.

The letter begins with, **Altum volare in tenebris...**

"You won't go it alone," Ivy says, hooking my elbow in gentle understanding, "I'll show you where the coffee cart is so we can be caffeinated while we explore the dump."

We turn for the door, but stop when a voice says, "You seriously have a death wish, new girl."

6

*P*iper stands in the doorway with Chase's shadow looming behind her. Before I can speak, she storms over to where I am, eyes blazing, and rips the letter from my hands.

She shrieks, "Who the hell do you think you are to go through my things, you perv?"

Though my heart's pounding at being caught, I respond mildly, "I'm the person whose *things* you dumped in the trash." I flick pages of the letter Piper's now holding. "Tit for tat."

Piper bares her teeth. "You little whore—"

"Now, now," a mild, low voice interjects. Chase comes up behind Piper, his head angled, his eyes sharp. "There's no need to start a fight, is there, new girl?"

"I haven't started anything," I say, but I direct my answer to Piper, since Chase's stare is causing goosebumps to spread down my neck. "All my stuff's been taken. Including my damn bookcase."

"Then there must be a mistake." Chase settles his hand on Piper's shoulder, drawing her to his chest while using his other hand to pluck the letter from Piper's hand and smoothly pocket it. Piper maintains her glare, but her body relaxes against him, and she gives me a closed-mouthed smile, as if she's won something I never had a chance of challenging her for.

"Your things got delayed at the airport, or, I don't know..." Chase gives an exaggerated eye-roll, "...the additional car carrying your luggage was caught in traffic. I hear there was a horrible accident on 95." Chase lowers his chin to address Piper, a slow, awful grin drifting across his mouth. "Terrible tragedy. Didn't you hear, babe?"

Piper settles herself against Chase and smiles. "Totally."

I glance between the two of them. "You expect me to buy that? There's no extra car, and I didn't come here on a plane."

Chase's grin fades, and a preternatural calm takes its place. "You must not have heard me, new girl. Your things got delayed. They'll be along shortly." Chase darts a glance at Ivy, who squeaks and drops the phone she was probably texting an SOS on. Then he centers back on me. "There's no need to report anything missing."

"But—"

"I'm telling you nicely," Chase says, "to shut up."

"And I'm *demanding* you return my things." I cross my arms. "Or I'll have Marron up here so fast—"

"Sweet, sweet new girl." Chase reaches over Piper and tucks a strand of hair behind my ear. I jerk back, my expression hopefully communicating repulsion and not giving away the scary-fast heat that shot to my core the instant he touched me. "You have so much to learn."

That scary-heat is now an inferno. I clear my throat, hoping I don't choke on the intensity.

"Enough of this shit," Piper says. "You're trespassing. Get off my half of the room and go live in the hovel that is yours."

"Bring me my stuff," I retort.

"Find and collect it yourself," she says.

"Callie, let's just go," Ivy says, pulling at my arm. "I can help you bring everything back up here."

Piper laughs. "Enter the squeaky little church mouse. You're always so helpful, aren't you, Freebie?"

Ivy's lips thin, but she doesn't clap back, which is odd, considering the Ivy I've been conversing with is the complete opposite.

"Let's go, Callie," Ivy says again.

I don't want to. These people don't know that my whole life is packed up in those two suitcases. They don't care, and it's with a frustrated growl that I tear my attention away from them and follow Ivy out the door.

"Don't be a Karen," Chase says as I pass. "That is, if you're hoping to survive more than a day here."

I whirl, sweeping my arm in the direction of my room. "You two immature assholes can have your win. I've survived a lot worse than you."

"Aw," Piper says, faking a trembling lip. "Are you gonna cry, babe?"

"It's so cute that you think we care about your life," Chase adds, cocking his head.

My mouth works, but Ivy gets to me first. She grabs me by the elbow and drags me out.

"I'm saving you," she says as we stumble into the hallway. "Before you get under their skin."

The word *fury* doesn't come close to describing what's crawling under mine. "I don't care."

"Callie." Ivy holds my shoulders and leans in close. "You do care. Do not get on their bad side, okay? Let them bat you around a little and get bored with you. It's the only way."

Ivy pulls me down the hallway toward the elevators, but when I risk a glance over my shoulder, I see Chase moving to stand in the center of the hallway, watching us, his hands tucked in his pockets, and his blazer flared out behind.

He catches my eye and winks.

7

We find my missing furniture exactly where I feared. The Dumpster behind the dorms.

Automatic sprinklers from the neighboring acre of lawn cast their spray across the mattress propped against the giant, stinking canister, soaking the material to the point that when it dries, it will forever smell like mildew. My drawers are stacked haphazardly beside it, some cracked, others missing knobs because of all the manhandling they experienced during their brief travel from the third floor to here.

But that's not the worst part.

Garbage bags were ripped, and their contents poured over my things. Spoiled food, rotten milk, used tampons, and the flat slugs of condoms drape over the contents of my suitcases, unzipped for all the putrid detritus to slip in.

"Christ on a cracker," Ivy whispers beside me.

I run a hand through my hair, clenching my fingers against my scalp as I take stock of the scene.

What Piper—and Ivy—don't know is, I'm not above searching through trash. There was a time I Dumpster-dived behind restaurants to collect their cast-off food when my mom was between jobs. It's amazing, the fresh, untouched meals one can find in an NYC trash bin, but something tells me these girls would never understand. My eyes grow hot with warning, but I bite down on the inside of my cheek, redirecting the pain.

"How are clothes cleaned around here?" I ask, hoping my voice is steady.

Ivy's expression becomes pained. "At Thorne House, they put their laundry in special fabric bags and leave it outside their door to be picked up and returned."

I can't imagine packing all my soiled clothes into a bag to have someone else pick through the mess, brimming with terrible hygiene.

I point at the pile of my shit. Literally. "Safe to say, my special Briarcliff laundry bag is in there somewhere."

"Yikes." Ivy bites down on her lower lip. "I guess that means your school uniform's in there, too."

"Yep." My lips pop against the *p*.

"Off-campus laundry is Thorne and Rose House policy," Ivy says. "At Richardson Place, we're normal folk. We have a laundry room with washers and dryers. Coin operated, even."

I breathe in deep. "I guess that's where I'm headed, then."

Ivy nods, and I sense her study of me. I won't buckle beneath her gaze. I don't want to see the pity there.

After a moment, where it's only the sound of the sprinklers between us, she says, "I'll get the luggage caddy. It's around here somewhere. Then we can start stacking."

A tug of guilt grows tight in my belly. "Ivy, thank you, but you don't have to. You probably have class or somewhere to be. I can handle this."

"Can you?" Ivy props her hands against her hips. "Because as a human being, I can't leave you to this mess. Besides, I have free period the rest of the afternoon, hence why I took a shift at Thorne House."

"Shouldn't you be out front, then? I don't want you to get fired because you're helping me."

"I'm absolutely positive the Briarcliff girls will be able to get themselves into their apartments without any help from me. I'm more of a mascot, anyway. Or a zoo animal. 'Look at the charity case, working at a job just like the hired help. How cute and interesting to watch. Look at the way she signs people in and out. What a unique way to use one's hand.'"

I can't help but smile. "Thank you, Ivy."

"Not a problem." Ivy throws an arm around my shoulders, which is somewhat awkward considering she's half a head shorter than me. But the comfort works. "I'll also track down Darren. He's the custodian around here. We are *definitely* gonna need some gloves."

"And maybe some bleach."

I lean into her shoulder. Despite the knowledge that the rest of my afternoon will be knee-deep in garbage, I don't feel so alone.

"That's the last of it," Ivy says, lowering the hose from the drawers.

Darren ended up being super helpful and provided us with goggles, forearm-length cleaning gloves, disinfectant, and directed us to the attached hose to wash down the furniture.

We also made three trips to Ivy's dorm with the rolling luggage caddy like you see at hotels, my suitcases dripping unidentifiable goo onto the walkway as we traveled, and we took over three washers and two industrial-sized dryers to try and salvage my clothes.

Evening has fallen, and I take one glove off and swipe the back of my hand against my forehead. "Good, because I think I've gone nose blind."

"Consider that a gift," Ivy says, then drops the hose to the ground and checks her watch. "My stomach's grown a giant hunger-monster. You ready for dinner?"

I glance down at my clothes, the front of my mom's old shirt dampened with water and ... brown liquid. My jeans haven't fared much better, either. "Does this place have room service?"

Ivy laughs. "That's where the luxury ends. We all have to eat at the dining hall regardless of status. We'll shower in my dorm, and I can lend you some clothes until yours are dry. If we hurry, we'll catch the last bell."

"Bell, huh?" I say as we begin our trek from Thorne House to Richardson House.

"Not a cowbell, if that's where your peasant mind is going." She says it as a joke, then points to the east. "See the bell tower? It'll ring at seven PM."

I pause and stare at the brick laid tower, at least five stories high, with an open, white-beamed cube at the top and a large brass bell in the middle.

"Is there an actual person that goes up there and rings it?" I ask.

"Ha, no. Briarcliff isn't hiding a hunchback. They've embraced the technology to build an electronic lever up there that moves the bell at specified times."

"Wow. Cool," I say, then rush to catch up when Ivy starts walking again.

"While I'm your tour guide, I might as well point out the line of trees over there. See?"

I do. It's sort of like a manmade forest at the end of our flattened landscape on the west, lining the school grounds for privacy rather than promoting nature. But it's thick, and I can't see through it.

As if she reads my thoughts, Ivy continues, "There's a huge cliff on the other side, called Lovers' Leap. We aren't supposed to go anywhere near it, but schoolkids are always hopping the gate. Certain people are known to go there. Those of us who haven't made use of it call it Fuckboys' Leap."

I find myself staring long and hard through the trees. Chase comes unbidden into my thoughts, his haughty, handsome face like a physical alarm for my body. "People like Chase?"

"How astute of you." Ivy elbows me as we dawdle. "Him and his crew, yeah. And Piper and hers. There's plenty of intermingling, if you know what I mean."

I remember the group of guys that were with Chase on the upper balcony when I entered Briarcliff.

"I can point them out to you in the dining hall," Ivy says with a secret smile, and this time I elbow her.

"I have zero interest in that clique," I say, and I'm half-honest, at least. I want nothing to do with Piper and her band of merry thieves. "Can I ask you something?"

"Sure."

We're drawing close to Richardson Place, so I make it quick. "Has anyone ever stood up to those assholes and won?"

Ivy's step slow. "Those people are bad for you. I hope you know that. They're alluring and have a ton of charm, but none of it is real."

I frown. "Did something happen to you? With them?"

Her throat bobs. "Something happens to everyone who comes across that group."

I whisper, "Like what?"

But Ivy blinks out of whatever memory she fell into. "My advice ... don't think too hard on it. Piper and her followers, they're drawn to shiny new things. But just like fickle, overly-groomed house cats, they'll get bored and move on to the next sparkly object."

"I may not be here by choice, but now that I am, it's to get into a good college, that's all. Not get caught up in a bunch of drama."

"That's a great attitude to have," Ivy says with a wide smile. But her lips are too stretched, and it doesn't reach her eyes. "I hope you can keep it going."

8

*I*vy's dorm, Richardson Place, is a one-story brick building stretched wide to hold about ten apartments.

Ivy unlocks door 5, smack in the middle, and she mutters about neighbors against both walls as she strolls inside.

I follow suit, and I can't say I'm shocked, but...

"Whoa," I say.

Ivy tosses her backpack onto her bed. "What?"

"This place is *nice*." And I mean it.

While not the opulence of Piper's dorm (which I refuse to call mine, too) with Persian carpeting, high ceilings, and an en suite bathroom, Ivy's apartment is still way better than any of the places my mom and I rented before she found a stable career.

Two twin beds have headboards with built-in shelving measuring all the way to the ceiling. Two nightstands with drawers are also attached and nestled between both beds. A pair of desks stand against the opposite wall.

"You think Briarcliff gets their furniture custom made?" I ask as my finger drifts across Ivy's desk. It seems to fit perfectly in its spot.

Ivy snorts. "I wouldn't put it past some alumni putting in

funds for it. You know, Piper's family owns the furniture conglomerate Comfy-At-Home. I bet it's them."

"Huh," I muse. "How nice for them, helping out the less fortunate."

Ivy snorts again. "Communal bathrooms are through that door there, and down the back hallway at the end. You can borrow a towel and some clothes until your stuff is dry."

"Thanks. I appreciate you helping me out."

"Have you found another orphan, Ivy?"

Said door widens to reveal a girl with long, damp hair, ample bosom wrapped into a towel, and a scowl.

"Callie, meet my roommate, Eden." With her back turned to Eden, Ivy adds an eye roll.

"So, you're the fresh blood, huh?" Eden looks me up and down.

"I guess," I say. "I had no idea I was this interesting."

"You're not," Eden says. "The bobbleheads around here are simply bored."

"Bobbleheads?"

"You know, the yes-men. And women," Eden says. She pulls on a drawer and starts rifling through. "That's all anyone is around here. I assume you're no different. Just like Ivy Dearest, over here."

I raise a brow. "You've known me for two seconds."

Eden raises her eyes from her underwear to meet mine. "I'm great at what I do. Watch out for Ivy. She may seem like an outsider, but she's not."

"*Anyway*," Ivy says, coming up beside me and holding a folded towel with some clothes on top. "You remember where I said the bathrooms are?"

"Yeah. Thanks." I take the stack from Ivy.

"It's just a plain T-shirt and leggings. Hope you don't mind. We have to wear our uniforms for breakfast and lunch. The one restriction at dinner is no jeans or flip-flops."

"Am I going to my school dining hall, or a formal restaurant?" I say with a smile.

"You're going into the wolves' den." Eden says it without cracking a smile, and my stomach flutters with the kismet of using the same comparison Chase did.

"I thought it was referred to as the Wolf's Den," I say.

"Off you go, Callie," Ivy says to me. "I'll put Eden back on her leash to keep her from biting."

Eden bares her teeth at Ivy but manages to do it without moving any other muscle on her face.

While it looks like *so* much fun having Eden as a roommate—about as enjoyable as being paired with Piper—I do what Ivy suggests and step into the hallway.

I find the showers, pleased they're deserted, and I clean and change within fifteen minutes. Ivy eventually joins me in the bathroom, and we make some friendly talk as we get ready and Ivy applies some fresh make-up. Asking Ivy to borrow some is overkill, since we just met, so I resign myself to going barefaced and wet-haired to my first dining hall experience.

I'm glad for the spare hair tie I always keep around my wrist, and finger-comb my brown strands until they're so fed up, they surrender into a top knot.

Ivy and I venture to the central building but use a side door. I admire the ease in which she floats from building to building, using side doors and shortcuts, and I hope to emulate it soon. They look like easy escape routes.

We cut through the foyer, and, as if my eyes are tugged on by an unseen force, I glance up. This time, no boys peer over the balcony's railing and into my soul.

"Is the Wolf's Den for all students?" I ask Ivy as we pass under it. "Or just the popular kids?"

"Technically, it's a lounge area for seniors, but the only seniors that tend to use it have connections to either Chase or Piper."

I snort. "You're telling me Chase calls dibs like a school bully on a playground?"

Ivy chuckles. "Still got a mind toward Chase, huh?"

"Ew. No," I say. "I saw him up there when I came in with Headmaster Marron and Piper."

I deliberately fail to mention how his stare bolted through me like lightning, so much so that my heart was singed upon contact.

I rationalize that this was *before* I truly met him and saw him with Piper. I can't help how my body reacts to a gorgeous guy, but I can certainly have my mind rein in my hormones once he proves what a jackoff he is.

Ivy pulls one side of large, mahogany double doors, saying, "You'll come to learn that Chase gets ample privileges compared to the rest of us seniors."

"Why?" I ask, but either Ivy doesn't hear me or chooses not to answer, because the moment we step into the dining hall, she gestures to the left. "There they are."

Across the multitude of tables, some seating six, others four, and the ones around the edges two, I find who Ivy's talking about. Four guys are clustered around a far table, the ones from the Wolf's Den, but an invisible magnet pulls me to the one in the center.

Damn it. Chase.

"From left to right, you have Riordan Hughes, Tempest Callahan, the infamous Chase Stone, and James Windsor. Commit those names to memory so you can avoid them at all costs."

"Ah, you lost me at Tempest."

Ivy gets my joke, because she laughs. "And you thought *your* name was extra. Let's go."

Ivy draws me to the side where a trussed-up buffet with a bunch of silver platters awaits us.

The dining hall is decorated with pure, unadulterated church-like excess. Four chandeliers hang in a row, centered in the arched, two-story high ceiling. Massive stone columns frame the stained glass-windows, but I don't linger on the details for too long, because people keep looking at me funny as we pass.

Maybe it's my sensitivity and hyperawareness at being the new girl. I suppose it's interesting to these people when a stranger walks onto territory they've been trampling since they were in diapers.

I'm ogling the table-side pasta bar containing noodles I've never even heard of when I hear my name whispered behind me. I throw a look over my shoulder just in time to see a girl turn back to her plate, with her five friends dipping their heads low to hear her better.

Hesitating, I swivel to the pasta bar and ask the chef for spaghetti Bolognese. He nods and gets to work.

"Ivy," I mutter. She's deciding between a Caesar or garden salad beside me. "Is something going on?"

"Other than Spaghetti Monday, my favorite dinner day?" Ivy picks up a premade Caesar and places it on her tray. "No, why?"

"Because ... people keep staring at me."

My instincts whisper their caution, and I lift my chin, searching for the source of that warning.

Chase.

He stares back, draped across a chair angled to see me better. His tie's askew, but that's because Piper is twisting it around her hand as she leans her hip against the table and tries to win his attention. His friends blur in my periphery, but I take note that Piper's entourage has also joined the table and made it a party of eight.

"Yep," Ivy says once she follows where my attention's landed. "And there we have the four witches of Briarcliff. Piper, Falyn Clemonte, Violet Tobias-Hayes, and Willow Reyes."

I purse my lips. "It's fitting there's four of them, you know, to round out the evil coupling."

Ivy smiles, then nudges me to accept the plate of hot pasta the chef's holding out. "You're not wrong. Emma Loughrey used to make it five, but she left a few years ago."

"Left ... as in dropped out?" I ask as I rebalance my tray, laden with too many fancy food items I couldn't resist. "Why?"

"You're always asking that question as if I have some kind of dark and stormy response," Ivy says, laughing.

Chase won't take his eyes off me, and curiously, the others stare me down, too.

"Can you blame me?" I say as we navigate to the scholarship table.

As we turn, I catch Piper's snake-like smile. She holds up her phone, waving it like she has a carrot on a stick. She gestures with her chin for Ivy to check hers.

"Maybe not," Ivy answers me, then, while balancing her tray with one arm, she cautiously pulls out her phone. "Emma ... left. There was drama. Nothing I should tell you on your first day, though. But ... oh, yikes."

Ivy's eyes pop wide as she stares at her phone's screen.

"What?" I ask, and when I get no immediate answer, I twist so I can see the screen, too.

"*Fuck*," I whisper-yell.

It's a picture of me plundering Thorne House's dump, my lower legs encased in two trash bags and tied with shoelaces so I wouldn't ruin my sneakers. My hair's in a messy top-knot. I'm wearing protective goggles and blue sanitary gloves, and there are streaks of ... glop ... on my exposed arms and chest as I'm stepping up to the dumpster to look inside.

Did I mention I'm also holding up a thong? My panties, found at the top of the pile.

It doesn't end there. I've been made into a meme, and underneath my beautifully stinky self are the words, **TRASH BITCH**.

Ivy swipes left to a .gif of an opossum screaming and baring its teeth inside a dumpster. Blinking scroll text reads, **MAKE YOURSELF AT HOME, TRASH BITCH**.

9

"Good Lord, she's lame," Ivy says as she blacks out her screen. Likely for my benefit.

I rub my lips together and look up. Phones that aren't switched to vibrate start going off. After reading their phones, heads pop up like groundhogs and beady eyes stare at me before students start laughing.

"Oh, God," I say, my stomach swinging dangerously.

"Forget it." Ivy presses her hand to my back and pushes me forward. "Just a stupid prank."

Ivy may be able to direct my feet, but she can't force my head forward. I glance back at Piper, who's got a hand to her chest and laughing. Chase, however, is unfazed, almost bored.

"Sit," Ivy says, and when I don't, she plants a hand on my shoulder and shoves. I land in my seat with a smack.

Ivy sits beside me, and though I feel like I'm as red as the spaghetti sauce I'm staring at, I can tell she's landed warning looks on each and every person at this table.

"The only trash bitch in this room is her," I hear someone mutter across from me.

It's Eden, Ivy's roommate.

"Eat your food," Ivy says, patting my hand. My arms have gone limp around my tray. "You win by ignoring it."

I blink. Swallow. Straighten my spine. If I can get through my mom's death, I can get through this shit, shit, *shit* of a first day. I just have to turn my luck around.

I say to Ivy while attempting a smile, "There's no way I can leave without eating the five-star cuisine in front of me."

Ivy raises her fork in salute. "That's the spirit!"

Smiling, I cheers my fork with hers and dig in, refusing to look behind me and at that table *ever* again. Like Ivy keeps reminding, no good can come from gaining their interest.

But Ivy isn't done talking. "Callie, meet the rest of my crew. You've met Eden, but this is Paul, Luke, Mercy, and—"

Someone's tray, filled with dirty dishes and smeared food, lands on our table.

I jump back at the sound, and Ivy flies against her chair.

"Seriously, dude?" she says to the student who did it. He just smirks and keeps walking.

Blinking rapidly, Ivy says to me, "What the heck was th—"

Bang.

A second tray lands on the original, used silverware and flat soda spilling onto our plates.

Mercy, a cute blonde with ringlets, jolts to a stand, hands raised as cola drips from her skirt. "Callie, what did you *do* to them?"

My mouth opens and closes. "Who? Chase? Piper? I've been here half a day—!"

Crash. More trays. More plates. More glasses.

This time, they're coming from a line of students, some cutting in and throwing their tray at us before scampering away.

"Screw this, I'm out," Paul says, and Luke throws his napkin down and follows suit.

"Thanks, *guys*," Ivy calls after them, but says to me, "They have the right idea. We need to leave."

I glance furtively at the table, noticing Eden is already long gone. During Ivy's and my brief exchange, Mercy and the girl I never got the name of left as well.

Throwing a sad, mental farewell to the delicious food I can no longer eat, I start to rise, but something heavy and wet forces me back down.

I yell. My eyes burn, and I rub at them, realizing warm liquid drips down my face. Something else falls from my head to my back with a wet, sucking sound.

"Piper!" I hear Ivy yell, but before she can follow that up with anything else, I stand, whirl, and shove my palms into the closest chest.

Piper laughs at my feeble, half-blind attempt to push her. "No need to get so angry, Callie. I'm putting my trash where it belongs."

"What's going on here?" an authoritative voice booms out.

I scrunch my eyes, trying to see better, then feel a napkin forced into my hands. I swipe my face, squinting through all the red sauce.

A teacher storms forward, his face lined with fury. "Girls! What is all this?"

"Nothing, Professor Dawson," Piper says. "Callie just had an accident and slipped and fell while holding her tray. Didn't you, Callie?"

Appalled, I answer, "No, I fucking did not."

"Language, Miss Ryan," the teacher says. "And in case it's not clear, that kind of rudeness is not the way to properly introduce yourself to faculty members."

Piper says to him, "It's all a misunderstanding, sir. I swear."

"Then explain the pile of trays on this table," I say, close to shrieking. I glance around frantically, searching for Ivy, for *someone*, to back me up.

But Ivy's held back by one of Chase's boys, his grip tight on her arm. The strawberry blond one, the one named James. Her eyes are steady on mine, but pleading. Her lips are a thin, white line.

The students who haven't exited the dining hall with tray-throwing flare don't bother with pretense and abandon their food, ogling in silence.

"Oh, in case you didn't know, Callie," Piper flaps her hand. "At the end of the evening, one table is selected to help clear and clean the dining hall. It's a way for students to appreciate our custodial staff. This table was selected for tonight, was it not, Professor Dawson?" Piper's question rises with innocence at the end. "Miss Ryan isn't yet aware of how things work around here. Are you, Callie?"

The double entendre isn't hard to miss. Except for this Dawson, who still has yet to choose a side while he studies the trays in grim silence. "Well, yes, Miss Harrington, but usually students are a lot neater than this."

"We're in a big rush, sir," Piper says. "What with the night run that's happening tonight."

"Mm." Dawson nods, resting an infuriating finger on his chin as he listens to this bitch.

"That's not even sort of true," I say. "Piper *threw*—"

"—I'm here to help with clean up," she cuts in.

"You're out of your mind!" I say, still wiping droplets of red sauce from my eyes.

"Callie," I hear Ivy whisper close by. "Stop."

"I saw it all," another girl says as she sidles up to Piper. Is it Violet? Falyn? The evil little sister? Who the hell cares.

"More importantly," this girl says, "Piper's been Callie's Student Guide all day, so it makes sense that Callie learn the kitchen rules from her."

Piper squeezes the girl's hand. "Thanks, Addy."

My eyes are close to bugging out. What I say is being twisted.

"Ivy saw it, too. Right, Ivy?" Piper asks.

Dawson asks Ivy, "Is this true, Miss Alling?"

Ivy's throat moves. I wait for her response, *certain* she'll have my back...

"Yes," she says. Then follows up, in a dull tone, with "Callie tripped. The students were in a rush to see the race and the table got overcrowded. It ... got out of hand."

Ivy's name bursts from my lungs, but she can't look at me. Or won't.

"Okay, then." Dawson smacks the sides of his legs. "Problem solved."

My jaw goes slack, and I'm ready to unhinge it when he adds, "It means you'll also be wonderful at showing Callie the rules of detention, of which you'll be joining her for two weeks' worth."

Piper's face blotches, her voice taking on the notes of an out-of-tune flute. "But Professor!"

I smile.

"I can fall for your stunts only so many times, Miss Harrington," Professor Dawson drawls. "As for the rest of you, you'd better hurry. Mr. Stone, aren't you leading the boats this evening?"

Ugh. I'm not surprised to see Chase on the fringes of this gathered group, observing from afar.

"Hell, yes," he responds.

"That settles it. Miss Ryan, you can be exempt from assisting in dining hall clean up tonight considering your ... appearance, but don't make this a habit, okay?"

I have no words. But what I lack in syllables, Piper makes up for with a blubbering defensive argument, appalled she's made to clean up the mess *she* instigated.

I leave her to it, storming through the gathered group and pass Ivy along the way.

"Callie..." she says, but my answer is my shoulder hitting her on the way out.

I'm a fool. I shouldn't have been so trusting, so fast. So *clingy*.

Ivy's been here a lot longer than me, and she has her own motives to make a priority. They all do.

I push through the doors and into the cool, empty air of the hallway, lights dimmed for the night. Trophy displays cast their glow onto the marbled floor, but I fly past them.

"Hey," I hear a voice say behind me. I don't stop.

"New girl," it says again, and my molars clench.

I throw a "fuck off" over my shoulder.

"Is that any way to thank a guy for bringing you a towel?"

My steps slow, but I keep moving. Unfortunately, Chase has much longer legs than I do, and he comes up beside me with smooth precision. "Here."

I bat the towel away. "I don't want your help."

"Aw, don't be such a *Carrie*."

I halt and spin so fast, red droplets scatter, some hitting Chase's perfectly pressed polo shirt. I'm glad for it. "What part of *fuck off* don't you understand?"

"Hmm. I understand the 'fuck' part well enough," he responds, a slow grin creeping across his face.

I raise my upper lip in disgust. "I don't want anything from you. Or anyone else in there. I just want to be left alone."

"Not gonna happen."

"Why? What did I do to piss you all off so much?"

"You're new." He shrugs. "And somewhat easy prey. Frankly, Piper's becoming lazy. I don't condone what she did in there."

"Yeah, right." I scoff. "If you for one second consider yourself a white knight, you can take your piss-poor armor and shove it up your dick. You didn't do anything to help back there. You just *looked* and enjoyed. Like the rest of them." Then I laugh. "You know, when I met Piper, I asked if she led a bunch of rats around." I give Chase the once-over, ignoring the twinges and pulls in my belly at the sheer length of him and the amount of muscle bunching underneath his shirt. "Guess I was right."

"So, what am I then, new girl? A dickless knight, a useless

bystander, or a rat? Choose one analogy, at least, if you're determined to insult me for offering you a towel."

"It's not just the towel," I spit. "It's that you do nothing. You just stand by and *watch*."

"That's where you have it wrong." Chase lowers his head, shadows from the hallway forming a tarnished demon over the angelic curvatures of his face. "I'm merely waiting my turn."

He moves before I can clock it. In an instant, Chase stands close, his nose inches from mine. I'm shocked to feel his finger trailing down my cheek, leaving sparks in its wake. My lips part of their own accord, and I'm drowning in the chocolate depths of his eyes, dark and bitterly sweet.

"For the record," he murmurs, angling his lips close, "you look nothing like a possum."

The word—the memory of the graphic image—snaps me from the reverie. Horrified, I harden my features, rip the towel from his grip, and continue stalking toward the exit.

His laughter follows me all the way outside.

10

It's when I hit the pavilion out front that I realize I have nowhere to go.

I'm in clothes that aren't mine, in a place I've never been before, and in less than a day, managed to attract the derision of the entire school.

Great job, Callie. I wish proving to Dad and Lynda I don't belong here didn't have to hurt so much.

As I walk in the dark, with tall, electric lanterns providing minuscule light, my phone illuminates in the thigh pocket of my borrowed leggings. I pull it out, thinking that at least my phone has survived this hell-pit.

Ahmar: How was your first day?

I stop in the middle of the walkway. The crashing waves half a mile from here are amplified in the silence.

Ahmar's been a shoulder I've often cried on, but there's not much comfort he can provide from New York City. I could call him and whine about my circumstances, but I've already done that. This is where I am now. Accept it and move on. Despite drawing Piper's inexplicable ire, I'm still a student at a world-class school, and my classes start tomorrow.

Great, I text back, the screen of my phone smearing with garlicky red sauce from my thumbs.

Ahmar: I love hearing that. Call me anytime, ok?

Sure! I text.

I've never been so fake with Ahmar. Ever. But what are my options? Tell him I'm currently standing outside, my things destroyed, kicked out of my dorm, and have no friends to speak of? Then ask him to please come over and arrest the bitch who started it all?

A smile spreads across my lips as I advance forward, picturing Piper screeching in handcuffs as Ahmar plops a hand on her flat-ironed head and pushes her into a police car.

I reach Richardson Place and file that fantasy away for a later date. I knock on Ivy's door. Eden answers with a frown.

"Ivy's not here," Eden says.

"I know. I'd just like to get my stuff from the laundry room."

Eden looks me up and down, refusing to move from the doorway. Just as I'm about to appeal my case, she mutters, "You need to use the showers again, too."

"Yeah," I say.

Eden steps aside, her expression unreadable.

I cut through the room, but pause at the back door when a sharp, humiliating realization hits.

"What now?" Eden says as she resumes sitting at her desk, a lamp lighting the textbook she's been highlighting.

"My luggage was destroyed. The bags, I mean." I can't even look at her as I say this.

"That sucks. But how's that my problem?"

"I, uh…" I close my eyes for this part. "Do you have some garbage bags I can put my clean clothes in?"

Silence.

I wait for the laughter, or maybe a highlighter to hit my head. I know nothing about Eden, other than she's overtly rude, whereas Piper hides her distaste until the minute she can wield it. And Ivy ... Ivy isn't who I thought she was.

Eden says, "Fine."

Her chair creaks as she moves, and I hear the rustle of plastic bags she's pulled from somewhere. "Here."

I turn to grab them—quickly, so maybe the humiliation will end faster—but also latch on to cushy-soft fabric.

"What's this?" I ask.

"A sleeping bag." Eden shrugs. "I hear things."

It wasn't even said that nicely, but the gesture makes my eyes sting with tears.

"Eden, I..." Oh, please, don't break down and cry. "Thank you."

Eden clicks her tongue as she waits for me to regain control. "You might want to use the back walkway behind this building that leads to yours. Since you'll be carrying trash bags and all, I doubt you're aiming to be photographed."

"That's true," I say. "Thank y—"

"Go away now."

I sniff. Nod. Then head to the bathrooms. Again.

※

I'm spinning my hair into a wet top knot when the sound of the bathroom door draws my head up.

An ice-blonde head appears. It's Ivy. "Hey," she says.

I meet her eyes through the mirror.

She fidgets with her hands at her sides, then continues, "I'm sorry about dinner and how I didn't help."

"It's fine." My hair tie snaps into place. "We just met. You don't owe me anything."

"Callie, I—"

I bend to grab my two garbage bags and swing both over each shoulder. "You helped out today. I'm grateful that you picked through trash with me. But what I most appreciate is how you educated me on the class system here."

Ivy's eyes soften. "Callie, I'm so sorry. I wish I could make you understand, but I…"

"You don't have to. Like I said, we're not even friends. I have no idea how you interact with those guys—"

"The Nobles," she whispers. "They're called the Nobles."

"Uh-huh," I say, staring at her sidelong. "I have no idea how you interact with guys who deem themselves royalty from centuries ago. God, it's like they've replaced compensating their tiny dicks with fancy cars to using royal titles instead."

One corner of Ivy's lips tics up. "They still have those fancy cars."

I resist warming to her smile, but it's harder than I thought. "Point is, you *did* help me today. You've been nice when you didn't have to. So, it's okay. I've got it from here."

I step closer, indicating that I need the space to get around her, but Ivy doesn't move. "Do you?"

"Sure." I put extra pep in my tone. "Avoid them at all costs. Keep my nose in the books. Literally. Survive two semesters here, then go to college like my mom always wanted. Easy peasy."

"They're bad," Ivy says, and I don't need to ask who. "Like really harsh. This could just be the beginning for you."

I lick my lips. "Then at least now I'll know to expect it. Excuse me."

"Where will you go tonight?" Ivy asks, remaining in place.

"I don't know," I say honestly. "But it'll come to me. I refuse to go to Piper's room."

"I could—you could stay with us."

I think of Eden and how much it pained her to even share garbage bags. She did provide me with a sleeping bag, but I doubt her kindness extends to a third roommate. Then I think of Ivy, and how she showed me just how easy it is to be super-kind, then super-silent, in just five hours.

"Thanks, but I'll be fine."

Ivy hesitates. When I don't show any indication of wavering, she steps aside.

"I hope we can be friends," she says.

I stop with my hand on the door. "I think we will be." I muster up a smile to toss over my shoulder. "Just give me the chance to survive twenty-four hours."

Ivy's answering smile is sad and hopeful, but it doesn't distract from the fear in her eyes before the door swings shut behind me.

11

The back walkway Eden suggested is better titled the *hidden* walkway.

Richardson Place is at the bottom of Briarcliff's sprawling hill, flush against the trees lining Briarcliff's property. The paved stones cut through a miniature forest as I trek along, aiming for the main building at the top and hoping I don't get eaten by a wolf.

Real or fake.

The crashing waves nearby are extra loud. I keep on the pavement, since I'm so unfamiliar with the layout and worried about wandering off track and ending at the bottom of an unexpected cliff. I'm one of those people who goes blind when night falls.

Electric streetlamps are scattered throughout, so I do have some light as my footsteps pad silently forward. I keep my eyes straight ahead, ignoring the random snaps of twigs and rustle of leaves.

It's not a wolf. It's not a bad man. It's just the wind.

Saliva builds in my mouth, and I swallow, the trash bags making squishing sounds against my back as they swing with my movements.

I'm lulled into a hypnotic pace and warm up to the sounds of the forest. I've almost convinced myself the echoing snaps and crackles and pops aren't a threat and just the former mascots of puffed rice cereal screwing with me like little elves.

It's why when I hear a whisper, I halt.

I set my jaw, searching the area with my feeble vision, positive I heard a human voice.

Over here.

My head snaps in the direction of the hushed speech. It's to the right, where the forest becomes deeper and the cliffs get closer.

Are they calling to me?

If so, are they living under a rock? I'm not about to follow some faceless asshole into the woods after having trash slung at me all afternoon.

Something flits across my vision, and I'm careful not to yelp.

It was a person, running, with something flowing behind them.

Oh, fuck. It's another prank.

I readjust my bags and start running, bending my head to go faster—I'd rather run into a tree than face whatever they have planned next.

As I run, panting and following the curves of the walkway, spurts of fire draw my attention, flickering higher the closer I get.

I slow to a hesitant jog, then to a creep, when I realize my poor vision's brought me deeper into the woods instead of its fringes. The forest bed is soft, fallen leaves and soil obscuring my sounds. I squint at the little fires ahead, formed into a circle with hands cupping their stems. Faces are obscured by shadows layered with the dark of night. I have no sense of whether they're twisted in glee or tense with wait as their prey—i.e., me—scampers around the edges.

Slowly, I set the two bags on the ground. Then I move, bending low, into a denser thicket of trees.

These people are in cloaks. Like, Red Riding Hood cloaks with the hoods pulled up and their voices murmuring in a low chant as they surround a bonfire.

I tilt my ear so I can hear better.

"*Altum volare in tenebris, altum volare in tenebris, altum volare in tenebris...*"

What the *what*?

I study harder, blinking just in case I'm seeing things, but the spooky imagery doesn't go away.

Some cloaks are black. Others are a color I can't tell in the firelight. Gold? White? Come to think of it, the black could be a dark purple or deep blue...

Ugh. Colors don't matter. What's important is that I get the hell out of here as fast as my sneakered feet can carry me.

I straighten to escape at a low run, but of course, hook my toe on an exposed root and faceplant into damp leaves.

Excellent, Callie. Now you can add rotting leaves to your rotten day.

I land with a muffled "*oof*," but stay on the ground, refusing to move until I'm sure I haven't been heard.

The chanting stops.

Crap.

"Rise," a voice booms, and I cower against the decaying leaves until my brain logic figures out it's not me he's screaming at.

"And honor," the voice continues. I keep still, one half of my face pressed against the slimy, rotting fronds. The sharp, distinct smell of soil, ripped leaves and damp wood makes me want to sneeze. I pray no creepy crawlies come along to add to this nightmare.

"You have been chosen. Our two chapters are gathered here for the inaugural initiation," the low, male voice says, "as extended by exclusive invite. Show your papers, and let the fire eat the truth."

I hear the spit and crackle of fire as something's thrown in.

"Now, lower your torches and let the fire of ambition grow."

A waft of heat hits my exposed skin.

"Are we ready for this year?" the voice asks.

"Yes," come a chorus of voices, both male and female. "We are ready. We await."

"Then let the sacrifice begin..."

Oh, man. I don't want to be present when whatever's being sacrificed shows up.

I scoot onto my elbows and knees, crawling through the underbrush as chanting begins anew. I jam my fingers on exposed roots, and my knees catch on some overturned stones as I move, but the pain doesn't hit my throat until I'm back on paved ground and I wheeze out a relieved breath.

Pushing upright, I grab my bags and run.

I'm in full-on sprinting mode, even though I've never joined a track and field team in my life, bags swinging as my arms pump side-to-side.

Unfortunately, my untrained gait, coupled with my poor night-vision, makes me plow into a firm, insanely hard, wall of a person.

"Ack—" I gasp, tripping back and landing on my butt.

A cloaked form stands above me, his face overcast by the large hood, but I'm sensing his study of me. I say it's a guy, since I did not fracture my face on soft boobs.

"I—sorry," I blurt. The form doesn't move. "I'm just—I'm going. Gone. I'm gone."

I right myself, with no help from this immovable figure, lift my bags, and skirt around him.

I don't look back to see if he's following me, and instead half-limp, half-walk the rest of the pathway and up to the academy.

Using the side door Ivy showed me earlier, I stumble in, dropping the bags and then spreading a hand across my chest as I pant.

I couldn't tell who was behind the hood, but he certainly saw me. I wonder how much time I have until he tells his friends and they come back to toss me into their cauldron.

What did I just see? Devil worship?

I wouldn't put it past the demons wearing human skin in this school to engage in nightly rites and rituals. Piper is probably in there somewhere.

Stairs to the Wolf's Den loom before me, its structure cast in the dim glow provided by the stained-glass windows, and I trod over, dragging my bags along. The balcony will be the safest place tonight. I can sleep, then live to fight tomorrow.

Once up top, I scope the loft-like space for a place to hunker down. Two couches are angled in the center, with a low table in the middle. The skeletal shapes of high-top tables perch against the back wall. There's a coffee cart, too, with an emptied-out pastry station neighboring it.

Sighing, I search through my belongings until I find my makeup bag, dry from being hosed down. I had to pick through a profuse amount of garbage to locate what was inside, but I ended up finding most of it. I tear at a pack of travel wipes and swipe the fragrant, damp cloth around my face to remove the rest of the Briarcliff woods from my cheeks.

In the silent gloom, I unroll Eden's sleeping bag (smelling suspiciously of weed) onto the couch and burrow in, bone heavy and tired.

My mind isn't ready to shut down. Instead, I lift my phone, bathed in its blue light as I scroll through Instagram, a place where I never post but always creep.

As soon as I tap on the app, my notifications *ping*. I've been tagged multiple times—bordering on over a hundred—and my thumb hovers over the heart icon. Most of me knows what I'll find, and I'm right.

Hashtag after hashtag of #trashbitch and #trashbitchgohome is tagged to my handle. I don't look at the images.

That's not why I'm creeping, anyway. I planned to scroll

through the posts of my friends back home and shift my mindset toward what kinship feels like instead of whatever I just witnessed in the forest. Except ... they're not my friends anymore. When my mom died, I'd become a different person, and Sylvie and Matt had difficulty keeping up. Sylvie especially. After what happened during our last night together, their parents got involved, and I'm lucky Sylvie's mom and dad didn't press charges.

I'm on Sylvie's account, and I suck in a breath when her pictures load. She's unblocked me.

I don't hold onto that hope for more than a second. Our friendship is over, but I'm thankful I can see slices of her life, and that she's okay. Her summer consisted of a greater number of pictures of her and Matt. Arms slung around their shoulders, linking hands in front of the Coney Island Ferris Wheel, sharing a Salty Pimp from the Big Gay Ice Cream shop ... and kissing. Lots of tongue action boomerangs.

I lower my phone until it's flat against my chest and stare at the ceiling until the sad smile drains from my lips, and I feel nothing. A fan *whirrs* its blades above.

The soft sound lulls me into a doze, and I close my eyes, trying hard to fall sleep, but familiar bodies keep forming, using the backs of my eyelids to come alive.

They're not my old friends. They wear hoods and move in a circle around a large fire.

Then, one turns.

He steps closer, and my heart kicks into an erratic beat.

His cloak is velvety soft and shifting with his long strides, changing shades in the moonlight, until he lifts it and settles the heavy fabric over my face.

And I go blind. All I see is darkness, black as a raven's feathers.

12

The pungent scent of coffee hits my nostrils, and I scrunch my nose, snorting at the smell.

I mumble, turn over, and plant my face straight into fabric that rubs the wrong way against my skin.

It's velvet. A cloak. *No*, my waking brain tells my racing heart. *Suede.*

I pry one eye open and cautiously twist until I'm not facing the back of the couch. Then, in an instant, the when, where, and how, all hit me.

I bolt upright.

"Shit, where's my phone?"

I'd set an alarm before falling asleep so this wouldn't happen. I frantically search around, within the folds my sleeping bag, in the cracks of the couch—

Someone chuckles.

Someone else clucks their tongue. "Looks like a bag lady broke in and tried to sleep it off. Fuck, she stinks."

I hold my breath and peer through the strands of my hair, noting the two figures idling near the balcony's overhang.

"Your phone's on the coffee table," one says.

I tuck my hair behind my ears. As soon as it's clear who's speaking, I sneer, then snatch my phone off the table and frantically tap against the screen as I register the time.

Son of a bitch.

No wonder I never heard my alarm. It's been turned off.

The horror must read in my expression, because the second voice laughs.

"Why the hell did you do this?" I ask Chase, ignoring the laughter of his friend, who I think is the one named Tempest.

Tempest's hair is as dark as the promise of his name, cut at an angled chop where some strands fall across his brow. His eyes are a bright green and at odds with his thin, jaded lips. He's laughing, but I'm certain his happiness will never match the natural spark in his irises.

"I believe you're on my turf, therefore, I can do what I want," Chase answers. He leans back on his elbows, resting against the railing behind him, exactly like the playground bully I predicted he'd be.

I have the vapid wish for the wood to buckle. Chase is too handsome for 7:30 in the morning, showered and groomed. His scent cuts through the freshly ground coffee beans in the air, a freshwater mix of pine and sage.

Like he's been tramping through the woods, my mind whispers.

"What, destroying my furniture wasn't enough?" I ask. "Soiling my clothes and trashing my uniform didn't give you the jollies you were searching for?" I throw off the sleeping bag and shift until my feet touch the floor. "Now you make me late for class, too?"

I swipe my make-up bag off the coffee table and scrounge through it, finding a compact. Flipping it, I check to see that these twerps didn't draw a Sharpie penis on my face while I was sleeping.

"I'm not the one who chose to trespass up here," he responds, the brown of his eyes shining amber from the stained-glass sun above.

"Then why are *you* up here? The both of you."

Chase pushes off the banister. "We've acquired the privilege."

"Damn it," I mutter, deciding to ignore the boys. I'm late, my uniform is somewhere and wrinkled, and I was hoping to get up at five so I could secretly use the gym showers and get ready. Now, I'll be lucky if I make it to class with my hair brushed.

In an effort to do that much, I start packing up my things.

"Are we too much?" Chase mocks. "Is your phone charged enough to call Daddy to come save you?"

I glance up from tossing my sleeping bag and necessities in a garbage bag. "Have you not left yet?"

"She has a point," Tempest adds, retaining his spot near the railing. He lifts his chin, as if to smell the air around him. "I thought we came to take her garbage and put it out in the rain to putrefy further. If we're not doing that, why are we here?"

I glare at him while pulling my bags full of clothes closer. "I don't have time for this. Or you."

"We make the time, not you," Chase corrects. "And if your aim is to make it to history before the bell, you'd better scoot that ass of yours out of here."

"Yeah, so we can get our caffeine buzz without a homeless chick shaking her cup for change," Tempest adds.

"You've used that insult twice in ten minutes," I snap. "I guess Briarcliff's best and brightest requirements don't include creativity."

"I don't need creativity to make you cry, Trash Bitch." Tempest cocks a brow. "Today's going to be so fun for you."

"Run along, Calla Lily," Chase adds, while he idly pours himself a cup of coffee.

I'm ready to oblige. It's unnerving they've been up here long enough to start a brew, fuck with my phone, and watch me while I slept.

And it's incredibly disconcerting to hear Chase say my full name. Where did he get that tidbit of trivia? Piper?

"Gladly," I say. "But first…" I storm over to the coffee cart and shove in front of Chase. He responds to the contact with a low chuckle.

I refuse to back down, so I let him press up against me—so hard, so firm, so *male*—as I pour the carafe into a to-go cup, dump in some cream, find a lid, then twist out of his unsettling hold.

When I turn, my front molds with his, the bumps and ridges of his muscular chest pressing against my chest.

His gaze drops, and I pretend I don't feel the length of him. Or how it's made my lower half stir with awareness.

There is not one soft spot on this guy.

My breathing quickens, but my stare holds steady, exuding an arrogance I don't feel. There are places—the wicked ones, the ones that delight in sinful pleasure—on my body that come alive with his presence, sending their request for more by setting off electric waves across my skin, goosepimpling my flesh.

Chase's pupils dilate, but his lips cut through the passion, cold as a steel knife. He says, "The coffee up here is for members only."

I point to my two bags, now containing my entire sorry life at this school. "Consider it an *earned* privilege. Now, if you'll excuse me."

Chase makes a low rumble in his throat but stands aside. He's backed me up against a wall, and it's cold where his body once was.

"It'd be in your best interest to run, not walk," he says. "Because once I give the go-ahead, the Den'll be crowded within minutes. Wouldn't want you caught with your garbage bags hanging out."

He glances down at my chest, appraising, before drifting over to Tempest.

My throat's tight, and I exhale to loosen the muscles.

"See ya, trash possum," Tempest says as I hitch both my bags over one shoulder, clutch my coffee, and head toward the stairs. He's munching on a cinnamon roll that I swear he must've pulled from his pocket, but it smells *divine*.

Chase must hear my stomach rumble, because he says as I hit the staircase, "Breakfast is over. Classes start in twenty minutes."

"I'm aware," I say, and start my descent.

"Piper keeps granola bars in the shared kitchen cabinet."

I pause. Chase sips his coffee with an expression that is anything but innocent.

"Why would I care about that?" I ask.

"Come on, little possum. You can't scurry around forever. Go to your room." Chase follows up with a feral smile. "Don't be afraid. Piper's not there. She's finishing up training at the boathouse."

"I'm not scared of her. Or you."

It's infuriating, but Chase is right. I can't sleep in the Wolf's Den forever now that *he* knows I'm here.

My feet pound down the stairs, but just as I break through into the foyer, Chase leans over the railing and calls, "Be glad I got to you first, new girl. I'm the only nice face you'll see today."

"I'm doomed," I mutter, and dash through a smattering of students out front, fat raindrops splattering both the plastic and my head.

13

I stroll through the public areas of Thorne House with my damp head held high, only a hundred snickers and whispered *trash bitch* insults trailing behind. No one offers to help.

A girl is at the front desk area, and she doesn't question me when I tell her my name and that I need a key to my room.

She hands it over without comment, but I don't miss the rush to her phone as soon as I head to the elevators and her snide glances at me as she texts.

Great. Trash Bitch lives in infamy.

My lips flutter with my exhale as I ascend to the third floor, and once the doors slide apart, I don't dawdle.

The key works on the first try, and I step inside with dread stretching its wings inside my chest, but I won't let them release to full mast until I know what lies in wait.

Lucky for me, it's blissful silence.

Chase was telling the truth. Piper isn't here, though she's left a heavy cloud of gardenia perfume (otherwise known as overly sweet entitlement) in her wake.

To be safe, I call, "Piper?" but the doorknob to her room doesn't move. Nor do I hear any scuffing sounds behind it.

Good.

I turn into my room, discarding my empty coffee cup in the kitchen bin along the way.

During my entire walk in the misting rain, I mulled over how I was going to dress for class, when despite multiple attempts at washing and ironing yesterday, I couldn't get my uniform to the pristine condition it once was, or for it to stop smelling like raccoon piss.

God, I'm so screwed.

My wet bags land on the floorboards of my room with a thud. On a positive note, the plastic is waterproof, and my clothes missed a second fate. I stare down at them, preparing myself for a thorough, desperate search, when—

Holy shit.

My attention centers on my bedroom, and I'm either wishing so hard that I'm hallucinating, or my room is fully furnished.

My desk has drawers. My nightstand has drawers. My dresser has drawers! I touch it all, the wood grain running up against the pads of my fingers as I glide them over the surfaces.

A thorough inspection confirms my suspicions—these aren't the drawers Ivy and I spent over an hour washing yesterday. They're too flawless, too unstained to have come from the dump. After receiving such a heavy dose of water, they'd be warped and hard to fit into their shelving, but these open and shut with ease, the movement bringing with it the sharp scent of freshly sanded wood.

Twirling, I move to my mattress, as white as the day it was wrapped up at the factory.

It can't be. None of this is mine. I haven't had the chance to report the missing furniture to Marron. There's no way the faculty could've known.

"What the..." I scan my surroundings, half-expecting Piper in full Briarcliff attire to leap from my closet and launch red paint on everything while she cackles.

Yet, the room is silent.

"Snap out of it, Callie," I whisper to myself. "You can solve this shit later. Get to class."

As I'm bending to sort through my belongings, something swinging on a hanger catches my eye through the crack of my closet door.

There it is, I think grimly. *The hidden snake.*

I pad over anyway and open the door further. Then step back in surprise.

A pressed uniform hangs from the railing, including a white button-down, maroon cardigan, black blazer, and a tri-color plaid skirt. White knee socks are thrown over the hanger, and my fingers slowly sift against the cashmere and cotton fabrics.

I lift the hanger, inspecting the uniform closely for hidden traps, but find nothing until I flip it around. I almost drop the clothes to the floor, but the instinctual clench of my grip prevents the immaculate outfit from puddling to the ground.

"Are you serious...?" I murmur, pulling the uniform closer.

A long-stemmed rose, its petals stained with black ink, is pinned between the shoulders of the blazer, tied with a golden ribbon.

※

No note.

Just a goddamned rose.

What am I supposed to do with that? Other than wear this uniform—which fits me perfectly, by the way—instead of the wrinkled and stained one on my first day of school?

There's no time to determine whether this is Piper's next curse in petaled disguise, or if this flower has something to do with the cloaks of last night.

I don't want to think about that last part, though. I did *not* attract the attention of weird ritualists in the deep reaches of the Briarcliff woods. Nuh-*uh*.

Before scampering out of my room, I throw the textbooks I'll need into my backpack, along with my laptop that survived the Dumpster delegation because it was nestled comfortably in my duffel I carried yesterday. Since phones aren't allowed in classrooms, I leave mine on my bed.

My wet hair is combed and thrown back in a ponytail, I've applied some cheek and lip stain and a coat of mascara, and my perfume of choice is *eau de raindrops*, because that's all I have time for before shutting my door—and locking it.

A benefit to these keycards is that they're specific to your identity. I can only lock and unlock my room, not Piper's, and vice versa, yet we can both access the front door to our apartment.

I have to admit, the added level of security against Piper is assuring, and I focus on that barricade instead of wondering how someone else redecorated my room last night.

It's with a full sprint under an umbrella (I need to send Lynda a thank-you text; she thought of everything when ejecting me from Meyer House) that I make it to the Briarcliff building, the clocktower tolling the start of class. I'm proud to only have gotten lost on the ground floor twice. I'm not counting the third time when I caved and asked a passing student where History with Dr. Luke was.

"That way," he said, pointing to the East Wing, and I fly past closed classroom doors until I find Classroom 110.

I stop in front of the door, staring at the frosted glass for a full minute before I twist the doorknob.

"—so you'll come to appreciate the importance of our roots before extending to the U.S. as a whole—Ah. I see we have a straggler."

"S-sorry," I say, clutching my backpack's strap hanging off one of my shoulders. "I got lost."

What feels like a stadium's worth of eyeballs shift in my direction, but I keep my focus on the teacher, Dr. Luke, and not on the growing grins and whispers spreading like a virus from the desks.

"You must be Miss Ryan," Dr. Luke says. He's perched on the front of his desk in slacks and a white button-down, with his blazer thrown over his chair.

What draws me to him is that he's young, but not trying to be hip. Shaggy caramel hair partially obscures his light eyes, and he sports a bit of scruff on his sun-aged face. He's handsome, disarmingly so, in that California surfer-by-morning, teacher-by-afternoon kind of way. I'm beginning to wonder if there's something in the water here that makes people at Briarcliff either stunningly gorgeous, or sinfully hot.

"Try not to make this a regular thing," Dr. Luke says, then gestures to the class. "Take a seat."

"Yes, sir," I say, and for some reason, that causes a wave of giggles.

Dr. Luke smiles. "You'll come to learn I'm not like the professors here. You don't need to call me 'sir' or stand when I walk into the classroom. Okay, history buffs." Dr. Luke claps his hands. "Let's get back to it. Briarcliff Academy has its own deliciously evil past..."

Thoroughly dismissed, I pick my way through the closest line of desks, scanning for an available seat. I briefly land on Piper two rows in, then glance away. It's when I do that I almost trip over a set of legs splayed out in the aisle.

I stop before I stumble, and I wait for the feet to move and let me by.

They don't.

They're crossed at the ankle, and they're comfortable staying where they are.

I sigh. Chase is attached to these damn feet, his arms crossed, and he arches his brows over his heavy lids, daring me to say something.

Move, I mouth, as Dr. Luke drones on behind me.

A grin drifts across his face. His lips part. *Nope.*

Fine. I step over his obnoxious kneecaps and continue down my path, working hard to ignore the muffled *trash bitch*, *possum breath*, and *rabies and scabies* comments. I reach an empty seat and collapse into it.

"You okay there, Miss Ryan?"

I nod without looking up.

"You sure?" Dr. Luke eyeballs the students in my immediate periphery. "Because I swear I heard detention-worthy slang uttered in this vicinity."

I resist, vehemently shaking my head. Chase, Tempest, and James surround me on one side, with Piper and her friends manning the opposite.

My first day of school already includes my first detention with Piper. I'd prefer that *none* of these people join us.

"All good," I say to Dr. Luke with too much enthusiasm.

"If you insist," he says. "But if I hear one more peep outta you peckers, instant lunch detention. I'll even add an additional two-thousand-word essay as a bonus, due at the end of the day. Got it?"

There's mumbled assent at Dr. Luke's threat. Satisfied, he goes back to his lecture, but as soon as his attention's away, acerbic glares turn in my direction.

All except for Chase. He maintains deep interest in what Dr. Luke has to say and traces his thumb along his jaw in thought.

I follow the trail over his sharp, clean curves, his thumb hitting his full lips and staying there. I swallow, thinking of how it would've been to wake up in the Wolf's Den to that thumb tracing my face, then landing on my lips.

Someone snorts.

I blink, then put my head down and take out my textbook, pretending like I didn't just ogle Chase Stone in plain sight.

I might as well just gift Piper a box of ammo to fill her pariah pellet gun.

But my attention won't stay on blocks of paragraphs. I'm all too aware of the shifting bodies and angled profiles of my fellow classmates, and whether or not they're for me or against me. I've been here less than a day, and already I feel like Piper's condemned my two semesters into loser status. If I wanted to make more than one friend during my stay, I'm screwed.

In search of a friendly face, I look for Ivy's with a nervous, agitated sweep. Being thrown into a full class of jerks and jerk-followers has made me rethink the whole being strong and leaving Ivy behind angle I had going on yesterday.

I don't find her, and my stomach sinks.

"Briarcliff has skeletons I want each of you to unearth," Dr. Luke continues. I start listening. "You were divided into groups of three and given a founder to study and write an essay on in hopes that the twenty-one of you will leave here with some local history under your belts. I know, I know, it's not the epic battle of the Civil War or the grotesque effects of the Spanish Flu, but let's see if I can't hold your interest with some small-town lore, hmm? Ah. Wait a sec. There's now twenty-*two* of you. Hello again, Miss Ryan."

Dr. Luke's focus is nothing but friendly, so I tentatively smile in response.

"Therein lies a problem." Dr. Luke raises his finger. "Any mathletes want to take a shot on what that is?"

"Sure, Dr. Luke," a low voice purrs. "Twenty-two doesn't make for even threes."

"And they say you get by on looks alone, Mr. Stone," Dr. Luke says. "Well done."

The skin under Chase's eye tics dangerously at the veiled insult, and this time, my smile is true.

"What a pickle!" Dr. Luke proclaims, and he lifts his tablet from the desk. "I assigned this topic yesterday, so breaking up a triangle shouldn't be a problem. Miss Harrington."

My stomach dips. Scratch that—my stomach finds the cliff called Fuckboys' Leap and throws itself off it.

"You can work with Miss Ryan," Dr. Luke says.

Piper's shoulders stiffen into sharp angles. "You can't possibly want me to work with her."

"Oh, but I possibly do." Dr. Luke's eyes twinkle, like he knows the exact kind of fuckery he's creating. "You're roommates. You're in the best position to explain the assignment to her as well as my best practices. And hey," Dr. Luke includes me, "you may even let Miss Ryan in on the rules all her professors want her to aspire to. First and foremost: being on time."

I give a stiff nod. I have trouble speaking when in the spotlight. Namely, Chase's, and how I can't shake the sensation that he's memorizing my face, searching for any flinch of weakness.

I am strong. I am my mother's child.

I sit straighter in my seat.

"Can't you divide the entire class into pairs?" Piper asks. She won't give up. "There's an even number now, and—"

"Sadly, that will not do," Dr. Luke says, his expression grave.

"Why not?"

"Uh, because that gives me more papers to grade." Dr. Luke tosses his tablet back on the desk. "The pairing's done, Miss Harrington. As you cool kids say, deal with it. Moving on."

Dr. Luke begins his lecture, and heads turn to him. I relax in my seat, content to get through the rest of class with as little a peep as possible.

Piper's eyes slide over to mine, turning into slits the instant she hooks my attention.

She mouths the word, *trash*, and I commit further into pretending she doesn't exist, well aware that throwing food in my face was a mere introduction to our newfound enemy status.

14

*T*hank God the rest of my morning classes don't contain Piper or Chase. English literature even manages to catch my attention for the entire period. So much so, that I stop thinking about either of them for the whole hour.

When the clocktower tolls, I collect my things off my desk and dump them in my backpack. I'm not looking forward to lunch, but I suppose I chose my destiny when I shoved Piper into a dining hall table yesterday.

I wish I'd pushed harder. Then, maybe, detention would've been worth it despite how unfair it feels.

Trudging out of English, I study the Briarcliff brochure, its corners already becoming worn. It's the only map I've found of the school grounds, discovered at the bottom reaches of my backpack where I'd carelessly shoved it before leaving Dad and Lynda. Since my roommate and student guide—I use both terms loosely—is nowhere in sight, I'm trying my damnedest not to be late by using it as a directory.

"Callie. Hey."

I glance up from the brochure, my shoulder brushing against the stone wall as I find my balance. I'd been sticking to the edges of the hallway, so I don't bash into anyone while I figure out where the hell I'm going.

Ivy stops in front of me, clutching textbooks to her chest.

"Hi," I say, carefulness lacing my tone.

"So ... how's your day?"

I fold the brochure. "Shitty."

Ivy winces, and guilt creeps its way into my throat. I add in a softer tone, "I'm surviving."

"I didn't see you at the night regatta yesterday," Ivy says, perking up.

"I ... don't understand the words coming out of your mouth."

"Oh." Ivy laughs. "Sometimes I forget that people have lives outside of this school. Outside of *crew*."

"Uh-huh." I'm still not getting it.

"Briarcliff lives for its athletes, the rowing team especially," Ivy explains. "Even though it's off-season, the boys' and girls' teams still train stupid-hard. The Night Ride is the anticipated opening head race. It kicks off the school year in the manmade lake, down through the south woods. The guys' and girls' eights are what everybody wants to see."

I purse my lips and nod. "I think I understood most of that."

"You didn't go," Ivy surmises. "I mean, I understand why, but it's too bad." A shy smile crosses Ivy's face. "You could've seen me whoop Chase's ass."

I give her an answering grin. "What's more badass? That you're on the rowing team, or that you kicked Chase where it hurts?"

"Well, okay. Maybe I didn't hurt him *too* much." Ivy grimaces. "He's good. And super strong."

I don't doubt it. But I say to her sincerely, "I'm sorry I missed it. You row in this eight that you speak of?"

Ivy nods. "Eight girls in a boat. One coxswain to direct us. You should come to practice. You're tall. Somewhat graceful." Ivy's stare rakes me from head to toe. "I bet you could make the team."

A peal of laughter escapes me. "No, thanks. I'm not a sports person."

"But that's the best part! It's a team vibe. If you fail or suck or whatever, the rest of us lift you up. It's amazing. I think you might like it, too."

"I, uh, I can't."

"Look, I know yesterday sucked." God, Ivy's relentless. "But I'd love the chance to show you the sweeter sides of Briarcliff. You know, the parts without mean rich kids and terrible roommates."

"Ivy, I can't."

"The good exists, I promise. If you open up to it, it starts with crew."

"I'm sorry, but it's just not for me."

"You won't even try? Callie—"

"Ivy, no."

"But—"

"I can't swim!" I yell, then lower my voice as soon as I attract the attention of passing students. "So, thank you, but no."

Ivy's staring at me like I've just been gang-banged by a passing alien ship. "You ... can't swim?"

I sigh. "I grew up in Manhattan. There aren't a lot of pools around, not where I lived. Never mind manmade lakes in our backyard. Hell, I can't even ride a bike."

"You *can't ride a bike?*"

"Would you stop?" I smack her in the arm. "You're the one friendly face I have here. Don't ruin it by judging my lack of a suburban childhood."

"Shoot. I'm sorry." Ivy shakes herself out of it. "I'm the last person who should be judging. My parents are Danish and like to watch me hitting the cat out of the barrel at Fastelavn."

I can't help but laugh with her. "All right, a compromise. I'll be at the next practice and take a look at you slicing waves through the water so long as you don't ask me to join crew again."

Ivy bats her eyes at me like I'm the cutest thing, then loops an arm through mine.

"Slicing waves ... that's not a crew term, is it," I say.

"Not even kinda." We settle into a comfortable walk. "Thank you for forgiving me."

She says it so faintly, I have trouble catching it. Once I do, she changes the subject.

"Where are you headed?" she asks. "I promise I'm way better than an outdated flyer."

"Shit!" I screech to a halt in the foyer. "Detention!"

※

"I see you've yet to embrace the term *prompt*," Dr. Luke says as I knock on today's assigned detention classroom.

I grimace. "I'm—"

"Sorry. I'm well aware."

Dr. Luke is propped in a chair with his feet crossed on top of the teacher's desk, a paperback spread open on his lap.

Piper's seated in front of him, reading a textbook by standing it vertically on the desk and hunching behind it.

We're the only two students here.

"Listen, being the new kid sucks," Dr. Luke says. "Winning over your classmates is hard. Try not to piss off your professors, too, all right?"

Nodding, I step inside. I'm all for friendly teachers, but it's ultra-weird when that teacher is ridiculously hot and close enough to my age that I want him to like me.

"I drew the short straw and got stuck with detention duty all week," he adds as I plop myself into a front-facing desk—the farthest one from Piper. "Take it from me. Don't be the short straw."

I nod again, avoiding his assessment by pulling out my English homework. From my vantage point, I notice that Piper's using the textbook as a wall to hide the smuggled phone she's texting on.

"Normally, this is a silent hour where you contemplate all the wrongs you've done to Briarcliff Academy," Dr. Luke says as I straighten. "But, since it's just the two of you, and I'm your detention proctor, why don't you guys start the history assignment? You have the added bonus of having me all to yourselves to answer any questions that might pop up."

"Can't," Piper says without looking up. Her thumbs are nothing but a blur over her phone.

Amazing. It's hard to believe Piper's so unaffected by Dr. Luke's looks *and* his unintended proposition of having him all to ourselves. Is that what it's like when you're that pretty? To have the problem of so many prospects that even teachers with movie-star jawlines don't keep your attention?

You dummy. She doesn't need to fantasize about Dr. Luke. She already has a god under her hands. She's had Chase.

The thought of Chase sprawled against her bed sheets, bare-chested and groaning under Piper's hands as they scrape down his pecs and abs, has me feeling uncomfortably bothered.

I clear my throat, forcing myself to think about Jane Austen.

"I have science homework," Piper says.

"Uh-huh. And what type of science would that be, Miss Harrington?" Dr. Luke asks.

"Chemistry."

"Then why do you have your math book open? Are the strange symbols helping you with new emojis to text your friends?"

My eyes widen at his flippant candor. Piper glares at Dr. Luke over the edge of her text. The phone drops to her desk with an obvious and pissed off clatter. She doesn't break eye contact with him when she does it.

"I could confiscate that, you know," Dr. Luke says.

"I dare you," Piper says with a devilish grin.

"Don't tempt me, Miss Harrington."

Their glares clash across the room. I should creep out of here and leave them to it. But Piper is the first to interrupt their silent war. She stands.

"Dr. Luke." She smiles coyly. "You and I both know my parents pay Headmaster Marron *way* too much money to be associated with such silly drama like lunchroom misunderstandings. Callie and I both consider it ridiculous we're even here. We made up, like, yesterday."

I may be mute for the moment, but I'm not dumb. I purse my lips at Piper.

"Is that so?" Dr. Luke crosses his arms. "Miss Ryan? Care to add to this dog-and-pony show?"

"I'd like to focus on my studies," I say. If I side with Piper, I'm an idiot, but if I side with Dr. Luke, I'm a brownnoser. Either way, I can't win.

Piper makes a sound of disgust. "I'm telling you to leave, too, Callie."

"What about the all-important chemistry homework?" Dr. Luke asks Piper. As he says it, his expression goes back to what I've come to recognize as his usual sexy and relaxed self.

"Take it up with Headmaster Marron." Piper swings her bag over her shoulder and sashays to the door, her short skirt covering her ass-cheeks by half an inch.

"Do not push me, Miss Harrington," Dr. Luke warns, but Piper keeps on striding.

Dr. Luke stares at Piper while she leaves, but it's not at the hem of her flapping, plaid skirt, like most red-blooded males would. It's directed at her shoulder blades.

I'm not as focused, and I hitch in a breath when I notice who's waiting for Piper at the doorway.

Chase.

He's not watching Piper saunter over. His attention is on me, unwavering, cat-like, *wild*.

It's like he's the magnet, and I'm the poor piece of broken metal that can't move out of his pull. His utter charisma creeps into my bones, and his expressionless face seems to have memorized every twitch, every blink, every heartbeat I emit.

I feel, deep in my bones, I'm supposed to recognize what he's communicating, but for the life of me, I can't grasp his request.

It's unnerving and ... hot.

Boys don't pay attention to me like this. Normally, they don't look twice, unless you count my old friend Matt's and my brief, drunken sexual encounter when sneaking into his dad's closed bodega last Halloween.

That was amateur fumbling compared to Chase's scrutiny. I've never felt *hunted* like this, but it's not like the physical target Piper's painted on my back. I can't say I hate the way Chase's lips part every time he lays eyes on me.

Piper glances over as she passes by, and once she notices where my attention is, she slams the door behind her, ensuring Chase's hardened, calculating features disappear behind the frosted glass.

15

My final period is independent study, and I use those minutes to get caught up on the day I missed, hoping to get out in front of the lengthy assignments and high expectations of each professor I come across.

Once finished, I head back to my dorm for some quiet before dinner. My gut feeling is that Piper's not there. She's too popular and involved in sports to be in her room much, even if she's determined to claim both bedrooms as her own.

Ivy isn't at the front desk when I arrive, and I'm coming to learn that during school hours, it's usually a hired employee—or a nearby college student hoping to make some quick and easy cash while they keep our dorms "secure" and study their own shit.

On a quick flash of my keycard and ID that the girl doesn't lift her eyes from her textbook for, I enter the elevators and let out a *whoosh* of air.

I did it. I made it. First day of school: check. And there's not one deliberately inflicted stain on my uniform, either. Bonus!

My backpack is heavy on my shoulders as I traverse the hallway to my new home. I don't trust using the student lockers available at the school yet, since it's on a combination lock attached to the door, therefore, anyone fluent in bribery can access the code.

My card *beeps* its entry, and I step into the central room, the beige sectional calling my name. Now that the adrenaline from constantly looking over my shoulder has faded, my bedroom seems too far away. And ... the rose is still there, on my nightstand, asking its unanswerable questions as to how it got here.

My bag lands by my feet with a thump, and I fall onto the couch, arms spread, and face the ceiling. I let out a long sigh.

"Ugh. You're here."

I slow-blink at the ceiling, having no urge to allow my head to fall forward and find the statement's source.

"It's my space, too," I say to Piper.

I hear Piper walk into the room through the door I must've accidentally left open. Clangs and rattles sound out as she fishes through our kitchenette.

"I need coffee," she mumbles. I'm not about to believe she'll offer me any.

"Rough day?" I ask, my voice full of sarcasm.

"No more than usual," Piper says on a sigh.

My head lowers. Is Piper initiating small talk?

I decide to take advantage. "Hey, do you know anything about the new furniture in my room?"

"You have new furniture?" Piper asks it with the flat tone of someone who Does. Not. Care.

"Yeah ... someone came into our apartment and set it up. I figured you'd be aware of it."

"Nope." Piper flips her hair off her shoulder. "I just assumed you whined to your daddy about all the mean girls and got him to shell out for new shit."

The way she baby-voices the word *daddy* sets my teeth on edge. She can't know about my lack of one, or how the one I'm unrelated to couldn't wait to be rid of me and start fresh with a baby.

In response, I'm desperate to shout, *you are such an ignorant, superficial bitch.*

Yikes. Even the logical part of my brain is shocked at my vitriol.

Instead, I latch on to Piper's mistake. "I thought you said you didn't know about any delivery?"

Piper's expression freezes for a fraction of a second before she sculpts it back to her uppity mockery. "I don't. But if you're talking about a new bedroom set, then obviously someone had to pay for it. That someone must be your father. Or heck, your mom." Piper shrugs. "I'm all for boss bitches. Maybe she holds all the cash and your dad has to beg for it."

My teeth scrape together. "You are something else, you know that?"

The Nespresso machine gurgles to life behind Piper as she faces me.

"Are we gonna do this assignment, or what?" she asks.

I'm pissed, so I say nothing.

"It has to get done some time," she continues, "which means I have to acknowledge your existence. Can we get this part over with so I can get back to the people who matter?"

"Wow." I raise both brows. "What a proposition."

"They're your grades, too."

"True," I say, shaking off the clinging animosity. Piper has a point. "How do suggest we go about this?"

Piper pulls her fresh cup of coffee out from under the machine, grabs her backpack, then wanders over and perches on the other end of the couch.

A waft of cologne comes with her, a mix of cedar and an indeterminable musk. I squirm when I realize what it could mean.

Sex.

Recent sex.

Recent sex with Chase.

For a veritable host of reasons, I *do not* want that image in my head, but Chase comes uninvited anyway, sculpted torso and all.

I grunt and rub at my eyes, hoping to erase what my imagination's conjuring up in front of the one person I don't want to give any evidence to.

Piper stills beside me, and I open one eye to find her staring at me. "You look more and more like a possum each hour that goes by," she says in awe, shaking her head.

"I have a headache," I snap. "And I'm in total agreement with you—let's get this over with so we can retreat to our designated sides of the apartment."

"Yes. Let's," Piper says tartly, then pulls out her laptop and gestures at me to do the same.

Once she wakes up her computer, she adds, "I suggest we do our paper on Rose Briar, Thorne Briar's wife.

"Waaaaait a second, a couple named Rose and Thorne founded Briarcliff?"

Piper blinks at me. "Yeah, why?"

My mouth falls open. "Can you not picture the shipping that would happen in this day and age with those names?"

"Oh-em-god." Piper rolls her eyes. "You are *such* a sad weirdo. They're not the *only* founders. Thorne Briar had two brothers, Richard and Theodore, and they had wives, too. Sophia and Martha."

"Not nearly as shippable," I observe while bringing up a blank document on my screen.

"We can't write our paper on the popularity of combining couple names, Callie."

"I'm aware," I say. "Which is why I'm looking up Rose Briar."

"Don't bother, I already have a whole list of bookmarked pages I can email to you. When I was paired with Violet and Falyn, I suggested Rose Briar, but they wanted Thorne, since his photo is hot." Piper shrugs. "For an old, dead guy, he is kinda cute."

I say, straight-faced, "And *I'm* the weird possum in this scenario."

Piper shrugs me off. "I'll send you what I've found."

"While I wait with bated breath, why don't you give me the Cliff Note's version of why we should profile her."

At this, Piper turns to me, eyes gleaming. I'm so thrown by the sudden activity to her usually resting bitch face that I recoil.

"I'm *obsessed* with this story. Have you ever wanted to know why the cliff nearest to us is called Lover's Leap?" she asks.

"No...?"

I mean, I assume it's because of all the co-eds banging there, but since I'm including Piper in that assumption, I don't want to say it out loud and risk offending her. I still smell like red sauce from "stealing" her dorm room.

"Rose was full of telenovela issues," Piper continues. "She was always fragile, sick as a child, and you know what that's like in the nineteen-hundreds."

"Not personally."

"*Obviously*, Callie. Jesus. So, she marries Thorne young—I have a theory it's arranged. Then, they try to have a baby. Throughout her entire life, all Rose wanted was a child."

"Oh," I say, and I have the heavy feeling I know where this is going.

"They couldn't conceive. Not initially. Then, when she managed to get pregnant, she miscarried. Six times..." Piper pauses for dramatic effect, then adds, "some at a later term than others."

"That's terrible." I'm so appalled, I can't even type notes as Piper speaks.

"One stormy night—and I'm talking brutal, with rolling thunder and insane flooding and blinding rain, Rose disappears. It's said that she jumped off the cliff."

"God," I say.

Piper nods, then flaps her hand. "In between all that, Thorne was accused of having an affair and further disintegrating his wife's mental state, but let's focus on the mystery. On the leap, if you will. There's something so cruelly romantic about it, don't you think? Like, why jump? Why not take a vial of poison or slit your wrists? Personally, I think she was *pushed*."

"You are darker and more twisty than I ever gave you credit for," I say. "And I gave you a bunch of credit."

"Well, it's way better than a hot, dead guy who died of a boring heart attack, isn't it?"

"I guess," I say. And because I haven't researched any founders to argue my case with, and the paper's due too soon, I suppose this is what we'll write about. "Why do you think it was murder and not suicide?"

"I've been looking forward to this paper since, like, last week. I found these old notes in the library that point to a completely different story than Rose's official obituary. Don't you get it? There's a piece of history the school doesn't want revealed, and it's a big one. Briarcliff Academy is hiding a scandal, and out of every professor at this stuffy library of a prison, Dr. Luke is the most open to out-of-the-box theories. I'm practically guaranteeing us an A. He wants to unearth some skeletons? We have one. So, listen close. I think Rose might've had a—hang on."

A buzzing sounds from Piper's bag, and she pulls it out. Her lips pull up when she reads the notification, then she sucks her lower lip under her teeth as she responds.

"Unless you're video chatting," I say dryly, "No one can see your Come-Fuck-Me face but me."

Piper ignores my remark, finishes her text, then drops her phone in her bag. "I'll take the mystery and questions surrounding Rose's death. You can do Rose's biography."

Piper smacks her laptop closed and stands.

"Wait a sec," I say. "According to you, we're about to write a scandalous exposé on Briarcliff Academy, and you're giving me the vanilla?"

"Oh, like you care that much, Callie. Rose Briar's background will be a breeze compared to the rest of the student load you didn't have the summer to prep for, and I don't need some new girl screwing up my life *and* my GPA. Got it?"

She doesn't wait for my answer and strides toward her bedroom.

I don't stop her. Piper's given me the easiest and most boring part of the paper, yes, and while it won't get me five stars from Dr. Luke, it keeps me away from tragedy and gore, something that's all too real in my flashbacks.

I decide to let Piper walk out of neutral ground and into her territory, thinking she's won.

"Don't breathe in my direction for the next hour, okay?" Piper says. "I have to prepare. There's somewhere I need to be."

When Piper shuts her bedroom door, I fixate on the wood paneling, my grip tight on my laptop. Piper can dissect poor Rose's sordid past all she wants.

Especially if it distracts her enough to never get to mine.

16

Falling asleep in a foreign room is hard.

I would've thought bunking in the Wolf's Den was worse, but I slept better there. The echoing sounds and ricocheting creaks were easily attributed to the cavernous space, yet the enclosed air felt fresh, the ceilings untouchable, the walls less likely to shrink in.

This morning, I greet my ceiling, hands behind my head, wondering if I blinked enough times last night for it to be considered sleep.

I skipped dinner in the dining hall yesterday, opting to sneak one of Piper's granola bars instead. After, I had a quick shower and debated starting my research on Rose Briar but opted for bed. Unfortunately, I was too attuned to Piper's noises once she came back from wherever she went, showering, then padding around for what I supposed was a midnight snack. Each shuffle made me afraid of my knob turning, of Piper and her friends filling my doorway, armed with their next attack.

Then, as the night grew darker, I worried about the people in cloaks and whether they were students who saw me, and if they wanted to make me pay for witnessing such a secret ritual.

Rolling over, I check my phone for the time, noting the missed text messages from Ivy asking where I was at dinner last night.

My phone feels hot in my hand, but it's not real heat. It's more because it lay close to a mysterious, hidden object all night.

I'd shoved the rose in the drawer of my nightstand, having nowhere else to put it. I didn't want to display it in a makeshift vase, nor could I throw it out. It's shrouded in too much mystery to toss it aside without understanding its origins.

I'd rather leave it to wilt in the closed-off walls of my drawer than have it be discovered by Piper. Why I don't want her to see it, I'm not too sure, so I chock up the passing chills on my skin to not wanting Piper to ever see anything of mine.

I slip out of bed, fixing my wrinkled, oversized tee, then unlock my door with a yawn.

My yawn turns abruptly into a choke.

"Morning, sunshine."

Chase lounges on the couch, bare except for his briefs.

I cover my mouth, swallowing, but it does nothing to control where my eyes go, straight to his morning wood.

Which I swear he makes twitch once he notices my attention.

Chase smiles, his blond hair in disarray, one muscular arm behind his head, and glasses on his nose. He's holding a book in the other hand.

He's sexy. So, so sexy, and I hate it.

"What are you doing here?" I ask, hovering in my doorway.

Chase cocks his head. "Nice stems, Calla Lily."

My bare thighs instantly clench together. "This is a girls' only dorm," is the one stupid thing I think to say.

A low quiet laugh sounds in his throat. "I'm known to work around that rule."

And sleep with Piper.

The thought doesn't sit well, so I busy myself by veering into the kitchenette and making a cup of coffee. I don't cover myself, since he's already seen me half-naked and isn't overly concerned about the erection between us.

I am, though. Oh *boy*, I am, because he's ... large in that department.

"I'll take one, too, new girl."

"Whatever," I mumble, then make a mental note to leave campus at some point and buy groceries. "Since I'm your unofficial butler today, does your girlfriend want one, too? Where is she, by the way?"

Chase's answering smile is slow and indecent. "I take mine with a splash of milk. And Piper isn't my girlfriend, and she's in the shower."

I can't ignore the strange leap of faith in my stomach before I smash it with a stern, *what the fuck is wrong with you, Callie?*

It shouldn't matter whether or not Chase is taken, because I refuse to be a girl who's taken in by him.

But, now that he mentions it, I hear the soft spray of the shower behind the closed bathroom door. I'm unable to fight the instant questions my mind flings at me—is Chase's hair wet? His body damp with steam? Was he in there with her?

He's not close enough to tell.

I say, "Does your fuck buddy want a coffee, then? It is her stash, after all."

"Such crass language from such a delicate flower." Chase moves to a sit, setting the book beside him.

I'm drawn to the movement, but we both hear the faucet shut off. He lifts his hand to his chin, holding a finger to his mouth. "*Shh.*"

As if we're doing something wicked behind Piper's back.

I'm oddly disturbed and turned on by the thought of getting into trouble with him, so I turn my back to Chase and finish the coffees. I make one for Piper, too, since it is her stash and it looks better for me if I steal and give at the same time.

I say, as airily as I can, "I don't care what you're up to over there, or if Piper'll be mad at you for it."

Chase's stare holds steady, and even though I can't see him, my body responds to his focus, growing achy and nervous.

"Aren't you curious as to what I'm reading?" Chase says behind me.

My spoon clanks against a mug as I stir. "Your notes for the history project?"

Chase's laugh becomes a growl: predatory and deep. "You could say it's historic."

"Well, it's nothing of mine, so I can't say I'm intrigued."

Chase considers this. "Does that mean you might have something I want?"

He says it with such a sexy curvature to his words that my kneecaps melt before I can yell at them to keep stiff as soldiers. "It's a toss-up on what's worse. Piper's in-my-face despising, or this whole mystery façade you have going on that you think is so sexy."

It's so sexy.

"Aren't you curious about what I think of you?" he asks, but the question mark lags, like he already knows the answer.

"Pretty sure I'm already aware."

"I wonder how I'm progressing in your head," he muses as if I haven't spoken. "Piper puts on a show, you know, that's completely unlike who she truly is. We've known each other a long time. Her opinion of you isn't what you think."

Damn him for piquing my curiosity. I disguise it by handing him his coffee. "You're not getting anywhere near my head, and the private thoughts of Piper sound like my personal nightmare."

Chase's finger curls against mine on the coffee mug's handle, its stroke so light and delicate, my breath follows its touch. I can't seem to pull my grip away.

"There are some things between Piper and me that go unspoken," he says, his finger still curved against my skin. "And there are ... operations ... at this school you will never understand. I'm looking out for her."

At my frown, Chase adds, "And I can't seem but to want to look out for you, too. I wonder why that is?"

His index finger moves, tracing my knuckle. Once my eyes meet his, he bites his lower lip. My attention drifts to his perfect Cupid's bow.

"Fine." I pull my hand away, breaking his strange, hypnotic connection. "Have whatever kind of obsession you want. I'm gonna be late."

I turn before he can notice how pert my nipples are, how exposed and aching they've become without a bra to protect them.

"How's your new furniture?" Chase asks.

Whirling to face him, I say, "How did you—?"

The bathroom doorknob turns. "God, my head." Piper sniffs as she steps out with a towel wrapped around her torso. Upon closer inspection, her eyes are swollen and rimmed red—like she's been crying. "I need coff—Chase, what the hell? You're supposed to leave before the rest of the dorm wakes up!"

Chase shrugs, and with that movement, he deftly knocks back the full cup of hot coffee. He lowers the mug, entirely unaffected by the burning, caffeinated flames that must've flared up in his mouth. "Relax. No one will care."

"That's not the point," Piper says. Her eyes snap to mine. "What the hell are you standing there for? This is none of your damn business. Scurry back to your room, rodent."

Her crabbiness sets me straight. I take one final look at Chase, but he ignores my silent prompt to answer my previous question just as easily as he dismisses Piper's name-calling.

"Thanks for *looking out*," I say to him, then force a fake smile for the both of them. "Have a nice day, you two."

I ease into my room, but I'm saddled with more questions, hormones, and *want* than any woman should have to experience before 7 AM.

17

*B*y the time the clocktower tolls its bell for lunch, my shoulders ache so badly from carrying a backpack laden with books that I'm close to crawling the rest of the way to the dining hall.

I tread through the hallways, thinking, *This is it. This is the literal straw that broke Callie's back.*

And there's only one solution: use my assigned locker.

I'm no dummy. A student's locker is open season for their enemies, and there's no reason to think it'd be any different at a private school. Maybe it's worse here, since these kids have nothing to worry about outside of their cushy, padded future. It allows boredom to take over, and with monotony comes the devil's work.

I heft my bag higher on my shoulders and dip into the West Wing, happy that by my third day here, I've come to know the school grounds better.

Locker 4323 is harder to find than I imagined, as the long, dark mahogany lockers (yes—they're fancy wood), don't vertically line the hallway. Instead, they're formed into 3/4 squares, much like you see in fitness center changing rooms. I peer into five of them before finding mine, nestled in one corner.

On the outside, my locker appears unharmed and lemony fresh. Not one scratch mars any of these doors. I doubt I'm in the type of area where students tag lockers with spray paint. No, these kids are crafty.

I'd unintentionally memorized my locker combination when I received the Briarcliff Incoming Student Paperwork, having inherited a knack for numbers from my biological dad—according to my mom, since she insisted there was no way it could've come from her.

My lips pull down in a wry twist. To this day, I'm stuck on the fact that Mom never gave me a name for him, but she gave me his penchant for numbers.

"It's not worth it, Calla," Mom's ghostly voice whispers in my head. "It was a one-night-stand. I don't remember him, and he doesn't remember me. Heck, I never told him I was pregnant…"

Mom never hid the fact that nineteen-year-old Meredith Ryan didn't make the best decisions in life.

I shake off the sad reminder, spinning the combination. It unlocks with an innocent click.

These lockers are much wider and taller than public school issued tin cans, and the door is heavy with quality as I pull.

If you could see me now, Mom, with a walk-in closet for school-work storage—

I scream as a wet, furry *stink* engulfs me.

Passing students freeze at my distress. The ones at their lockers around me jump and scatter back.

"Get them off, get them *off!*" I yell, but no one wants to touch me.

Dancing backward, arms flailing, I fall into someone's chest before I stop writhing. Strong arms wrap tight, and as I struggle, I think I hear, "Calm down, Callie. You're fine."

I fight against the hold, freeing myself and spinning around.

"I'm not fine!" I shout. "Someone put fucking dead rats in my locker!"

I catch my breath and realize I'm shouting at Chase. He's the one who caught me. The one who held me and murmured words of comfort.

He also could be the one that did this. Or knows who's behind it.

Piper.

Chase's face hardens as he takes in the scene. He snaps his fingers at the dawdlers, some laughing, others retching in horror.

"Get the fuck out of here," he says, so faint there's no way they'd hear.

But they do. And like proper, terrified sycophants, they scatter to the wind upon Chase's command.

I trip back, my heel landing on something squishy, and I yelp.

"This is so overboard." I can't stop gasping. "You people are so fucked up in the head, you know that?"

And I was too lost in the haunting of my lifeless mother to remember any caution when unlocking my damned locker. A mind-fuck of its own accord.

"I didn't do this." Chase's voice doesn't rise in tone.

"I don't care," I seethe. "We both know who the mastermind is. I'm reporting her to Headmaster Marron so *she* can be the one to clean up these corpses—"

Chase hooks my arm in an iron grip as I attempt to pass. "Don't."

"Like I'm going to listen to you," I hiss. "This has gone too far. There's ... God ... there's like seven dead rats here."

"Ten," Chase says, his eyes flicking back and forth as he counts in his head.

I wrench my arm away. "Is that supposed to mean something?"

"Not to you," he murmurs, his attention still on the poor rodents on the ground.

"Piper needs to pay for this," I say.

He shakes his head. "It wasn't her."

"Oh, no?" I'm on a roll now. "Do you know anyone else who's chosen to make my life hell? Any other girl who's thrown trash over my head, destroyed my room, and given me the name of a rodent? Anyone? Come *on*, Chase, even you can't be this dense."

He crosses his arms, meeting my stare. "Piper wouldn't touch a rat, even if she had one of those grabber tools for old people."

I'm about to argue, but sadly, in my brief time of knowing Piper, I can believe that much. "Then who did?"

Chase's chin lifts, his intense scrutiny changing to one of languid survey. "Don't know. Don't care. All I can say is, it's a mistake to report her to Marron." Before he turns to leave, he says over his shoulder, "This is me looking out for you, by the way."

"Leaving me among a bunch of rat bodies?" I say. "Yeah, that sounds about right."

Chase's strides don't slow as I launch my retort. I don't expect them to.

Sighing, I turn back to my locker, pinching my nose at the smell. I use the back of one of my books to usher the rest of the tiny, mauled bodies out, and decide to leave my locker door open and empty so the stench can dissipate.

"Gross," I mutter to myself. "Gross, gross, gross."

Once the last of the furries leaves my space, something shadowed and bunched up in the bottom back corner catches my eye.

I lean back—not in—just in case it's alive. When I don't see additional movement, I tentatively reach in and bat it out, just in case it *really* is alive.

A rose falls onto the marbled flooring. Wilted white petals hang off a stem tied with an ebony bow.

"Miss Ryan?" a voice asks from behind, and I startle to attention.

Dr. Luke strides toward me, his stare roaming across the tiny, rotting bodies scattered on the floor.

I step forward. "It wasn't—" but can't finish my sentence. Something wet squelches under my sole, and I yelp before leaping into his arms while kicking the corpse away.

Dr. Luke's arms tighten to catch me, then release as soon as my forehead hits his chest.

"I'm—I'm sorry," I stutter, but he's shaking his head.

He says softly, "Don't bother with detention today. Go to the headmaster's office. *Now*."

I don't argue.

How can I, when there are a bunch of rotting rats at my feet?

I do as Dr. Luke asks, but not before grabbing the rose and hiding it my bag.

※

"If that heinous shrew wants me out of here," I say, slamming my lunch tray onto the table. Ivy and the scholarship kids jump. Eden doesn't react. "She needs to do better than becoming Briarcliff's pest control Employee of the Month."

"I heard," Ivy says as I slump down across from her.

"Judging by the stares and pinched noses as I passed the dining hall's tables, *everyone's* heard the latest," I say.

"That was some twisted shit," Mercy says beside me. "The whole school's buzzing about it."

Eden lifts her attention from her food, her expression bland as she picks at her truffled mac and cheese. "Any idea who it was?"

"Piper," I spit. "It had to be her. Or her minions."

I don't mention the rose, its presence the one uncertainty in an otherwise flawless argument. Piper may not have wanted to touch poisoned rats from the basement cellars, but one of Chase's guys would. My money's on Tempest, the one most likely to have killed kittens as a toddler.

I twist in my chair and observe Chase and his buddies—these

Nobles Ivy speaks of, lounging and belly-laughing as they enjoy their lunch, content in their own, isolated world. Thinking they're better. Royals among peasants.

Chase must've let his royal court out to play, because he's strangely absent from the scene. Piper's also gone, probably finishing detention with Dr. Luke, while I was given a reprieve from it by Headmaster Marron. He considered being reamed by him out a suitable substitute.

"They think they're invincible." I seethe through my teeth. "Someone, at some point, needs to do to them what they do to us."

"Callie..." Ivy pleads, eyes wide when I turn back to her. "It's in your best interest to just ride the wave until they get bored."

Mercy, Paul, and another person I can't remember the name of, nod their agreement.

Eden murmurs her dissent. She says, "Wake that inner beast, Callie."

I say, "I was threatened with expulsion because of them."

Ivy gasps. "But you've only been here three days!"

"I had to sit through an entire twenty minutes of Marron's tirade." I gesture with my fork. "When he stopped yelling to take a breath, I managed to convince him I had trouble remembering where my locker was, never mind where the pest traps are in this building—oh, and the slight logical problem of me vandalizing my own locker with rat corpses."

"To put it simply, Miss Ryan, we've never experienced a vileness of this sort in all our one hundred and seventy years of education," Marron had said. *"By process of elimination, you're the single variable we've added recently, and these 'injustices,' as you see them, keep happening to you, and you alone."*

Injustices, I realized, when Marron's computer went to screensaver mode and I saw the photo, that Marron will never believe Piper and her cohorts are behind.

On the pixelated screen, Marron had his arm slung around

Willow's shoulders while holding a fishing pole. Willow grinned widely at him, strands of her auburn hair flying into her face from the wind. Sections of an expensive, white yacht and an exquisite, foreign coastline painted their background with white and turquoise dream colors.

Willow must be his kid or a close relative, since she doesn't have his last name. Either way, she's besties with Piper. There's little chance Marron would side with me over those two. I'm the unchartered variable within this mess.

So why the hell am I targeted with these roses?

"Ivy," I say, "Did you know Willow Reyes is related to Headmaster Marron?"

Ivy starts at the statement. She swallows then sets down her fork. "Shit, I didn't think it'd matter, but yeah, she's his daughter."

"That settles it." I slouch against my chair, folding my arms. "I'm screwed. They can do whatever they want to me without any consequence. God, that *pisses* me off."

"From my perspective," Eden says, keeping focus on her plate. Her hair becomes a curtain around both sides of her pockmarked face. "That also means you can do whatever you want without getting in trouble. Black ops were invented for a reason."

I blink at her. "You're right. I can be as devious as them."

"Now, now," Ivy says, placing her hand on the table between Eden and me. "I don't think escalating this war is the answer. I swear to you, Callie, Piper has the attention span of an indoor Persian cat. She'll move on as soon as you stop reacting."

"Do you know what cats do to their prey?" I ask. "They bat them around, flaying them with their claws and teeth until their prey can't strike back. Then, the cat shakes the animal until they break their neck. And the poor thing isn't even dead yet."

After a beat of silence, Eden says, with her mouth full, "I'm gonna like you."

Mercy's plate scrapes as she low-key shuffles her chair away. I ignore her, because if Mercy's offended by my grotesque description of a cat's meal, then she'll have a hell of a time surviving outside of this preppy-ass school when she graduates.

"I don't want to be Piper's mouse, Ivy," I say.

Ivy holds up her hands. "Fair enough."

I've lost my appetite and push my lunch away. Maybe I should've just let Marron expel me. Then I'd be able to go back to my old school and my old friends … who want nothing to do with me and are now #couplegoals on Instagram. Not to mention, I'd leave here with no luggage and a big, bold EXPULSION written on my transcript.

If my aim is to go to a good college, then staying here and weathering this garbage storm is my only choice. With *them*.

"I'll be in my room until classes start again," I grumble, and push to a stand.

"Don't go, Callie," Ivy says. Her face grows serious as she thinks. "I know … let me take you on a tour of the boathouse down at the lake." When she sees me wince toward a *no*, she adds, "It's a nice day. You can shake off some of that negative energy before afternoon classes."

I waver at her words. Should I stew at the injustice in my room, or enjoy a gorgeous walk of the school grounds, something I've yet to make time for?

"You win," I say.

Beaming, Ivy stands. "Excellent! Plus, there's the added bonus of fresh air, beautiful landscaping, a bright sun in a cloudless, early September sky—"

"Relax, Ivy," I say, laughing as she rounds the lunch table toward me. "You had me at 'cooling off.'"

"Let's go," she says and weaves her hand around my arm to pull me through the aisle. "Before you change your mind. Bye, guys!"

I offer a weak wave to my table of sort-of-but-not-really friends, but it's Eden I notice, watching us closely as we leave.

18

The sun is out in full when Ivy and I step out, the September air bringing cool ribbons of wind to help dissipate the remaining summer heat.

I sniff, my nostrils tingling with salt.

"The eastern breeze must be bringing some ocean with it," Ivy observes as we head down the staircase.

"Is there any way down the rocks to see the ocean?" I ask. "Like, a cliff walk or something?"

Ivy shakes her head. "Not that I know of."

"Too bad."

On the rare weekends my mom took off, sometimes we'd head upstate in pursuit of hiking trails. We'd never stay overnight in the woods—we laughed that we weren't *that* boho chic—but would book an overnight at a local bed and breakfast, then hit the trails. After, we'd try the popular restaurant in whatever small town we chose that weekend, trying out the local fare.

And, to be honest, I was more about the eating part than the trekking one.

The memory brings expectant sadness, which I push away by

using the subject to ask Ivy, "Is there a bus or anything that takes us into town?"

Ivy turns us left, skirting around the massive school building and bringing us closer to the ring of trees at the bottom of the hill.

"Nah," Ivy says. "Nobody goes into town."

"But what if somebody wanted to?"

"Like you?"

Ivy's question isn't judgmental, but it's definitely flabbergasted.

I respond cautiously. "Yeah. I need groceries. Piper will have my head if she realizes a rodent's been gnawing at her food. It'd be cool to also explore the town—"

"We get our groceries delivered," Ivy cuts in, then motions for me to veer left with her.

My chest tightens when I realize the path we're taking, but Ivy doesn't give me time to peer through the trees and see if remnants of the bonfire are still there, or maybe a discarded cloak stuck in the branches and flapping in the wind.

The memory of the man under a cloak, standing above me as I fell to the ground without offering a hand, comes to the forefront, the hood's folds obscuring his face...

"All you have to do," Ivy says, unaware that I've craned my neck around her to better look through the copse of trees, "is fill out an online shopping cart on Briarcliff's website. Groceries are taken out of your stipend and delivered Saturday mornings."

Her information makes me glance back at her. "So, no one leaves campus, like ever?"

"Well, I didn't say *that*." Ivy's shoulders shake with indulgent laughter. "I've yet to tell you about the parties."

"Parties?" I echo.

"Being on the fringe of the social ladder, I don't go to many, but we all know the types of parties Chase and his friends throw. Sometimes at the cliff, other times at the lake houses owned by various rich parents nearby. Usually on Fridays, but any day of the week is fair game."

I hum in acknowledgment, but given my current situation, joining their fun and games doesn't seem too fun for me.

"It's just through here," Ivy says, and I'm forced to walk behind her as we take a thin, dirt path through the trees.

"Are you sure there's a boathouse and not a labyrinth at the end of this?" I ask through stiff lips, since my focus has gone to avoiding errant branches. I'm forced to dig up long-ago buried memories of exploring trails with Mom in order to navigate foreign terrain without face-planting.

"You should try doing this at five in the morning," Ivy says over her shoulder, "during season when training is in full effect."

"Please tell me flashlights are involved." *And you don't encircle a campfire.*

Ivy laughs. "Some use the flashlight on their phones, but I could navigate this in my sleep."

"I bet," I say as she nimbly avoids exposed roots in the trail.

I'm so focused on scattered stones and slippery, damp leaves blown onto our path that I almost stumble into Ivy's back when she stops.

I lift my head to notice we've reached a clearing with a sparkling, flat lake in front of us. It's *unbelievable* that this is manmade, a special body of water created for Briarcliff's wealthy and elite. Adding to the glamour is what most people would think is a lake house for the rich and fabulous.

Those people would almost be right.

"Welcome to Briarcliff Boathouse," Ivy says cheerily, and grabs my hand to pull me closer. "A gift from former crew alumni." Ivy notices how I'm catching flies, and adds, "Rowing has been a dedicated sport of Briarcliff since it debuted in 1820. As you can imagine, there's been some sizable alumni wallets passing through."

I'm in awe of the size and architecture. If I thought Briarcliff's campus resembled a gothic church, this mere house perched on a lake is like a ski resort mansion without the snow and laid with brick and wood three stories high. Four or five garage-like doors face the water, with wooden docks sprouting from each.

I'm not fluent in boat-talk, so all I can say to Ivy is, "Hot damn."

"Shoot," Ivy mutters. "You see him, too. Jeez, he trains any chance he gets. I hope he hasn't spotted us."

That grabs my attention. "Who?"

But Ivy doesn't have to answer. I notice Chase lifting himself from a thin, vertical boat, pushing onto the dock with his arms, then deftly landing on his feet. He lays his two oars aside, then pulls the boat from the lake, twists it effortlessly, and balances it above his head.

With a frickin' boat for a head, Chase strides from the docks and into the boathouse, his body's profile in full, detailed effect. He's wearing some sort of maroon and black spandex short-and-tank combo, so tight I admire the perfect melons of his ass-cheeks and the sculpted muscles sprouting underneath. The shorts stop at the knees, and after that, it's just golden skin covering bulging calf muscles as he walks.

"Is he carrying an entire boat?" I whisper, and Ivy elbows me at the waist, stopping me from ogling. "And what is he *wearing*?"

"That boat is a scull—it's what they call single shells when we're out training on our own. And he's wearing a unisuit," Ivy informs. We start toward the boathouse again. "The mean girl version of a uniform. You have a flaw? It'll show it."

"Got it," I say, and blink rapidly before my vixen mind can show me what Chase's front must look like.

Ivy pushes on a red, wooden door at the side of the building. I follow her inside while she drones on about the boathouse, surprised Ivy has to turn on the lights, since Chase came in before us.

"Where'd he go?" I ask.

Chapter 18 | 117

"Probably the showers," Ivy says offhand.

Her tone clues me in to shut up. I shouldn't care what Chase is doing or where he is, and Ivy will start to think I care if I keep at it.

"If he's here, then Coach is in her office upstairs," Ivy says, "I've got to talk to her for a sec. Go that way." Ivy points to one of the boat bays overlooking the water, where shells are stored on racks bolted to the walls. "The view's insane if you step out onto the dock."

"I, uh…" I say, but Ivy's already dashed to the back, her motion flickering on the overhead lights as she passes by. When she opens a door, I inwardly shrink at the sight of water tanks. They are goddamned giant fish tanks with eight-person rowing machines in the middle of them. Getting stuck in one would be my worst nightmare come to life.

As soon as the door shuts behind Ivy, my vision clears, and I wander far away from them and through the sitting room of the giant space—the Club Room, Ivy called it— with fabric-covered patio furniture in Briarcliff's colors—white, black, and maroon. There is a line of windows overlooking the lake, showcasing the wild forest across the water.

As if on instinct, I'm drawn into the sunlight instead of the shadows. I step through one of the four boat bays lined parallel to the water, my hand trailing across one of the "shells" hung up at waist-level. It's wet, and I assume it's Chase's boat. My fingers touch the seat inside, still warm to the touch.

I walk across the thin platform to the dock outside, attuned to the lapping water below. I assure myself that an expensive structure like this would be safe and sturdy. I'll just stay away from the edges.

My shoes make hollow sounds as I pass over the floorboards. I pull at the hem of my skirt when I look down and see spaces between the wood, the water flowing underneath.

Why did I let Ivy bring me here again?

"For God's sake, Callie," I mutter. "You're in a mansion they call a boathouse. You're fine."

A noise sounds out, and I startle at the echoing clang.

It's just Ivy, I reason. *Or Chase, skulking around in the corners—*

"The fuck are you doing here?"

I cry out when the voice registers at my shoulder, then whirl, my hands up in defense. The movement sends my feet in a tangle, and I topple sideways—

Strong arms hold on and drag me to the safety of the dock.

"Christ, new girl," Chase says as we disentangle.

Gasping, my throat tight with stress at the mere thought of my lungs filling with lake water, I stare up at Chase, whose relaxed pose is the complete opposite of a boy who just saved a girl from certain death. He smirks.

"I was..." I gulp. "I mean, I was exploring." I catch my breath, but my hand stays at my throat.

Sunlight beams onto Chase's head like a fallen angel's unearned halo.

Droplets of sweat shimmer on the exposed parts of Chase's chest, lifting rhythmically as he breathes. When he'd grabbed me, and I held on, his arms were damp and sticky, but the scent of him, though similar to the boathouse, wasn't as cloying. It was ... indescribably addicting.

Conscious of how obvious I must look, I tear my gaze from his torso and meet his calculating, metallic eyes.

Chase's golden glow doesn't meet his intentions. He asks, "You interested in crew?"

Chase looks me up and down. I feel naked, even though I'm dressed in Briarcliff uniform. The sun warms me, but I shiver.

He continues, "Because you need more grace than that."

"I'm—that's the last thing I want," I say, and move closer to him, if only to get farther away from the dock's edge. "Ivy said something about the view being nice..."

"You like what you see?"

My back is to this allegedly epic view, and I'm focused solely on the boy in front of me, who looks nothing like the boys my mother would want me to get to know.

And yeah, the front of him is precisely what I pictured it'd be in the unisuit.

In an effort to release this ridiculous hold Chase has, I say, "What I don't like is what your girlfriend's doing to me."

Chase's cheek tics. "I told you, she's not my girlfriend."

"Then whatever she is, tell her to stop. This morning was epically fucked up."

"Ah yes, the famous rat infestation." Chase raises a brow. "What makes you think she was behind it?"

"Because she has all of you," I spit. "You asshole Nobles who think you can *hurt* people the way you do and think there won't be conseq—"

"What did you just say?"

Chase closes the space between us with such viper-quick movement, I'm caught off-guard. My heels scrape back, dangerously close to the edge.

I sense where the dock ends and the depthless water begins, so I cling to his arms for balance. Chase's eyes tunnel into mine. There's no savior here now, fallen or otherwise.

My fingers dig into his bare arms, his muscles hardening beneath, yet he doesn't shake me off.

I respond, keeping my voice level, "I said, you Nobles are assholes."

Thunder rumbles in Chase's chest. "I'll ask you one more time. How do you know that name?"

I've rankled him, and I decide to keep going. "Isn't that what your immediate fanbase calls you? What about the girls you sleep with? Don't you let them in on your cool clubhouse name—?"

"Shut up."

He says it with such succinct poison that my teeth clank together.

Chase lowers his head so we're nose-to-nose. I can smell his breath—spearmint—I can smell *him*, sweat and freshwater sweetness.

I refuse to buckle, but my hands don't leave his arms. I doubt they'll do it of their own volition until I'm well off this fucking floating wood.

He says, "Don't mention that name again, to anyone. You understand?"

My brows smush together. "Why? You'd think you'd be proud of the title. I was positive it's what you and your buddies put in front of your name when you present your dicks."

Chase snarls, but it only brings our lips closer together. Electricity sparks between us, a tingling spread that will dissipate if one of us backs away.

Neither of us does.

I stop breathing, and Chase takes my air as his own.

He rasps, "And you wonder why there were dead rats in your locker. Your big fucking mouth'll get you in trouble. Consider this your one warning."

I resist the temptation to grasp the back of his neck and ram my mouth against his, the craving to taste him unlike *anything* I've been brought up to do with a boy.

"So, you jerks did have something to do with it," I snarl.

Chase backs off, his upper lip lifting in a half-cocked grin. "We don't dabble in pest control."

"But you dabble in something," I persist. "Does it involve cloaks and roses?"

Chase steps away, leaving my hands bereft as I'm left to face my vertigo on my own. He turns on his heel and starts down the dock, leaving behind no clues as to whether I'm right.

"Chase!" I call. "What the hell? We were having a conversation!"

"No, we weren't," Chase says, his voice fading with the additional distance he's putting between us. "And I never saw you here, either."

"What the...?"

But Chase disappears into one of the boat bays, and that's the last I see of him.

Lake water *glugs* against the dock, the noise of the waves making me scurry into the boathouse, oddly chilled despite being greeted by the warm September sun when I got here.

"Sorry, Callie, but I've never heard of this craziness you're talking about."

I decide to fill Ivy in on my secret roses on our way back to campus, our school-issued shoes plodding along the dirt trail as we walk uphill, Ivy leading the way.

"Really? Nothing?" I ask. "I thought you were all about Briarcliff's gossip."

"Well, I am. But I've never heard of a student receiving black or white roses. Not even on Valentine's Day."

Drat. I'd hoped Ivy of all people could shed some light on my mysterious admirer ... or enemy. I suppose it would depend on whether I'm talking about the gift of furniture or the rat presents, and I've informed Ivy of the latter. At the moment, I keep the unexpected nicety close to my chest. So far, it's the one unsullied memory I have at this school.

"But you know of the Nobles," I say.

Ivy comes to an abrupt halt, keeping her back to me. "The who?"

"Ivy, come on." I climb to a stand beside her, but she won't face me. "You know what I'm talking about."

"No." Ivy glances at me briefly. "I don't."

She starts walking again, much faster, and I scramble to keep up. "Yes, you do! Remember, in the bathrooms, when I was cleaning up all that damn spaghetti sauce—"

Ivy wheels around and latches onto my arm. She coaxes me to meet her eye before saying, "I didn't say anything, and you didn't hear anything. Okay?"

I'm witnessing fear in her expression. Real trepidation. "Ivy ... you told me that's what they are called. Chase and his friends. Remember?"

"You heard me wrong. I said that their reach was *global*, and for you to be careful. Yeah, they're our age, but their families are rich and powerful. Their influence is never-ending." Ivy squeezes my arm and says, "Do you hear what I'm telling you?"

I shake my head. "That's not—"

The deep, echoing ring of the clocktower reaches our ears, and Ivy releases my arm and shoots forward. "That's our warning—we're gonna be late to class."

"Ivy, wait."

"Can't!" Ivy throws a wave in my direction as she kicks into a run. "We'll talk later!"

"I'm not done with this subject!" I call in a warning, but at this point, I'm yelling at her butt as she sprints up Briarcliff's stairs and runs into the building.

Jeez. That's two people in less than an hour who've pulled a disappearing act on me.

I think of the wilted white rose, crushed at the bottom of my backpack by my books, and I know, with resolute certainty, that I'm not finished with either Ivy *or* Chase.

Ahmar always joked that if my mom was going to pass me down anything, it would be her dogged tenacity. His sobering voice adds inside my head, *Yeah, Calla. The trait that got her killed.*

But I brush that thought away and stride to Briarcliff Academy, my thumbs digging painfully into my backpack's straps.

19

I'm starting to enjoy moonlight more than I appreciate the sun, since the moon's face is the friendliest I see by the time the week is over and a fresh one begins.

Ivy is missing from the dining hall Monday evening—a girls' crew meeting, she said—so I brave the masses alone, without the confidence to join Eden and the scholarship kids when Ivy's not around.

At first, it doesn't seem so bad.

The few students also enjoying an early dinner don't notice me walk in and head to the serving station, grabbing my tray and choosing between steak or chicken cordon bleu. No shoulders bump into mine, nor are there any hisses or jeers behind my back.

I relax, thinking I avoided the worst, since Chase, Piper, and the rest of their posse aren't here yet. The timing was deliberate on my part—I didn't think they'd be so pedestrian as to arrive for 5 o'clock dinner service, crew meeting or not.

Then, a hush falls upon the room, its obviousness exacerbated by the echoing vastness in the uncrowded dining hall, conversations trailing to whispers, then echoes, then ... stares.

Clutching my tray with both hands, I move away from the serving station, a plate of steak with peppercorn sauce and broccoli steaming the underside of my chin.

Piper, Willow, Violet, and Falyn pose at the dining hall's entrance.

I'm starting to differentiate them by hair color, since they stand in order of their ombre hues. Violet is on the left, with her ebony hair. Piper has the darkest brown, then Willow with auburn waves. Falyn, with her hip cocked at the end, is the most (bottle) blonde.

After she finishes scanning the room, Piper's stare knifes into mine.

I pretend not to notice, though my teeth bite down hard as I find a vacant table and sit, grabbing the napkin from the place setting and unrolling it to get to the flatware.

The sound of my fork and knife clanging together when they fall into my palm is the loudest in the room.

Then, the scraping of my knife against the porcelain plate as I cut my steak.

I'm honestly at a loss as to why I've attracted Piper's animosity again. We seemed to have come to a silent truce of sorts during our lunch detentions with Dr. Luke, but I don't think too hard on the reasons why I'm back on her hit list. What I'd like to do is eat my dinner, then escape to the frivolous protection of my bedroom.

Two palms slam down on my table, rattling the place settings within their vicinity, as well as my heart. I startle, my knife and fork dropping from my hands.

Piper stews above me, her cheeks flushed and eyes sparkling with rage. She sneers. "Stay away from him."

I take a moment to finish chewing my mouthful, using it to regain calm and school my expression. I swallow, then buy time by lifting my water glass and sipping. "Who?"

Piper's eyes narrow. "You know who, possum."

"Well." I set my water down, then smooth the napkin resting on my lap, emitting an assuredness my heart isn't mimicking. "Considering you've made it impossible to make a ton of friends, never mind talk to guys, I'm not sure what—or who—you could be talking about."

"You *bitch*."

The insult hurtles around the room before smashing into my face, a hiss of massive proportions. The entire room, already quiet, falls into a thick silence.

I'm confused. "Piper, I've never—"

"Don't lie, rodent, or I'll have the whole school call you a rat instead of a possum," Piper interjects.

"You mean like the rats I found in my locker?" I ask, bolstered by her admission. "A little obvious, isn't it, to threaten me *again* with vermin in public."

"I saw you!" she shouts, and frankly, it sounds unhinged.

I search behind her for her friends. Surely, they want to drag Piper out of here and calm her down. Yet, none do. They watch the show, various expressions of concern, interest, and vindictiveness etched across their faces. Violet is the singular soul that seems reluctant to watch.

I ask Piper slowly, "You saw me what?"

"Showing your slutty tits off. Practically begging him to fuck you when you're alone with him."

I laugh at the absurdity of the situation, but Piper takes it the wrong way.

"*Fuck* you," she hisses, her elbows shooting out like a praying mantis, her face darting close. "You don't get to have him. You can cling to him all you want, plead with him to stick his dick in you, but he won't. He's as disgusted with you as I am."

I admit, the last part hurts, but I avoid the poison arrow to the heart. Piper's accusation flashes me into to the warmth of Chase's arms, the dappled sunlight beaming onto his skin as he smelled of lake water and mint, and his stare, for that one moment becoming a savior's, flickering with warm emotion before he tamped it down.

But that happened a week ago. Why is Piper bringing it up now and not the many times we've been in detention together since?

Because now she has an audience, my suspicious head-voice whispers.

"You're threatening me for nothing," I say. "I promise you, Chase would rather kick me off the dock than screw me."

Piper flinches at the use of his name, and all she can come up with is, "You're *lying*."

"Oh my God, which is it, Piper? Am I so desperate for him that he can't stand me, or are we screwing behind your back?"

Piper's face goes red.

I roll my eyes, but I'm shaking inside. "He broke my fall into the water. That's it."

"Bullshit. You have an agenda involving your tongue and tits to take him from me."

I sigh in an effort to coax my heart to stop racing. I hate being the center of attention, but Piper's forced my hand. I take comfort in the fact that nobody can see the erratic, untamed beats.

Standing, I mutter, "You're taking this too far. We can talk about it in our room, but—"

"You're no roommate of mine," she snaps. "Tomorrow, I'm going to Headmaster Marron and reporting your ass."

On cue, Piper flutters her lashes, thickened with crocodile tears.

Dread drips into the empty rumblings of my stomach. "Piper, stop. You're being ridiculous."

"This has gone too far, Callie. Your repeated abuses have to stop!" Her desperate shriek reaches the ceiling.

At this point, nobody's eating. My appetite has disappeared, and part of me wishes I'd evaporate, too.

I throw my hands up, matching my voice with hers. "Take what? I haven't done anything to you!"

"Oh, so you think hurling insults at me was nothing? Refusing to do your half of our history essay? Vowing to ruin my GPA and my life? What about vandalizing my bedroom? Smearing my lipstick all over our bathroom mirror? You're fucking nuts, Callie! Fucking *certified!*"

"What the f—?" I temper my voice before it turns into a banshee screech, because I'm not seeing Piper's statements as accusations. I'm seeing them as...

"Piper," I say in an astonished whisper, "Are they doing this stuff to you, too? Are you getting roses?"

For a brief second, Piper's eyes snap to mine, but the movement is invisible to anyone else. A smile replaces any recognition, growing wider with malice the longer she stares. "Like I said, *rat*, you're as dumb as the brain God sized you with. I wasn't going to say anything, since I figure you're acting out because of your mom's murder—"

The entire room gasps, and I feel blood leaving my face.

"—but it's gone too far. Fucking with my room, then trying to steal my boyfriend ... you're messed up, and you need help outside of this school."

"You're not his girlfriend," I blurt, instinctively surrendering to the constant unwelcome loop in my head. *She's not my girlfriend.*

My face rings with a slap, sending me stumbling. Students murmur, but no one stands up to do anything.

I hold a hand to my cheek, as hot and stinging as my eyes. "What's going *on* with you?"

"Which part confuses you?" Piper mocks, but unlike me, appears to the entire dining hall as sleek, collected, and entitled. "My bedroom? My clothes? My boyfriend? Or your mom getting decapitated?"

My mouth works. I'm bent over and clutching my cheek. "All but one," I admit in a sickly whisper.

"Uh-huh. You're so done, Calla *Lily*." Piper bends so she's at my level and whispers so only I can hear, "I warned you. I've tried to tell you to stay away from him, from me, from all of us. This is my last attempt at being kind."

Her baseless threats, coupled with the torrential humiliation in front of the entire school, *again*—and the never-ending rage boiling at the tip of my heart from losing my mother, without choice, without a goodbye...

Yeah, my flip-out is inevitable.

I rear up on a roar, clipping Piper in the face with my elbow and sending her sprawling onto my table. The plate falls to the floor and shatters. Blood bursts from Piper's nose. She screams, and her friends come running.

"You have *no right!*" I scream at her. "To bring up my mother, to threaten me, to think you can control what I—what *all* of us in this room do, like you're some kind of false queen. And why? Because you *think* I'm after Chase? You're desperate to ruin my life based on a pointless rumor! How savage *are* you to do that to a person you don't even know?"

Piper scrambles up on the table's surface, clutching her nose. "It was a mistake to come here, Callie! I will *ruin* you!"

"Hey!" an older male voice calls.

Great. The delayed, biased Professor Dawson is here to save the day.

"Girls! Haven't I told you—"

This time, I'm not waiting around to be framed.

I sprint from the dining hall, Piper's theatric wails and captive audience keeping well behind.

20

"Have you thought this all the way through, Calla?"

Ahmar's calming voice flows through my phone and into my ear as I continue tossing clothes onto my bed. I throw a look to my bedroom door, assuring myself that I indeed shut and locked it.

"I don't belong here," I say, getting back to adding to the pile on my bed by rifling through my dresser drawers. "There are things going on that I ... that I have trouble putting into words."

"New schools are like that, kiddo." Ahmar's voice takes on a fatherly tone. "It's hell fitting in, but you don't get education like this anywhere else. Briarcliff is the school your dreams are made of. Your momma always wanted you to go to college, and this is your golden ticket. If you throw it away based on a fight with your roommate, I promise you, you'll look back and regret it."

"It wasn't just an argument. It was..." I pause and stare at one of my bare walls, my folded T-shirts dropping from my arms. How can I define the clash as just "girls being girls"?

The malice. The vapid hatred. The physical assault, of which I reciprocated ten-fold.

Yeah, Ahmar would be *so* pissed I used force and focus on how I overreacted and possibly broke a girl's nose over a slap and accusation of stealing her boyfriend.

God, just thinking about it that way makes me lose respect for myself, never mind what Ahmar would think.

"Trust me on this, Ahmar. I don't belong. These students are unlike any other humans I've ever encountered."

Ahmar laughs. "You're talking like you're on some sort of safari."

"Maybe I am," I say. *A jungle with nothing but poisonous predators waiting for their chance to bite my head off.*

"Okay, say I indulge you for a moment," Ahmar says. "What are you going to do once you leave? Where will you go? You no longer live downtown. I hate to say it, but you can't go back to your old school. Not after…"

Ahmar lets the rest of his sentence go unsaid, but the missing words ring their wicked truth in my head.

I was close to expulsion once. I can't experience the threat of it again.

"Easy." I add a positive punch to my explanation, though none of it registers in my gut. "I'll go back to Dad and Lynda's. If I show up on their doorstep, they'll have to take me back."

"Kiddo." The pity in Ahmar's voice hardens my jaw. "You're not something they've tossed aside."

"Oh, yeah?" I gear up for an argument, somehow craving it, regardless of how misguided it is. "Where are their phone calls? Or text messages? Or any sort of communication to see how I'm doing? You call me, Ahmar. They don't—they have a family to start, and I'm the dead weight."

The poor joke falls flat on both our ears.

"I didn't mean that," I say. "All I'm saying is … they can't send me here and think I'll be happy. Not with the elitist favoritism that goes on. These kids even have the headmaster in their pockets. I'd rather deal with Dad's cool dismissal."

Ahmar sighs. "It's your choice. Lord knows I can't stop you. But take the night and think about this, okay? This is a big decision you're making—possibly life-changing. And I think you've had enough of those. Maybe, you can see the time away from your stepdad as a good thing. It allows for you and him to start fresh—"

"Dad and Lynda put me here because they didn't want to deal with a problem child." I stop with my one-handed folding, deciding to put Ahmar on speaker instead. Once I press the button, I place the phone on my pillow, so it doesn't get lost in the detritus on my bed. "Hey, Ahmar?"

"Yeah, hun?"

"What would you think of ... I mean, if Dad and Lynda are furious I've left Briarcliff and refuse to let me stay with them ... um, can I stay with you?"

There's a long pause. Too long and deafening in its answer.

"Calla, I would, honey, but ... I'm in a one-bedroom." He laughs in an attempt to lighten the denial. "I can barely fit myself in here. And I'm messy as fuck. This isn't the proper housing for a seventeen-year-old—"

"I get it," I cut in, unfolding a long-sleeved shirt with a sharp flick, then refolding it again for no reason. "You don't have to explain. It was too much to ask."

"No, I don't think you do. I fought for you, honey. But it wasn't in the cards for us. I'm so sorry."

Again, with the pity. I reach for my phone. "I gotta go. Thank you for the talk."

"You sure you don't want to keep chatting? What about this friend of yours, Ivy? What's she think of you leaving?"

"She's—it's complicated," I say, because I haven't told her yet.

"Promise me you'll take the night. Don't be calling a car at midnight and travel with a stranger."

That brings a smile to my face. "I won't. Briarcliff has personal drivers."

"Jesus. And you want to leave that place? I love you, kiddo. Stay safe. And strong."

"Yeah," I say, but trail off.

Ahmar hangs up, and I'm left alone with my thoughts. Piper hasn't come home yet, even though it's been four hours. She's probably bunking with one of her friends, lest Crazy Callie do something vicious to her vulnerable person.

What the hell was that dining hall confrontation about? Earlier this week, we joined forces on the creepy historical project, and I'd believed we'd tolerate each other from there. We had to live together. We could ignore one another just fine once I purchased my own coffee.

Why does Piper hate me so much?

And to accuse me of trying to be with Chase...

She has it so wrong.

I don't know this guy, yet I'm drawn in, despite my current problems always circling back to Chase. My dreams contain him. I remember the feel of his muscles and skin like they're my own. And I've merely touched him once.

But, you've touched him.

Oh, yeah? I sneer to my subconscious. *Now watch me leave him.*

I'm going to escape this place, whether or not Ahmar approves, but I refuse to call it running away.

It's inevitable: Piper will take her fabricated story and real bruises to the headmaster.

Now my packing is spurred by anger. I reach deeper into the mountain of clothes on my bed, and latch onto something sharp. Cursing, I pull my hand back, gripping the object despite the trail of blood traveling down my palm.

It's the inked-dipped rose, the one I'd hidden in my nightstand, but was unearthed when I emptied my drawers. One of its thorns nicked the pad of my thumb.

My lips peel back. I break the stem in half, black petals ripping free with my sharp twist.

In doing so, I curse Chase, Piper, and each of their friends, wishing them all the bad luck a dying, poisoned rose can give.

21

The sun's rays stream through the single window in my room, and I sit up blearily, rubbing my face awake.

I must've fallen asleep on the heap of clothing on my bed, which surprises me, since the last thing I remember is deleting all my research on Rose Briar.

Piper can suck it. There's no way I'm gifting her with the information I found before I leave campus. She can start the project from scratch for all I care.

But something seems off. I woke up with an abrupt start, and not with my usual cat-like stretch and slow-blink habit.

Rapid knocking sounds at the front door, and it's sharp and impatient.

I mutter a curse, then peel out of bed. I'm still in my school uniform, with my wrinkled white shirt unbuttoned and plaid skirt askew.

My door unlocks with a sharp click, and I plod into the central room, hazily registering that Piper's room is unoccupied. Her bed's made, and there's no air of perfume from any recent departure, so I suppose she didn't come home.

Good.

Maybe that's why I slept like a baby—there was no one to storm through the apartment and take her unfair intimidation tactics onto domestic territory.

"Callie?" a muffled voice asks through the door. "Are you there? Please say you're there. *Please.*"

"Ivy?" I call, moving faster to the front door. "What's wrong?" Ivy doesn't normally sound so high-pitched and desperate.

I'm hoping it's not to convince me to stay. I sent her a text last night, promising I'd call her today and explain, but that I was done with this school and the snakes it nurtures inside it.

"Oh, thank God," she says, then flies into my apartment and glances around with skittish awareness. "They're not here yet."

"Who?"

"The police."

That gives me pause. "Um. What?"

Ivy spins to face me. Splotches of color rise high in her cheeks, and her eyes are abnormally wide. And wet.

"Ivy, are you crying?"

She sniffs, then pulls out a tissue from her bag and dabs at her eyes. "Have you not heard? Is your phone not blowing up?"

"I mean, it could be." I gesture vaguely to my room. "I've been busy packing, and your knocking woke me up. I haven't checked my phone yet."

"Oh, Callie." Ivy's knees turn to liquid as she glides closer and grasps my arms. "It's bad. It's really, really bad."

I'm so sorry, Calla...

"What's bad? Ivy, you're freaking me out."

Don't see your mom like this. Come with me. Please, kiddo...

Tears pool in Ivy's eyes. She parts her lips, and her despondency unearths a stirring inside my head, a slithering awareness that until now, was slumbering in the trenches of my mind.

Kiddo, Your momma...

I've been here before.

She's...

Ivy's expression is an exact replica of ... Ahmar's.
"Callie," Ivy says. "Piper was killed last night."
Dead.

※

"W-what?" I stutter. Automatically, I glance past Ivy's shoulder into Piper's room, though I know it's empty. "No. She's not. I just saw her..."

"Last night?" Ivy's grip tightens on my upper arms. "Omigod, Callie, did you talk to her before she fell?"

My eyes flick to hers. "What? No. I saw her at the dining hall." I study Ivy closely. "You didn't hear?"

"No. I do know she missed the crew meeting, though. But listen, there's no time. I came to prepare you."

"Prepare me for what?"

I hate that I keep repeating things back to her, but my brain's in a jumble and my body's going into panic mode.

"They found Piper at the bottom of Lover's Leap."

It can't be. This can't be happening a second time...

I fight through the pulsing muscles of my throat. "Ivy, yesterday at dinner, I—"

"What the *fuck* have you done?"

The deep, masculine tone causes the hairs on the back of my neck to rise.

"Chase," Ivy gasps, releasing my arms. "I-I'm so sorry. I'm so sorry about Piper."

"Get out."

Chase's words are clipped, but lethal. I have no idea if he's talking to Ivy or to me, but either way, he doesn't own this fucking apartment.

I swivel to face him. "You're the one that's unwelcome here."

When I register Chase's expression, I'm shocked I got the

words out. Never before have I seen features so flat yet exuding such rage.

"Ivy," he says, without tearing his gaze from mine, "I said get out."

I grab Ivy's arm. "She doesn't have to go anywhere."

He grits out, "Yes. She does."

"Callie, it's fine," Ivy says in a small voice, "I can meet you in the lobby."

"You can wait in my bedroom," I say to her, keeping my stare on Chase's. "Whatever Chase has to say to me, you can be a witness."

Chase arches a cold brow. "You want a second ear for what I'm gonna say? Fine. Where were you last night? What did Piper do that got you so enraged you made her bleed?"

I guffaw. "Are you—is this what I think it is? Are you accusing me of killing her?"

Chase flinches at the word 'kill.' I don't blame him. It's a hard word to swallow when it starts relating to your life. Worse than 'death.' I recognize the pain behind Chase's fury, and the grief. But I doubt my kindred spirit will mean anything to him.

"Who the hell do you think you are?" he says, and for a brief moment, his eyes gleam with unshed tears. "To come to this school and fuck it up the way you have?"

Chase steps closer, his large body overshadowing mine. I don't cower. I hear Ivy back up a step, then two, but she slides my hand off her forearm and into hers. And squeezes.

"I've done *nothing*," I hiss in his face. His anger billows over me with hot breaths. "You're hurting, Chase. You're furious and upset. I can understand that. I'm sorry Piper's gone"—it still sounds so unreal coming from my throat—"but I won't be your punching bag."

"What, you think you know me now?" His eyes transform the tears into glimmering animosity. "Because your mom's been killed and Piper's dead, now we're warm and fuzzy friends?"

I flinch. "I don't give a shit what you think."

Sliding my hand from Ivy's, I storm to the front door, but Chase catches me by the elbow and spins me into his chest, his other hand cupping the back of my neck and pulling at my hair until we're eye-to-eye.

Ivy shouts a warning, but it does nothing to stop him.

This is nothing like it was at the docks. There's no sunlight streaming down, no hint of an angel now.

I'm in the grip of a demon.

"She'd still be alive if you never came here," he snarls.

"You're the one who was supposed to be her boyfriend," I retort. We're both heaving, and a fucked-up, secretive section of my heart wonders if he's pulsing with twisted heat the way I am. "Her protector. What was it you said to me when you splayed yourself across that couch over there like an entitled prick? You *look out for her*. Well, look where she is now."

I've hurt him. I see it in the flash of rage that washes across his overly schooled expression. His hand clenches on my hair where he holds me, and his eyes grow so everlastingly cold.

I may have gone too far, but with such burning confusion inside me, there's no other way to release it. It's all too much, too soon.

The silence between us is thick and nauseating, but neither of us will break.

The weight of Ivy's hand comes down on my shoulder. "Chase, please. Callie, come on. We need to..."

"You have no idea. None." Chase tightens his hold, and an unwilling gasp leaves my throat. "If you thought this is done—if not having Piper around would give you a reprieve—you're wrong. I'm about to get started with you."

I snap out, "You can watch me tremble another time. Now get the *hell* out of my room."

A light knock startles us both, and our heads whip to the

sound. A plainclothes detective stands there, with a shield around his neck. Two uniformed officers are behind him.

The detective with the gray hair and rugged face looks between Ivy and me. "Is one of you Calla Lily Ryan?"

"Yes," I say, and disengage from Chase like he's coated with snake venom.

Surprisingly, he lets me go, but he saunters back with a malicious grin maligning one side of his face. What he wants to do to me is obvious in the shape of his lips. He wants to devour me. Destroy me.

"It starts now," he says, then twists to the police. He points at me. "She did it."

My mouth falls into an *O* as the policemen part to let Chase through. The detective doesn't take his attention off me as he steps aside.

"Miss Ryan? We have some questions for you regarding the death of your roommate," he says, and a lump forms in my throat.

A lump the size of a rock at the base of a cliff.

22

Detective Haskins wants to question me? I tell him he can, so long as I have a guardian present and it's conducted on neutral territory.

That's when he informed me Dad and Lydia were on a babymoon in Tahiti and couldn't be present for any questioning. And Ahmar was too far away of a drive for Haskins to wait.

Faced between dealing with Haskins's stern face alone or having a teacher present in substitution of a legal guardian, I asked for Dr. Luke to sit beside me in the empty classroom they directed me to. He seems the friendliest of the faculty, and the one likely to take my side if things go awry, since I doubt Professor Dawson, who knows me second-best, has bonded with me enough to want to say anything in my defense, should it come to that.

I sit at a school desk and Haskins takes a seat across from me. Dr. Luke stands at my elbow, his arms crossed as he studies Haskins.

I can feel my heartbeat in my fingertips. The silence in the empty classroom doesn't help. It brings back memories of being sat down on my bed and Ahmar bending in front of me, holding on tight to my elbows.

We did all we could. She's gone, kiddo. She's gone.

My breaths patter in my throat like a bird's wings clipped for a cage.

None of this is my fault. I'm not in trouble.

Or so I thought. Yesterday's fight with Piper is glaringly present in my mind's eye, blurring the shining floors beneath me into a transparent movie screen where I elbow Piper in the face and she screams, blood pouring out of her nostrils.

I swallow. I want Ahmar here.

Don't go back in there, Calla. Stay with me. Cry it out. I'll hold on tight.

I scrunch my eyes shut.

A hand comes down on my shoulder and squeezes before retreating. It's Dr. Luke.

"I'll keep this brief, Miss Ryan," Haskins says. He flips through a notebook on the desk, his pen poised as he starts by taking down my basic information. Then, he asks, "When did you last see Piper Harrington?"

"At dinner," I whisper, but force my voice to come forth to admit, "We had a fight."

"That's a start," Haskins says as he scribbles something down. "We know about that from Piper's friends. I'm glad you're being honest."

I nod, aware that being truthful about any friction with the victim is the fastest route to clearing my name and having them move on to someone else.

"Where were you this morning between one and three AM?" Haskins asks.

"In bed," I say. "I fell asleep packing."

Dr. Luke's head tips in my direction. "Packing?"

"I'll be the one to ask the questions, Doctor, thank you,"

Haskins says. "So, Callie, you were in the apartment you shared with Piper? All night?"

"Yes."

"You didn't go to the party at the cliffs like the rest of 'em?"

I lift my head up. "Huh?"

Dr. Luke's hand squeezes my shoulder again. "Miss Ryan's new to this school, Detective. She might not have been made aware of the mischief these kids get up to once the moon's out. It was a small gathering, anyway, kids Piper Harrington ran around with. I was the professor who found them and broke it up. I'd come from the professors' lodging at around one, and for the record, I didn't see Miss Harrington there. The kids assured me she left the party early because she wanted to go home to be alone."

The longer Dr. Luke's friendly explanation goes on, the more Haskins's features harden. "I'll get to you in due time, Doctor. If you'll let me do the talking?"

Dr. Luke clears his throat. "Apologies. Go ahead."

"Dr. Luke's right," I pipe up. "I'm not cool enough to be invited to those kinds of things."

"Yes, you and Piper rubbed each other the wrong way, didn't you?"

"We didn't become instant friends upon meeting," I admit.

"So, did you see her at all? Did Piper come back to your room after your argument at dinner?"

I shake my head.

"How about after the party?" Haskins glances down at his notes. "Those kids have corroborated Dr. Luke's statement that she left early because she didn't feel well."

Probably because I'd recently bashed her nose in. I flinch at the thought but cover it up in hopes Haskins doesn't read any guilt on my face.

"She refused to be accompanied back, so the rest of the students dispersed around 1 AM," he says.

Again, I shake my head. "I didn't hear her come back. I had my door shut, though." *And locked.* "She could've come in and left and I wouldn't have known."

"Tell me about the altercation between you two. Why was Piper angry and upset?"

At last, the petty reason behind our fight comes into good use. "She accused me of stealing her boyfriend."

My words have their intended effect. Haskins lips lift briefly in what appears as a tired sigh. Dr. Luke frowns.

"And you assaulted her," Haskins says.

I'm talking to the bald spot on his head, since he hasn't lifted his attention from his notepad. "I was defending myself. She threatened me."

"And yet, this is not the first time you've been involved in similar conflict. Your friend from back home—Sylvie Teegarden—you were with her when she overdosed, correct?"

Acidic drops of unease *plink* into my belly. "That has nothing to do with ... Piper and I started off with a misunderstanding. Piper explained it that way when Professor Dawson found us. And again, during detention. Right, Dr. Luke?"

"Miss Ryan's telling the truth." Another shoulder pat, though slower this time, as news of my checkered past sinks in. "Miss Harrington also expressed to me they worked out their differences."

"Mmm. Until new differences came up." Haskins lifts his gaze. "Who's the guy?"

"Chase Stone," I say, without hesitation. *She did it*, that bastard had said.

"The boy who...?"

I give a sharp nod. "The one who was in my dorm room when you arrived and accused me, yep."

"Looks like you have some differences with him, too."

"Of a sort." I pick at invisible lint on my cardigan. My face is too pinched and vindictive to look at Haskins head-on. "Are you questioning him, too? He and Piper were close for a long time."

"I plan on talking with him." Haskins cocks his head. "You can relax, Callie. You're not in trouble. Right now, we're going through all the steps of an investigation, but it's appearing that, well, Piper was the last one at the cliff. Dr. Luke may not have seen her, but all the kids we accounted for insisted she was with them at the beginning. She may have gotten turned around. I hear visibility isn't so good around there at night."

So, she either fell or she jumped, and no one noticed, is left unsaid between us.

I'm practically digging a hole in my sweater, so I drop my hand. "I'm sorry. This whole thing has me ... upside-down. I can't believe it's real."

"I pulled your history," Haskins says, his voice sobering. "I apologize for dragging you through this again, but you understand why it's so important we chat."

Chat. Like we're old friends catching up on death. "I do."

"Any other reasons why Piper might've been upset, or was this just about boyfriend stealing?"

"I've known her for a little over a week, sir. And I wasn't stealing Chase. We're not—we were never together. Piper and I may not have liked each other, but I'd never hurt her."

"Indeed. Well, so far, we have witness statements in your favor, and they line up with what you've told me this morning. Piper threatened you, and assaulted you, on both occasions as well. You were the victim, too. We also have video of you coming into your dorm yesterday evening, and no video of you leaving, so that lines up with your statement of not being at the illegal gathering. But you can see why that may not be sufficient." Haskins crosses his legs. "Briarcliff Academy is known for its hidden passages."

All of this is news to me. My stomach curdles uncomfortably at the realization that Haskins doesn't know I was the last one to throw a punch ... because no one's told him about Piper's accusations about me vandalizing her room or scribbling lipsticked threats on our bathroom mirror. All concocted by Piper's scheming mind, but Haskins wouldn't know that. And it's nothing I can prove as fake, especially when I've done the opposite of endearing myself to the Briarcliff student body.

So, why hasn't anyone told him of the last words she'd said to me?

"Who are the witnesses?" I ask. The dining hall was sparse when I was there. "Piper's friends?"

"Technically, it's confidential, but..." Haskins waves his hand like I'm getting close.

I frown.

Why would Piper's friends ever want to help me?

"Am I under arrest?"

"No, and I'm hoping we've established the type of rapport for your continued honesty."

I nod as if a puppeteer holds my strings, and move to a stand, assuming that was my dismissal.

"We're done here for now." Haskins closes his leatherbound notebook. I stand, the hollowness widening in my chest.

I'm not about to mention the roses, or Piper's continued harassment, because I have the uneasy certainty that it'll be used against me as motive. And I have no idea if Piper's responsible for the secret messages, or if the Cloaks have something to do with it ... should I tell Haskins about the bonfire I witnessed?

I'm questioning the relevancy of it when Dr. Luke chimes in.

"There's an assembly in the large lecture room, Miss Ryan. Headmaster Marron and the guidance counselor will be discussing Piper's tragedy."

It's weird, yet inevitable, that Dr. Luke is using Piper's first name. It makes the finality of her death more apparent, and I'm nauseous at the thought.

"You're all right?" he prompts.

Again, I bob my head, but it's a mechanical motion.

"You and her didn't get along, but the school would understand if this affected you," Dr. Luke says. As he walks over, he lays a light hand on my forearm. "If you need to take the day, I can let the headmaster know, and you can see Mrs. Maisey in private, when you feel comfortable."

"Thank you, but no," I say. "I'll go through the motions today. It ... it doesn't seem real yet."

Haskins clears his throat. "Thank you for your candor, Callie. Here's my card if you think of anything else."

I take it automatically, shoving it in my inside blazer pocket.

Haskins says to my retreating back, "Don't stray too far with that luggage you were packing. I expect you to be available."

With the way he says it, I wonder if Haskins reads more into Piper's and my friction than I initially thought.

"Of course. You have my number," I say, then retreat out the door.

My worries over further questioning from Haskins fade the faster I take the path away from the main building and in the opposite direction to the Assembly Hall.

I'm leaving this place, this school with too many ill intentions weaved between its textbook lines. Piper's tragic death solidifies it, as if the roses, rats, and bullying didn't already. I pick up speed, prepared to bag the rest of my things and drag them out front until an Uber comes to get me.

As I take to the path, I notice lights flashing a quarter-mile away, in rough proximity to Lover's Leap. I've never been there, so I can guess, but chances are there isn't any other reason for police vehicles to be parked nearby.

Oh, Piper, I think, unable to tear my attention away from the blinking lights through the rising fog of the morning. *What happened?*

My feet keep moving despite my distraction, and I'm in front of Thorne House before I register the distance I crossed.

I'm surprised to find Ivy behind the front desk when I enter.

"Callie!" she says, and flies to the front, gripping me in a tight hug. "Omigod, are you okay?"

"Fine," I say, but it comes out shakier than I intended. "It was just basic questioning."

"Thank goodness. I thought you were under arrest, after what Chase said."

My eyelids lower, my vision darkening with held-in frustration. "Unfortunately, it takes more than a flippant comment to solidify me as a suspect. I also think they're ruling it as an accident or suicide."

"Oh. Gosh. That's terrible."

We pull apart, and Ivy walks with me to the elevators. "Hey, while you were out, you got a delivery."

I think of my previous "deliveries," and my steps slow. "Do you know what it is?"

"Some boxes," Ivy says, then hits the UP button. "Return address was from NYC, though."

"Oh." I exhale the remnants of tension. "That doesn't sound too bad."

Ivy laughs as we step into the elevator together. "You poor thing. No wonder you're desperate to leave this place."

We fall into silence once we stride down the hallway to my room. My keycard clicks us in, and I focus on the tower of boxes sitting in the center room, instead of the commotion in Piper's bedroom, cameras clicking and low-voiced mumblings of cops clogging up the atmosphere.

I count three boxes, and notice a note stuck to the top one.

Hey, Callie!

Here's the winter clothing I promised. It's supposed to get cold a lot sooner, so we've sent you proper gear. Did your dad tell you? We're headed to Tahiti for two weeks to celebrate your baby sister. Six months already! Can you believe it? I'll be loaded on virgin pina coladas before you know it.

Anyway, enjoy the clothes. We hope you're having SO MUCH FUN at school and have made a ton of friends, just like we knew you would.

We'll touch base when we get home. Talk soon, hon!

Xoxo, L.

I release the letter from between my fingers, the note fluttering to the ground.

"What did it say?" Ivy asks behind me. "Who's it from?"

"My parents," I say dully. Then, I say it again, with forced pep. "My *parents*."

"Girls?" A policeman ducks his head out of Piper's room. "You can't be here. Not until we finish processing."

"Yes, sir," Ivy says, then obediently cups my elbow and leads me into the hallway.

My lips spread wide in a vacant grin. "My fucking *parents*."

Laughter bubbles up, uncontrollable, and soon I have to clutch my stomach, I'm giggling so hard.

"Uh, Callie? Are you all right?"

"My parents!" I screech through my laughter. I lift my head to the ceiling and cackle.

"Callie ... hey." Ivy comes up beside me, peering closer at my face.

"MY PARENTS!" I laugh again, laugh and laugh until tears start streaming down my face.

Ivy starts rubbing my back as I buckle from mirth. "Callie, you're scaring me. Tell me what's going on."

I throw my hand up, signaling for Ivy to give me a sec. Through my gasps and hiccups, I manage to say, my lips salted with tears, "They have no idea."

Ivy asks, "Who? Your parents?"

"Yes!" I cry, my arms splaying out as I straighten. "They have no fucking clue what's going on!"

"I ... I guess that's true." Ivy tries on a tentative smile.

"I'm-I'm bullied, harassed, then my roommate dies, and *they want me to have fun!*"

My knees turn to jelly as I laugh harder than I've laughed before, and soon, Ivy's clutching me, because I can't stand on my own.

The laughs turn to chuckles.

Then, morph into quiet giggles as I turn my face into her shoulder.

Then sobs.

"Callie," she whispers in my ear. "Shh. It's gonna be okay."

"I don't belong," I say in a hitched whisper into her neck. "Anywhere."

"You do," Ivy says. "You're my friend. You belong with me."

I sob into her shoulder. For Piper or for my mom, I can't be sure. Maybe it doesn't have to be one or the other.

Ivy rubs circles on my back. "You're not alone, okay? We'll get through this. We'll get answers."

No, I want to scream. *The answers will never come.*

23

*I*vy is an expert at the guilt game. Somehow, she convinces me to stay at Briarcliff, at least until Piper's investigation is completed.

Maybe the "somehow" should be better explained. The boxes of clothes Lynda sent me made my reality a lot clearer. She and Dad are off living their lives, Ahmar doesn't have room for me, as much as he wants to, and the place I have now is … one I shared with Piper.

There aren't many options, so until I clean up my life a bit more, I'm stuck at Briarcliff.

Since I'm not allowed back into my room yet, I scrub my eyes dry and we head to the assembly. The lecture hall is packed when we arrive, but Ivy finds two vacant seats toward the back. Headmaster Marron is well into his speech about student safety and mental health availability, as well as the dangers of drinking, essentially cementing the idea in all our minds that Piper either committed suicide or became so drunk she fell, before the investigation is officially concluded.

But having heard this all before, I use the time productively and scan students' heads, searching.

I find Piper's girlfriends, seated in the front row, just off center. Willow and Violet hold tissues, their eyes and noses bright red from crying. Falyn is pale—colorless—and stone-faced as she listens to Marron, her hands clenched so hard in her lap, they match the unhealthy white of her face.

Some friends they are. Did they really leave a drunk Piper to walk alone by herself back to the dorms?

Nearby, I see James's strawberry blond mop of hair, Tempest's textured ebony locks, and Riordan's close-cropped one. They sit, stoic and serious, their uniforms buttoned and pressed, the epitome of Briarcliff representation and not the least bit hungover during such a tragedy as they display themselves, front and center, while Marron waxes on about the importance of reaching out for help.

It's who I don't see that grabs my attention the most.

Chase is nowhere to be found, and my mind ponders the reasons why. He was severely incensed in my room, desperate to unleash his fury on the nearest victim. I'd think he'd make himself present, if only to rake his stare across the entire student body, as if someone in this room has reason to know why Piper toppled off Lover's Leap.

"Do you think there are pictures?" someone mutters to their friend in front of me.

"What, like of the crime scene?" the friend asks. "Or is it even a crime scene? She offed herself, right?"

"Yeah, but, like, someone must've taken pictures of the body. How fucked up do you think it is?"

Bile spreads in my throat, and I cough with disgust. Both pairs of eyes glance back, ashamed, until they realize who they're looking at.

"Maybe the possum did it," one sneers.

I sneer right back, surprised at my defense of Piper, a queen whose subjects are ready to turn on her as soon as news hits that she's dead.

Movement in front redirects my focus, and I notice Tempest leaving the lecture hall. I rise to follow him.

"Where are you going?" Ivy whispers loudly.

"I missed an assignment. Need that guy's notes. Don't worry," I say, then duck out the back exit as Ivy whispers furiously, *"What guy?"*

I catch Tempest in the foyer, just as he's about to hit the steps to the Wolf's Den.

"Tempest!" I call, sprinting to catch up to him.

His head turns, his unsettlingly green eyes meeting mine before sliding away in disdain.

"You," he says, once I skid to a halt in front of him. "What do you want?"

Up close, it's easier to spot the hangover. Purple crescents mar his unblemished skin and his hair isn't stylishly messy as usual. More like one side of his face laid flat against a forest floor all night.

Did you watch Piper fall?

The incredulous question rattles my bones, and I gnaw on my lip to cover my thoughts.

I ask instead, "Have you seen Chase?"

Guile replaces the disinterest in his expression. "Why?"

"Because he's a dick," I say, and my frankness makes half of his mouth tilt in a smile, stretching what I thought was a large freckle in the lower corner of his lip. Turns out, it's a hole for a piercing. I add, "And he needs to explain to me why he accused me of murder this morning."

Tempest's eyes flare, but he regains his languid composure. "Nobody knows why Chase does what he does. You might as well ask a fairy godmother for an explanation."

My hand tightens on my bag's strap. "I'd prefer to ask him."

"Well, he's not up there." Tempest's eyes drift upward.

I exhale and bite down on my lip again. "Hey, I'm sorry about Piper."

Tempest's hand freezes on the banister. "She made your life fucking hell, possum. Why are *you* sorry?"

"Because she was a person?" I respond, but I take a closer look at him. He seems so emotionless, so unaffected by the death of someone who—"Wasn't she your friend?"

He shrugs. "An acquaintance, but yeah, it sucks she died."

I set my jaw, but I stay silent, reluctant to agitate Tempest's icy calm.

Tempest must take pity on my inability to properly converse with him, because he adds, "Chase goes one of three places. Here, his room, or the boathouse."

Incentivized, I nod thank you, then turn for the exit.

"Possums are blind during the day," Tempest says.

"Uh, excuse me?"

After an offhand shrug, he replies, "Just a fun piece of trivia for you."

After a pause, I say, "It's their night vision that's limited."

Tempest raises his brows.

"And here I thought someone with *pest* in their name would be more familiar with their species." I add, "See? Creativity has its benefits."

I shoulder through the front doors, having no need to witness Tempest's resultant, vengeful glare.

24

Navigating the trail down to the boathouse is a lot harder when Ivy isn't in front directing my steps, but I manage to make it without breaking an ankle or getting my hair tangled in any branches.

It isn't hard to locate Chase once I hit the clearing, since the broad-shouldered figure seated at the edge of the dock could only be him.

I take the path Ivy showed me and enter the boathouse through the side door. Anger provides the bravery to walk through the clubhouse and equipment room until I'm through a boat bay and onto the docks.

Chase's legs hang over the side of the dock, water lapping at his knees as he lifts something that glints against the light and puts it to his mouth.

Unable to quell the good girl instinct, I glance up at the windows, conscious that a coach or a teacher might be watching. Though, when it comes to Chase, it's anybody's guess how little it takes to turn a blind eye to his blatant disregard of school rules. It doesn't take a genius to notice no one at this forbidden party is being overtly punished. I wonder how much money it took to keep Marron from expelling each and every one of them.

Yeah. Like that would ever happen.

Or maybe, the families and Marron see Piper's death as punishment enough.

I stanch the morality of my thoughts as I approach Chase, my shoes sounding against the wood. His head turns at the noise, showcasing his strong profile with his straight nose and sharp jaw. When he registers who it is, he goes back to gazing straight ahead at the view, lifting the bottle again.

My shoes stop at his back. Chase doesn't react.

"It's not even lunchtime," I say.

"And?" He scans the lake before him.

"You're getting drunk."

"What an astute nose you have, rodent."

The barb doesn't hit its mark. Instead, I volley one of my own. "It's funny, you never lowered yourself to Piper's insults when she was alive."

His back goes rigid.

I involuntarily gulp. I'm poking the beast. But it's too tempting to disturb him like he did to me this morning.

"You're so fucking clueless," he mutters, tipping the beer bottle to his lips.

I drop my bag and sit cross-legged beside him, ensuring no part of me hangs over the edge. "Then why'd you finger me to the cops?"

Laughter bubbles into his throat, and a genuine smile crosses his lips. "Did you actually try to sound like a crime show just now?"

I frown. "No, because that's what you did. You told them I killed her, Chase. Even your overly-entitled ass has to know how screwed up that is."

He allows his head to fall to one shoulder until he's staring at me with his depthless brown eyes, rimmed in thick lashes that he bats adoringly at me. I dismiss the flutter at my core as fast as it comes. "Relax. Nothing's gonna happen to you."

"Oh, so now you *don't* think I killed your girlfriend. How kind of you to be so wishy-washy. It's not like we're talking about a real death here."

Chase winces at my words. He says into his bottle, "I'm aware of the reality of the situation. And it's my fucking fault." He tosses the empty, and it lands in the water with a clunk. Squinting, I notice the few friends floating with it.

"How is it your fault?" I ask.

"I could've walked back to school with her." He shrugs, then reaches into the six-pack beside him for another beer. "Didn't, because we got in a stupid fight over her drinking too much."

"Don't go there. The rabbit hole of despair is a deep one. How could you have known she would turn around? Or get lost on a campus you all know by heart?"

His gaze slides back to mine, but it lands uncertain and unfocused. "I should've taken her back to the dorms. I should've looked for her. Should've searched harder and made sure no one was left behind before I walked away."

Chase's lips clamp shut, and he turns to the lake. I decide to sit with him a while, because he's not telling me to go. A quiet truce settles onto my shoulders as light bird chirps sound from the trees and water laps against the dock.

The reflection of the sun breaks into shards against the soft ripples of the lake, mesmerizing, meditative, and takes my mind off the horror of broken things.

I take advantage of this placid moment to study Chase's features, beautiful in sadness. His arched brows are lowered enough for his lashes to touch, and he's pensive, staring at the water as if the floating leaves can tell him why Piper fell into its depths.

I startle when he throws his arm out toward me. "Want one?"

"Um. No. Thank you."

"If you're here to tell me you've been through it, that you know how I'm feeling, you can kindly fuck off," he says.

"That's not why I found you."

"No?"

"I came here to yell at you."

Chase snorts.

"It's terrible, what Piper must've gone through before she died," I say. "But that doesn't give you the privilege to come into my room this morning, when I'm still registering the news, and yell and threaten to make my life hell."

"Poor Callie, you don't know how it works around here. I did it because I could."

"And now you're lashing out," I say. "Which is, again, unfair."

"Oh, is life unfair to you, sweet girl?" The brown of his eyes resembles sharp chips of wood. "Too fucking bad."

"How did you know my mom was killed?"

He jolts, then glowers upon realizing his tell.

"You said it to me this morning." I hesitate, but barrel on, "Piper said it to me before she … How did you guys know?"

Chase's shoulders move in an unconcerned shrug, but his hardened features tell a story he intends to keep hidden. "We looked you up once we heard you were coming here." Chase glances at me sidelong. "It helps to be aware of who's stepping onto our turf."

I roll my eyes, but the implications sit heavy on my soul. "You don't owe me anything."

"You're right. I don't."

I glare at him. "While this is clearly a tough time for you, I'd appreciate it if you'd keep the details of my mom to yourself."

"Don't want the school to see you as a murder victim's kid, huh?"

Chase says it so callously, I reach out to smack him in the arm.

It's with cat-like reflexes that he catches my wrist mid-launch, and his resultant glare would freeze this hell I'm in if I let it.

"I'd second guess that decision," he rasps, then pushes my arm back against my chest.

The force makes me wobble, and I slam a hand onto the wood to keep me level. Yet, the rising indignation in my belly won't keep in balance.

"Piper isn't like my mom," I say, hating that my voice is uneven. "But it's still an unfair death. Being angry at something you can't change isn't worth it."

With similar reflexive force, Chase twists and grabs my chin, holding my jaw between his fingers and thumb. "Oh, yeah? So, you're okay with your mom's murder never being solved? You're fine finishing the rest of your life without her? Dead is dead, right? Finding the killer won't change shit."

"You didn't let me finish," I say, wrestling against his tight grip. The pulse at the base of my neck pounds. "I managed to define that anger into seeking justice. I'm determined to meet her killer before I die."

Chase's fingers loosen on my cheeks, but his grim stare keeps its focus.

"It hasn't made it easier," I continue. "My anger just means I have all this love for a person no longer here, with nowhere for that love to go."

Chase lifts his upper lip, but it's not a sneer. It's an indicator of the inner battle he's waging upon himself.

Chase leans in. "Don't take me for a drunken fool. I've recognized my anger, too. I know where it needs to go. What if I told you I don't think Piper's fall was an accident or that she jumped?"

My surprised inhale causes a sharp whistle between my scrunched cheeks. For the briefest of moments, Chase's attention strays to my lips. It stays there, his penetrating gaze seeming to plump my sensitive skin all on its own. His tongue strokes across his lower lip, as if in thought, before he releases me abruptly, twists back to the lake, and tips his beer back until he finishes the whole bottle.

"Neither do I," I whisper.

Chase stills with the rim to his lips.

"I've had a bad feeling ever since I was told she died," I admit.

Chase whips his head around. "Why?"

The question is sharp and accusatory, giving life to the dull-eyed stare he aims my way.

"You have every reason to hate Piper," he continues.

"And what about you?" I dare to ask. My heart leaps into my throat, conscious of prodding the devil with his own pitchfork. "Why would you want her gone?"

Instead of the reddened fury I expect, Chase chuckles as he stares at the water. "Sweet possum, I did *not* hurt one of the few genuine friends I have in this school, I promise you that."

The way he says my deplorable nickname, prefacing it with a sugared compliment, shouldn't have me wanting to savor it, but it does.

I say, adding flint to my voice, "I have a passion for the truth. I'll always search for it."

"That's fucking fairy-tale thinking," he mutters, then lifts his legs and swings them onto the dock.

As he rises, Chase offers me his hand. I hesitate at the unexpected chivalry.

Chase crooks his fingers. "Chill. I'm not about to toss you into the lake."

The sarcasm doesn't ring true, and Chase's expression crumbles for the barest of seconds at his comparison of a body and water so soon after hearing about Piper.

It gives me faith that he's more human than demon, even in his own kingdom.

I fold my hand into his own, and he pulls me up with graceful ease, the strength of his rower's arms obvious with how weightless I become in his one-handed pull.

It's enough strength to fling a girl over a cliff's edge.

I'm appalled at the thought. Two hours ago, Detective Haskins all but concluded Piper jumped or fell. And what, all it takes to flip the switch is Chase's unbacked but passionate theory to make me question it? I'm better than that. I come from cop stock.

But, my subconscious whispers, *no one's explained Piper's reason to want to die.*

Piper isn't someone I got to know well, and her expressions and attitude were merciless and mocking. But the vibrancy with which she directed her malice forces me to admit that above all else, she was alive and determined to leave her mark on whoever crossed her path.

That is not the attitude of a person who wants to die.

Was she drunk enough to fall? Piper's familiar with Lover's Leap. She'd know where the edge was, even while sauced. Wouldn't she? And would she really wait for the party to end to linger near a cliff face?

The answer to my question clicks into place twelve hours too late. I gasp.

"You coming?" Chase asks.

His glowering form has moved closer to the boathouse. During my space-out, he also rolled down the legs of his pants and pulled his shoes on.

"Piper died the same night as Rose Briar. September tenth," I blurt.

Chase goes quiet. He licks his lips. Then, he asks, "And that's supposed to be relevant to me how?"

"Whose idea was it to hang out at Lover's Leap last night?"

His stare narrows. "Piper's. Why?"

I spur forward. "She was was hyper-focused on our history project. Piper fell in love with Rose's story. I just … the timing doesn't sit well with me."

"We're always at the cliffs, so her idea to go there last night isn't a new one. But, Briarcliff history is a fucked up one, that much is true."

"Why do people keep saying that, but don't give examples?

Rose's husband, this Thorne guy, he and his brothers founded the school. That part, at least, seems innocent enough."

Chase says nothing, choosing to regard me in that eerie, unmoving way of his instead.

I notch my chin up. "I'm going to look into it. With or without your support."

Chase's lashes twitch, but he keeps his tone bland when he responds. "Do whatever you want."

Despite all the beers, Chase's gait is steady when he turns. He stalks down the dock, and I follow a few steps behind. When he halts at the base of the path to the academy, I slow my pace.

"Tell me what you find," he says without looking back.

I don't respond, since I doubt it's a question, and when he resumes walking, I do, too. But I stop short of catching up to him. Whatever shaky alliance this is, it's bound to crumble as easily as the soil beneath Chase's shoes.

25

With assembly over, some students go to class while others take the opportunity to skip afternoon subjects in order to "grieve."

Their reasoning is dubious, since the halls I pass through are cluttered with students whispering about taking off to go to the emptiest vacation home. As soon as they catch sight of me, though, hands get tighter around mouths, and lips get closer to another's ear.

I'm antsy at the silent, targeted attention, but try to walk it off and focus on my classes. It kind of makes me sad, the way Piper's death is being used as an excuse to gossip or get drunk, and I think maybe she wasn't as revered by her pupils as I'd initially thought. When I pass by Falyn and Willow with their heads together in discussion, my pity is confirmed. Falyn's vouching that her parents are still in Boston and her lake house is free.

"What are you looking at, *rodent*?" Falyn sniffs.

I jolt, realizing I must've paused in the school hallway to hear what they were saying.

"Nothing interesting," I say, then decide to throw them a bone as I resume walking. "I'm sorry about Piper."

"Sure you are." Willow twirls a curly strand of reddish hair around her finger as I pass.

I slow to a halt at the implication in her tone.

"Judge us all you want," Willow continues. "We're holding a vigil for our best friend at Falyn's lake house."

"That's ... great," I say. "But why do you feel you need to explain yourself to me?"

Falyn laughs, but her eyes are puffed and swollen from crying. "Maybe we're studying your reaction, Callie."

My brows come down. "What?"

"You don't seem upset," Willow says. "Your roommate *died*, Callie, and you're skipping through these halls like it's just a regular day."

"I'm not." I'd love to argue further, but I tamp down the impulse to defend my case. I shouldn't need to convince these witches of anything.

"Did you ever consider that maybe the whole school's talking about you because we think you did it?" Falyn asks, her eyes, so pale they're almost gray, are calculating and cruel.

I cough out a laugh, but even to me, it sounds tight and anxious. "Then why not tell the detective what Piper said to me? About all the 'terrible' things I did to her?"

Falyn's lips twist. Willow sucks in a breath but keeps her cool. Both won't stop glaring at me.

"Maybe," Falyn mumbles, "we weren't given a choice."

"What's that supposed to mean?" I ask.

Willow pipes up. "It means, watch your back. You're protected until you aren't anymore."

I cover up my unease by turning my back on them in an attempt to find the nearest classroom.

Something pulls at my shoulder, and when I'm spun around, Willow's freckled, angry face looms near.

"Piper was fine before you moved in," Willow hisses. "But then you come along, and now she's dead—"

"Stop with the accusations!" I wrest out of her hold. "I never did anything to her. Ever. If you wanted to fuck me over, you should've just told the detective the truth. But you didn't, so don't come after me now."

"Yeah, well, have fun with that while it lasts," Falyn says as she comes up behind Willow. "Because we're all against you. We're positive Piper would be alive if it weren't for you. Whether she did it herself, or *you pushed her!*"

Falyn's yell bounces off the walls. Students slow at her words, and stares that were curious before narrow with conviction.

She did it, I hear someone whisper.

It totally makes sense, another mutters. *Thirsty as fuck.*

Isn't jealousy, like, the number one reason why people kill?

My lips tighten over my teeth, but I peel them back to counter, "Your lies are so much easier to swallow, aren't they? Since the truth is, you left your friend alone to die."

The accusation sits bitter on my tongue and I'm so disappointed in myself for stooping to their level, but it's much too late to take back.

Falyn's face trembles in outrage.

She breathes out enough to hiss, "You bring up *such* a good point, possum. Maybe the police *should* hear all about what you did to her."

"Falyn, don't," Willow says, "We're not supposed to..."

I don't hear their further conversation, because I've widened the space between us and stride down the hallway, their voices nothing but beetles hissing in my ear.

I'm desperate to get as far away from Piper's friends as possible and reach my destination in record time. I enter the classroom, and Dr. Luke lifts his head in surprise.

"Callie," he says. "I didn't expect you here today."

"I, uh, wasn't sure if my detention still stood," I say, and lower myself into a seat.

My attention strays to the seat Piper occupied during our

punishment, and a concrete heaviness weighs against my heart. It's not grief, but ... she'll never sit there again.

"I wouldn't have held it against you if you didn't show," Dr. Luke says kindly. "In fact, I'll nullify the rest of your detentions. Consider your punishment stayed because of the circumstances."

Dr. Luke leans back in his seat, arms folded as if he expects me to stand and sprint from the classroom, lightened by a lifted sentence.

"If it's okay with you," I say without moving, "I'd like to stay here."

I pull out my textbooks before Dr. Luke can respond. I'd rather catch up on homework or read ahead for classes than deal with any additional hallway confrontations. The stares and accusations will grow, and the *last* thing I want is to run into Chase in that kind of crowd.

"Well," Dr. Luke says, and when he sees me pull out my history text, his eyes soften around the edges. "You don't have to worry about that project. I can assign you something else or put you in with another group."

"Actually..." I splay my hand across the text. "I'd like to keep writing the paper."

"On Rose Briar? Can you handle her?"

I glance from the pages to him. "I can. I'd like to understand Rose." *And maybe I can also understand Piper* is a statement left unsaid between us, but Dr. Luke isn't so out of touch that he can't decipher my motive.

"Well," Dr. Luke says after a beat, "I never want to tear students away from an assignment they're passionate about, but given the circumstances, if it becomes too much, or you no longer feel comfortable with the subject matter, you let me know, okay? We'll figure something out. I hear Edward Briar is a maniac."

My lips twitch in a smile. "Isn't he the grandfather who lived a full, uncontroversial life before dying of consumption in his seventies?"

Dr. Luke's eyes crinkle. "Yes. Dusty as a chalkboard, that one. But like I said, if you'd prefer to pivot and do a piece on him, you have my permission to go full throttle. Got it?"

Nodding, I open my laptop, and soon, the sounds of my fingers hitting my keyboard are the only noises between us.

I spend the afternoon with my head down, studying hard, and avoiding the catcalls and heckling still going on in my head. What I also hear, though, is my conscience asking why I decided to stay at Briarcliff, when breaking into my Dad and Lynda's empty Manhattan home and living there while they get high on sugar from virgin daiquiris seems like *way* more of an accomplishment.

Because, I reason, I'd be more alone there than I am here.

It's with that crushing thought that I say goodbye to Dr. Luke and plod to Thorne House.

I key into my apartment, staring at the floor as I wander in. A noise sounds out in the direction of Piper's room, and I look up, then drop my bag.

My heart forgets to beat when I see Piper, digging through her drawers.

26

The coffee mug rack clatters when I stumble into the kitchenette's counter.

"P-Piper?" I stutter.

The girl turns, and as soon as she does, I note the differences. This girl has a pointier chin and angular cheekbones on a thinner face. But she has the same stormy blue eyes and long, brunette hair held away from her face with a fabric headband.

"Jesus." I bowl over while holding a hand to my heart. "You're not Piper."

"No." The girl sniffs and slowly withdraws from Piper's room. "I'm Addisyn. Her sister."

I vaguely recall mention of Piper's younger sister when I moved here. Something to do with the furniture-stealing and the initiation of every wrong thing that's happened to me since. "Oh, yeah. Addy."

"Only my friends call me that," she says, but it's not said with any venom. She seems tired. Sallow and deflated. "My parents will be here soon to help pack up my sister's things. I wanted to be here when they arrive."

"That's fine," I say, but with the way her gaze slides over me, I doubt she would've changed tactics if I'd said no.

Someone pushes in from behind, clipping my shoulder. "Here, babe. I found some chamomile tea downstairs."

The boy Addy accepts tea from isn't in Briarcliff uniform, but ripped jeans and a dirtied white tee instead. He gives me a brief study before laying a kiss on Addy's lips and massaging her shoulder.

"Thanks, Jack, but you'd better go," Addy says as she cups the tea close to her chest. "I don't want my parents catching you here."

"I get it." Jack smooths Addy's hair—though it's as stylishly sleek and flat-ironed as Piper's always was—and kisses it. "But I didn't want to leave you without one final goodbye. Text me when it's over, okay?"

Addy nods and falls into Jack's embrace before he releases her. He doesn't give me any sort of acknowledgment before he leaves the apartment the way he came.

As soon as he shuts the door, I turn to Addisyn. "Is that your boyfriend? He seems ... nice."

Addisyn's response is to cast her red-rimmed eyes over me before heading back into Piper's room.

"I'll be in my room if you and your parents need any help," I say, manners getting the best of me.

Piper's door shuts with a smart *click*.

The idea of sitting nearby while all of Piper's things are boxed up and transported to a place where a person doesn't need them anymore doesn't sit well.

While Addy is shut in Piper's room, I grab the books I need and choose to wait out the packing in the library.

I work in blessed silence among crisp books and the smell of hot-off-the-press paper—strangely fresh for what should be an old, stuffy library—for a few hours before the clocktower rings the dinner bell, but can't summon up the motivation to dig into the history project I asked Dr. Luke to keep working on. The clue is in my finding calculus more interesting than a nineteenth-century soap opera: I'm scared of what I might find between the lines of Rose Briar's death. It's so similar to Piper's in so many ways.

Did heartbreak cause Piper to jump, too? Or was she pushed?

Was Rose *pushed?*

At the bell, I go straight to dinner instead of dropping my bag off at my dorm. The feeling of being unwelcome in my own room is stronger than ever and won't go away until Piper's family finishes what they need to do.

I'm so deep in thought, on Piper, on Rose Briar, that it never occurs to me to avoid the dining hall, too. I push through the doors with my head down and beeline to the serving station, raising my chin enough to notice that today is pasta day.

I choose Alfredo this time, due to my complicated relationship with red sauce.

"*Killer*," someone hisses behind my back.

I twist to catch the source of the whisper, clenching the serving tongs in my hand. White sauce drops from the metal and onto the floor, splattering like ethereal blood at my feet.

"*Murderer.*"

This time, I hear it to my right and whip my head to the sound.

"*Jealous bitch.*"

On my left.

Despite my hand aching from how hard I'm gripping the tongs, I'm prepared to meet the angry expressions that must follow those words, yet the students around me are benign or relaxed as they fill their trays, almost like I never heard the whispers.

"*You're next.*"

I swear that was muttered by the girl beside me.

"Next for *what*?" I ask loudly. "To fall victim to an accident? To suicide? Be specific if you're going to threaten me about Piper's death over spaghetti."

The girl startles, her eyes wide behind her glasses. "Um ... what?"

"I heard you," I say.

She shakes her head, confused. "I didn't say anything."

"You did," I snarl, then look up at the students watching. "I had nothing to do with Piper!"

Dead silence meets my words as they echo throughout the hall.

"Why don't you all focus on *why* she did what she did?" When no one answers my question, I cry, "What *is* it about this school that turns people into Greek tragedies?"

Someone hooks onto my elbow and starts dragging me through the dining hall.

Automatically, I struggle against the hold, but his hand clamps down harder. I glance up. My insides shrink at the sight.

"Chase, let me go."

Chase's cold gaze stays straight ahead, but he mutters, "Not a chance."

"I said *let me go*." My voice gets louder. "You don't have the authority to control—"

"Do you see who's watching?" he asks through one side of his mouth. "Take a look, then you can tell me whether or not I should drag you out of here by your ass."

I look where he directs, and my lips thin upon seeing Detective Haskins leaning against the wall, arms folded as he witnesses the spectacle.

"Why do you care if Haskins sees my meltdown?" I ask Chase, but he ignores my question and walks us faster.

Chase pushes us through the double doors into the deserted hallway. When they shut behind him, I jerk out of Chase's hold.

"Why are you trying to save me?" I rub my arm where his grip was, a spot that's sore from his touch ... and pulsing hot. "I thought I was nothing but vermin to you."

His stare becomes his surname as he strides past me. "Because you're no good to me in a holding cell. You're going back to your room."

"I'm not one of your loyal subjects. You can't tell me what to do."

He continues eating up the marble floor, pulling me with him.

"Someone in this goddamned school needs to *answer me!*" I scream, then push at his back and drag my feet until he stops.

And turns.

And in the space of a second, closes the gap and claims my comfort zone.

"I'm not saving you, Callie," he says, and it's so low, so threatening that it's seductive in its menace. "I'm keeping you to myself. Because if you have any answers about Piper's death, *I'm* going to know about it. You'll tell *me*, not some podunk detective who thinks true gumshoeing is pulling kids over for a DUI. Isn't that what we agreed to at the boathouse?"

I bark out a laugh, and his spine jerks upright. "Did I just say something *funny* to you?"

"No," I say with a grin, but hold my stomach, nonetheless. "It's just ... you think you have the power of God. That you have the right to information about a suspicious death simply because you demand it. Fuck, maybe you do." I step back from him and rub my eyes. "What universe have I fallen into where a seventeen-year-old can influence my future?"

"Eighteen," he clips out. "And get used to it. Things don't work the way they do in the big city. My family has connections. *I* have power over this school and all the professors here. *My* family gifted the current library. Headmaster Marron? He's golf buddies with my father, a top criminal defense attorney in this *country*. That should make your tits shrivel, considering the school's current opinion of you. And I can use both my father's and my stronghold over Briarcliff to save you, or I can break you. Understand?"

I will ruin you!

Piper's voice rings in my ears.

I gather the courage to say, "Tell me about the roses."

The muscles in Chase's jaw goes tight. "What?"

"Tell me," I repeat. "Because if anyone knows if Piper's death is suspicious, it's the people behind those flowers."

"Those fucking plants have nothing to do with it."

Chase seems so certain, and yet... "So, you admit they exist."

Chase's lips peel back from his teeth. His eyes narrow to a glare. "What part of *go to your room* are you not comprehending?"

"I'm not forced to follow your rules."

"You better follow someone's, because after what you pulled in there, the cops will look at you harder."

"Why would they?" This time, *I* step up to *him*. "It was an accident. Or Piper jumped. Isn't that what you're so confident these hick cops are concluding? Case closed."

One of Chase's eyelids tics. "You said you were willing to get to the bottom of it, anyway."

"Yes, but I'm doing that for *me,* not you. And I'm not listening to the gossip, which you could stop with one use of that flinty glare of yours. Everyone in that dining hall looks to you, their *ruler*. You told me at the boathouse you don't think Piper committed suicide, and now people are calling me a killer, a murderer, unhinged from my mother's death. That all *stinks* of you Nobles coming together and letting the rumors swirl—"

Chase's hands clamp down on my shoulders. He rasps, an inch from my face, "What have I said to you about that word?"

"It has something to do with the roses, doesn't it? This whole thing, it comes down to the cloaks I saw, gold and black..." As I stare into the murky depths of Chase's eyes, the answers become clear. "They weren't pranks, were they? Replacing my furniture, then filling my locker with poisoned rats ... they're warnings."

Abruptly, Chase releases me, his hot breath leaving my lips. "Shut your mouth, Callie, or I swear to God."

My vision turns into two slits. "You want my help? Give me some answers so I look elsewhere. Are you part of it? Of the cloaks and roses? Is that who the Nobles are?"

"I said, shut up!" he roars.

I wince, his echoing shout slamming against my ears. His chest rises and falls with his deep breaths, but he's not moving. He's not tearing his gaze away from mine.

I whisper, "Ask your inner circle about Piper. She and I weren't friends. We were closer to enemies, but I never hated her."

The memory of me tearing up the rose and wishing Piper and Chase bad luck floats to the surface, but I shove it back down. Wishes can't be granted. They're nothing but envy put into words when people don't have control over their own lives.

"Or," I surmise, "Are your friends thinking Piper killed herself, too?"

I don't think Chase will answer me. I'm confident he'll stomp away like he always does, this infuriating boy who sends me all the wrong signals, but my heart argues is so right.

Chase's lips part. "If you're so smart, you'll figure out why you're in the spotlight soon enough."

I laugh dully. "Shocking. Chase Stone giving me a cryptic answer instead of the truth."

"Just be happy you're not in there having a screech-fest in front of the fucking noodle bar," he tosses out.

"You're such an asshole."

"Thank me later," Chase says as his parting shot, then shoves his hands in his pockets and leaves.

Half of me wants to grab him by the shoulder and drag him back here, because I'm not finished. Most of me wants to punch him in the face.

But part of me knows he's doing the decent thing, and I'm better off in my room, behind my computer. Students can't insult me if I'm not there to hear it.

My chief concern is whether Piper Harrington's sudden death will fall on deaf ears, too.

27

My stomach rumbles as I crouch over my desk and force my eyes to keep reading the document on my computer.

I lean back, absently rubbing my belly and wishing I'd gotten in a mouthful of fettuccini before being carted away by His Highness, King Chase.

The dorm room is utterly silent with me as the sole occupant, and I've left my bedroom door wide to get some air, because the longer I sat at my desk and worked on the history essay, the stuffier this room became.

Piper's door is open, too, but it's completely empty, save for her ghost. Her parents and sister stripped her bed, emptied her drawers, and cleaned out the center room and kitchen pantry, leaving nothing behind but empty food packets they'd shoved into our mini trashcan.

If it weren't for the scent of gardenia in the air, it's as if Piper had never set foot here.

My stomach growls again, with wet, bubble-bursting sounds.

At this point, I haven't memorized the campus well enough to search for late night snacks, but perhaps there's a vending machine in Thorne House's lobby. I vaguely recall Ivy mentioning a coffee bar set up there.

Or, if all else fails, I can scour the Wolf's Den for tossed-aside pastries, but that involves traveling Briarcliff's paths at night.

I'm not up for that, cloaks or no cloaks. And there's also Piper's fall into watery depths to consider, and whether someone hides in the shadows to do it to someone else.

Damn you, Chase, for getting into my head.

In more ways than one.

Ignoring my stomach for a little longer, I turn back to my research on Rose Briar, this time containing notes unlike the first round I deleted when I was determined to leave Briarcliff. I'm trying to read between the lines, as if an answer to Piper's demise is linked with Rose's. But with all I've read, the issues surrounding Rose's death are benign, nineteenth century issues. I click onto Briarcliff's library website, attempting to look up texts from that era, but keep getting "NO RESULTS FOUND."

It's freaking strange. Wouldn't Briarcliff Academy's library, of all places, have original founding documents, or copies of it? Didn't Piper say she'd found original papers?

Yet, other than a brief, transcribed obituary, there's nothing much on Rose, never mind any link to Rose and Piper, save for the same cliff, one hundred and seventy years later.

The two couldn't possibly be related. But this was the last assignment Piper was working on. The final subject in her head. Then, she fell off Lover's Leap—*Rose's* leap.

Piper loved the story and fed off Rose's heartbreak, but ... what am I missing here?

Brrrrrrrrrrrrruuup.

Ugh. Stupid stomach.

My chair scrapes against the floor as I push it back and wander out of my bedroom, chancing a search through the kitchenette, even though I know what I'll find. Again, I curse my lack of groceries and tell myself I'll carve out some time Friday to grab some snacks, meaning I'll only have to prowl for food one more day.

Like the rat they think I am.

My heart shrivels at the thought. It's infuriating, how I'm giving proof to Piper's moniker of me even after her death.

Sliding on my shoes, I peer into Piper's room, wishing her parents had left some of her binders behind, or that I'd had the forethought to take her notes or emailed them to myself somehow. She never did send me her findings on Rose Briar. And if any clues existed, it would've been in Piper's own interpretation of Rose's history.

Figuring that ship has sailed, I turn for the door and—

Wait.

I squint at the tiniest strip of red peeking from out of Piper's stripped mattress.

Like the brownnoser I am, I glance around on instinct, as if there's someone there to scold me for wanting to step into someone else's room and invade their privacy, but this dorm room is deserted, save for me. Piper's presence was permanently lifted when her family removed all of her things.

Technically, this room could be considered my property now, at least until Marron assigns someone else to it, which he has yet to mention.

Despite my rationalization, I hesitate in my steps. This space shouldn't be invaded so soon. It's as if the air itself contains sacred artifacts from Piper's life that will dissipate as soon as I disturb it.

"Don't be silly," I mutter. I was forced to live in my mom's space for a while after she died, my stepdad not having the funds to move us until he met Lynda. Her artifacts of life were around me constantly, whether they ripped my soul apart or not.

I can enter Piper's room and see what the ribbon is. Now that I'm closer, I confirm it's red satin and attached to something—not a rose, *please*—that's pushed into the mattress.

The ribbon's slipped free from a tear in the cushioning, likely from all the jostling when packing up Piper's life at Briarcliff. But it's a straight cut ... and clean. It's not a hole that happened by accident.

I touch the opening, then after a breath, push my fingers through the padding and hit something hard.

Frowning, I stick the rest of my hand in, grab the object, and pull it out.

It's a hardback book, with a cream background and red roses painted across it. The pages are trimmed at the edges with gold foil, and if I didn't know any better...

I gasp upon flipping the pages to a random section.

Pages and pages of handwritten notes greet my vision. In my brief scan, I see words like *Chase,* and *my heart's broken,* and, *Callie shouldn't be here,* before I close the book with a snap, splaying my hand across the front.

Oh my God.

I haven't just opened Pandora's box by finding this notebook.

I've stepped into a viper's nest.

This is Piper's diary.

28

*N*aturally, I go straight to the end of Piper's journal and read her final entry.

01.08.05.Ha
Nobody knows that Mr. S and I are back together, and to keep it that way, I'm not going to use his true name, not even during my private thoughts. Plus, he likes that I call him Mr. S when I'm naked. He wants me to moan it before my mouth goes around his dick and I take all of him in. He wants me to plead it when he buries himself inside me and won't let me come until I beg with his nickname on my tongue.

He likes the power. He gets off on it.

And I'm drunk off desire for him, my Mr. S. I missed him so damn much.

I wish he'd let me tell the world about our love. I want us to be real, to go out in public, but he says to wait until we're done with Briarcliff and both of us can leave. But I crave him. I need his arms around me, and the one person that's preventing us from always being together is Callie. My surprise orphan of a roommate is ruining our plans.

. . .

Holy. Shit.

My cheeks are hot by the time I finish, my fingers clenched around the notebook.

Mr. S sounds so much like Chase Stone ... but why would he want to keep their hook-ups secret?

My conscience roars its disapproval. Piper's death is likely an accident, so would the police even care if I gave this to them?

Unless there was something in it to indicate she didn't fall or jump. Like ... a secret affair Mr. S didn't want Piper to reveal.

My breaths level out, and I shut Piper's diary. I have to give it to Haskins...

I don't want to be implicated because I gave them Piper's private thoughts. I'm her supposed enemy. They would wonder, why do I have her diary?

"Argh!" I let out a frustrated growl. What would my mom do in this situation?

My inner villainess thinks to plant the diary on Falyn or Willow, but I'm way too clumsy to pull it off and my fear of authority and getting caught trumps that idea pretty fast.

Then, it comes to me.

I'll anonymously mail the diary to the Briarcliff precinct. Being caught with her diary would cause way more of an issue than mailing it. I'm innocent, but ... sending the notebook to them in an unmarked envelope seems like it'll keep me that way.

...There's nothing to stop me from taking pictures on my phone of each page before handing it over, though.

"I'm one of the rare few who believe there's something suspicious to your death," I whisper to her diary. "Me ... and Chase."

I was shaking by the time I finished Piper's final entry, picturing Chase and Piper doing all the things she outlined. And what's most appalling ... I'd wished I were Piper, begging for Chase to undress me.

God, when did I become so twisted with dark desires? He could be Piper's killer.

I reopen the book and turn the pages, snapping photos with my phone as I go along, reading snippets. Piper goes into visceral detail about what they did in private. How Mr. S found her during the day, then whispered hot promises in her ear as he thrust into her at night—until I came along.

My cheeks go hot again. They were doing dirty things in this dorm room, and it's *definitely* why Piper wanted to keep the apartment a single. There's a perverted urge inside me that wants to read more. And picture it.

Most of all, I have to *know*.

I switch to the strange date written at the top of her last entry, the only entry that has this combination of numbers and letters.

It can't be an actual date of the year. In 2005, Piper was 2 years old. Even reversing the numbers doesn't make sense.

I decide to copy it down on a sticky note as well as take a picture of it, thinking I might as well show the string of numbers to Ivy to see if she might know what it means.

"Allow me access this one time," I say, Piper's fragrance lingering in the paper. "I'll find out the truth."

To my surprise, I get midway through her notebook and find a section of torn-out pages. I run my finger along the remnants. Did Piper do this? It could be the simplest reason—she misspelled words, or her handwriting got messy, or the entry was stupid.

Or ... it could be incredibly important.

Where are the missing pages?

I leap out of bed and do a thorough search of her barren room but find nothing. Once back to mine, I finish up the photos, then shove Piper's diary into the nightstand's top drawer, but it doesn't feel safe there. This room has been violated with its gifts of roses and wood. Someone has trespassed with the intent of ownership and a display of power, and if they come back ... if they find this book...

It may never get into the proper hands. I *have* to get rid of it once I get the chance.

But I'm the person to read this. I know it deep in my heart.

Piper's soul needs to be put to rest, because I can't have two ghosts rivaling for my thoughts, demanding justice on their graves.

29

I spend two days wondering how the investigation into Piper's death is going.

On the outside, I'm the perfect student, paying attention in class, avoiding confrontation, and ignoring the sweeping accusations I hope fade as the gap of time between the shock of Piper's fall and campus visits from the police get wider.

There hasn't been a chance to get rid of Piper's diary anonymously, so I use the time to read more. And yet ... I can't find anything suspicious. Piper goes on and on about how she hates her parents' hounding or how annoying her sister is now that she's in school with her. She also thinks Falyn's getting too fat for crew. And Violet has an eating disorder. And Willow's getting too involved with Mr. S—*did they fuck without me knowing? Are they fucking with me? He will be so, so sorry if I find out it's true. He's mine, even when we're not together. Even if our parents refuse our relationship. It'll always be him, my Mr. S. Always.*

It's such drivel that I often have to shake myself awake to finish. So far, the sole intriguing entry is the last one. There are further graphic depictions of Mr. S and Piper's sexcapades. I haven't found much else about Mr. S, other than he could be

Chase, and I'm halfway through her journal. I mean, maybe I could make the mental leap and think it's Chase's father because of the "Mister" part, but that would be *crazy*. And Willow sleeping with him, too?

Yeesh, wtf kind of erotic novel am I reading?

My thoughts are yanked away from the journal when Dr. Luke enters the classroom, his expression grim.

"I have some news, class," he says.

The morning chatter falls silent as he leans forward on his desk.

"This morning, the official statement was announced. Barring further evidence, Piper's fall was an accident."

The quiet becomes a pause as we all process Dr. Luke's statement.

Falyn speaks. "But ... how? She's been up there before. I mean —Piper knows the layout of Lover's Leap."

Snickers burst out from students with a tenuous relationship with Piper, but Dr. Luke silences them with a death glare.

"Miss Clemonte, I know you're upset. You have the right to be. We all want answers, but it was especially dark that night with no moon," Dr. Luke says. "There were too many scuff and shoe marks in the dirt. Ultimately, there was just no way for her to tell where the edge of the cliff was."

"But what about her phone? Wouldn't she be using her flashlight?" Falyn persists. Her eyes shine with desperation.

"I don't believe she had her phone," Dr. Luke says, his forehead wrinkling with thought.

"But *why*? She doesn't go anywhere without it. Ever. Why was she up there alone?" Falyn's voice hitches, and Violet moves to comfort her. "Why didn't she go *home*?"

Any empathy I feel toward Falyn disappears when she turns and lasers into me. "In my opinion, the police haven't done an adequate job. There's at least one suspect in our midst."

"Then you have my full support to take it up with Detective

Haskins or read the statement yourself," Dr. Luke says tiredly. "Now, this is a terrible subject for all of us, so let's get lost in a little history before real life smacks us in the face again."

Dr. Luke launches into the economic state of Rhode Island when Briarcliff was built, but the buzzing in my ears overtakes his voice.

Piper fell. It was an accident.

But the police don't know about Mr. S.

Chase makes my paranoia worse. His silence on Piper's death propels rumors faster, and I'm having to duck and weave in the hallways in order to avoid the glares and insults cast my way.

Even now, I study the back of his head as we both sit through history class, attempting to decipher through the effortless styling of his hair why his face sports a shiner this morning and his knuckles are cut and clotted over with blood.

"Don't forget, your essays are due Monday morning," Dr. Luke says as he concludes the class. "Just because you're my favorite students ever doesn't mean I'll give any of you extensions."

Doting sarcasm fills his voice, and I offer up a smile along with some other students as we pack up our things.

"Callie."

The tone doesn't match Dr. Luke's and I glance up from my bag. Chase stands in front of me.

His face is flawless, save for the purple-red crescent under his left eye. A cut mars his lower lip, and there are fingerprints on his neck, scarlet marks that frame his jugular.

After a quick hitch of breath, I deploy the most annoyed eye-roll I have.

"Let me guess," I say. "I should see the other guy?"

Chase's brows flatline and his expression follows a similar iced-over state. "It's nothing you need to concern yourself over."

"Oh, don't mistake this for concern." I trace a circle around my face. "Color me shocked that you're talking to me in public."

Chase arches a dark blond brow, a wisp of amusement drifting through his dark cloud. "Only because I have to."

I toss my bag over my shoulder, and it lands against my back with a thump. I'm conscious of what's in it. "And why have you deemed it so important?"

"Did you find out anything?"

His question is direct, biting in its cadence.

I swallow but refuse to shrink under his focus. "About what, Chase? If you're here to accuse me along with the rest of the student body, get a clue. Detective Haskins hasn't spoken to me since, meaning I'm not on his hit list, so why should I be on yours?"

Now, both Chase's brows rise. "Easy. Because I want you to be."

My lips flutter with an exasperated huff.

"I'm watching you, Callie. You keep anything from me, I'll catch it. And I won't take it to the cops. I'll use it for my own weapon."

"You heard the latest. Stop being such a creep," I say, and move to get past him.

His arm blocks my way, pressing into my stomach ... and dangerously close to the underside of my breasts. An astonishing sensation happens around my nipples, and I glance down, horrified, but cover it up fast with a sound of disgust.

"I asked you a question," Chase repeats. "Did you find out anything about Rose Briar?"

A wave of relief passes through me at the mention of Rose. Chase doesn't know about the diary, or my suspicion that Mr. S is *him*. I push on Chase's arm, but it doesn't move. When he speaks to me, his bruised profile comes all too close to my cheek. A simple turn, a quick dip, and he could be kissing me.

No, Chase wouldn't kiss. He'd ravage.

Mr. S uses his tongue like a man, possessive and strong. When he strokes my mouth, I moan...

My molars clench, a painful warning to my brain to stop this bizarre fantasy.

I meet his eyes. A millisecond of movement separates our mouths, but Chase isn't fucking around.

I'm aware of my surroundings and notice the classroom has emptied, including Dr. Luke. Chase has me alone.

I don't back down, and I do not, under any circumstances, let a hint of what I know pass over my features. "If you're asking if I completed my paper, yeah, I did."

"Good for you. I hope you get an A. Now tell me what I want to know."

Under his intense scrutiny, I falter, just a little. "There's a ton of information on Briarcliff's founders. You did Theodore Briar, right? A nod to the odd man out?"

Chase's eyes shrink into slits. "Don't change the subject. It makes me want to pursue this harder."

"Read between the lines, Chase. I could research tons on the men. But Rose? I found zilch," I lie. "Enough to write a basic essay. If Piper knew anything, it'd be in her notes, which are on her laptop, which her family now has." I attempt to push past him again. "So why don't you go intimidate Addisyn?"

This time, Chase backs up a step. And his expression is oddly flat. "That's too bad."

"Too bad?" I echo. "I'm so sorry my research into Briarcliff's catacombs wasn't acceptable for you, Master Scholar."

"Not even close. There's a reason Piper wanted to be at the cliff on the same date Rose Briar disappeared. You're the one who pointed it out to me. But now you find nothing? I guess your usefulness ends there. I'll do the rest of the heavy-lifting."

"Oh, fuck you, Chase! I'm invested in this, but you of all people can't blame me for not knowing who to trust."

He pauses in the doorway, his shoulders leveling. "My, my, Callie, are you saying you don't trust me?" Chase lays a mocking hand on his heart. "I am shooketh."

"The official statement's out. It was an accident to everyone except you and me. So, unless you stayed at Lover's Leap with her that night, or, my bad, Fuckboy's Leap—"

Chase stiffens. When his eyes find mine again, they blaze copper fire. "I'd be careful choosing your next response. Accuse me again, and I'll have you tossed off this campus so fast, you'll lose the granny panties currently cupping your ass."

"Joke's on you," I snipe before thinking. "Because I prefer thongs."

Chase's eyelids flare. Heat snakes into my core, coiling its scales. My response to him is frightening, venomous ... and daring.

I hold a silent breath.

The urge is so sudden and *there*, that I'm desperate to think of something else. To get back to Piper and the mystery behind her fall. To do anything but meander into Chase's clutches.

Chase's focus dips to my skirt, as if he can see the building dampness in my panties. I'm desperate to cross my ankles, but that would accelerate the swelling need, so I clench my hands instead, so hard my nails dig crescents into my skin.

Ire builds in my belly, and wars with this unspeakable craving for Chase. Sheer exhaustion weighs heavy on my expression each time I leave my dorm, because to the rest of the school, theories, rumors, and gossip are easier than checking the facts. Hurled insults contain the satisfaction needed.

Cap all this off with Chase's weird and cold dismissal and his refusal to help despite our private talks, always after *he* seeks me out, it's natural that enraged stupidity spirals its way into my throat.

"I know enough, Mr. S," I say.

Chase's attention comes back to my face. Any passion I ignited disappears with that single flick. "Excuse me?"

"Mr. S," I repeat shakily.

His expression smooths. "Maybe I was wrong about you. Keep

your head in your books. You're better at that than any Nancy Drew bullshit you're attempting."

My hands unclench as I watch him leave, my arms trembling with the effort. Chase manages to get under my skin by uttering a simple syllable, and I hate how I can't manage the same effect on him.

Maybe I shouldn't have shown my cards so soon and called him by Piper's secret name. Or perhaps I damn well should've, because I need *something* other than casual coolness from this bastard.

If that flicker of flame in his eyes at the mention of my underwear is anything to go by, perhaps I'm getting there.

Which means, I must identify why it was so crucial to Piper that sex with him had to remain under wraps this time around.

30

That evening, Ivy comes over to study for our English Lit quarter-term exam.

Yup. Quarter-term grades are a thing here.

We're sprawled at either end of my twin bed, our textbooks and laptops between us as Ivy quizzes me on *Pride and Prejudice,* and I resist the temptation to relate the assignment to its modern twist, *Pride and Prejudice with Zombies.*

"I doubt Professor Parker will appreciate your addition of the apocalypse to a literary classic," Ivy observes as she flips a page.

"Hey, I can't take credit for that kind of originality, but it's unfortunate Parker won't widen his horizons." I stick my pen between my lips as I type out notes on my computer.

"Any other potential questions you can think of? I gotta leave in like..." Ivy checks her watch. "Ten minutes."

"Really?" I pull my computer onto my crossed legs, settling back against the wall. "Where are you off to so late?" I let out a mock gasp. "Are you meeting a paramour, Elizabeth Bennet?"

Ivy laughs, but there's a hesitant pitch to it. "I wish. I promised Eden I'd go over chemistry with her tonight, too."

"Jeez. That's adding some contrast to the night."

"I gotta keep the scholarship alive," she says airily, then runs a hand through her hair. "Unlike many of the privileged douches here, if my GPA drops below a three-point-seven, I'm out on my ass."

Accuse me again, and I'll have you tossed off this campus so fast, you'll lose the granny panties currently cupping your ass...

I wriggle against my mattress, static electricity raising the hair on my arm at the thought of Chase picturing me in the thong I'd told him I preferred.

"Might as well give the privileged douches a name," I say to Ivy, internally begging this extra energy to go to anyone but Chase. "You call them the Nobles."

Ivy's pen stops scratching against her spiral notebook. She doesn't look up.

"Right?" I prompt.

"Not this again," she says.

"You tried to get me to forget about it with that *global* bullshit, but Ivy, you told me about them on the night my entire scholastic future was written on the wall. In garbage."

"Yeah..." Ivy collects her white-blond hair at the nape of her neck, twists it, then lets it fall. "I realize that was a lame cover-up, but is there any way you can pretend I never told you that?"

I angle my head. "You want me to shut up."

Ivy raises her chin, pleading. I hold up my hand. "You're doing a much better job of it than Chase did, basically threatening to have my head if I ever uttered the name again."

Ivy hisses in a breath, and I swear, color leeches from her face in less than a second. "You told *Chase*?"

"It's not like you told me to stay quiet!" I defend. "Not then, anyway."

"Oh my God, *Callie*." Ivy covers her face with her hands. "Why?"

"Why not?" I push my laptop off my legs and slide closer. "I'm so tired of this game where I toss out an innocuous word and the person I'm talking to flips out. Can someone please be straight with me? As my friend? Explain to me why the Nobles send Chase into a rage and you into a tizzy." I slide a look to the opposite end of the dorm. "And while we're at it, do they have something to do with Piper?"

Ivy doesn't hesitate. "No." She follows my gaze. "Doesn't it freak you out? Living in a place Piper used to make her home? It's so lifeless out there now..."

"It is," I admit. "Which is why, tomorrow morning, I'm going into town and grabbing a few things to make this space my own. Marron says that barring any new students, there won't be anyone filling up her side of the room, so..."

Ivy tucks a strand of hair behind her ear. "It's just you? From now on?"

"I'm not sure how I feel about it, but—hey! Don't change the subject on me!"

Ivy offers a sheepish smile, but color hasn't returned to her cheeks. "A girl had to try."

"Tell me." I lean forward. "Give me something, Ivy, or I'm going to annoy it out of you every minute of every hour, I swear I will."

Ivy sighs, her attention straying to my doorway. "I can trust you, right?"

I grab her hand, and it's cold and clammy in my grip. I squeeze, letting her know that she can.

"Then you can trust me. Don't go to Chase," she says. My hold goes slack. "Drop it, Callie."

I lean back, releasing her hand as a signal that I'll listen to her. For now. Tomorrow morning brings its own stressful complications, so I can leave the subject of the Nobles for later.

"Fine," I mutter. "I won't talk to Chase about it."

"Good. Thanks for the study sesh," she says, and her smile isn't as tight. "I'll see you tomorrow? Maybe I'll join you on this field trip you have in mind."

"I'll text you."

"Sounds great," she calls as she exits my room, color back in her cheeks and a skip to her step.

As soon as my dorm room door shuts with a click, I rifle through my nightstand, pull out Piper's diary, and hold it up.

I glare at it.

"What the hell is the point of a secret diary if you don't write down any of your secrets, Piper!"

31

The following morning dawns with a dreary rolling fog across Briarcliff's picturesque lawn. It's Saturday, which means I should be sleeping in, but I can't get comfortable enough to fall back asleep.

Rereading Piper's diary wasn't the best bedtime storybook before crashing, fully clothed, on my bed. She invaded my dreams, visions of Piper dressed in a nineteenth century ivory nightgown running toward Lover's Leap. Chase ran after her, screaming for Piper to take his hand, until at last, with Piper's long, brunette hair cascading behind her, she takes the leap, without hesitation.

Without looking back.

Trailing behind her, where her footsteps should've been, are black and white roses.

My stomach rumbles when I sit up. Rubbing it, I convince myself it's because of the lack of food in my dorm and not two tragedies intertwining into a sleepless nightmare.

I peel off yesterday's uniform and pad into the bathroom naked, keeping my shower brief, and I decide against eating breakfast in the dining hall. On weekends, seniors are allowed to leave campus, and I can't believe it's taken me close to a month to step away from this cursed school.

A quick blow-dry and make-up application later, I choose basic straight-legged jeans and my mom's college tee. I hug myself once the soft cotton hits my chest, the familiar feel realigning my heart for the time being.

My phone's where I left it—tangled in my bed covers, and I send Ivy a text to let her know I'm headed into town for breakfast, exploration, and groceries, and I'd love a buddy. She responds immediately, and we agree to meet in front of the school in an hour.

I'm early, but it's never relaxing hanging out in my dorm room, so I swing my tote onto my shoulder and step out.

The hall is quiet, girls taking advantage of no classes and sleeping in. The usual "guard" from the local university is at the front desk, glasses perched on her nose and typing on her laptop. She grunts a greeting as I walk by.

Outside, the cool air brushing against my cheeks brings the promise of fall as my feet tread on the path. I'm looking forward to all these trees turning sunburnt orange, bright reds, and chocolate browns—all the colors social media posts promise. Living in Manhattan, I didn't get much fall, New York City basically leveling out into two seasons—winter and construction work. Trees don't change from green to anything. Instead, they turn into skeletons reaching their bare branches toward gray skies. If I ever wanted to immerse myself in autumn, I suppose I could've strolled through Central Park, but it's so overloaded with tourists, cyclists, and joggers, I could never find a moment's peace.

Here, though, at Briarcliff, I could appreciate fall in the quiet.

My head tilts to the left, and I picture my mom walking beside me, as excited about the changing season as me, since her hikes were planned around September and October for this reason.

Picture it, Calla-baby, the colors of painters' dreams. Peek through the fog with me. Go on, look. See, baby.

My throat goes thick, and I pinch the skin of my forearm to drive the sudden pain somewhere else. But my daydream has pointed out how foggy it's become, like the clouds have dropped from the sky to lay their tired forms on Briarcliff's bed of grass.

And ... I'm somewhere unfamiliar.

In my daze, I've gone in the opposite direction of the school, towards the cliffs. My nightmare clung to my subconscious with such tangible firmness that it propelled me in the direction of Lover's Leap.

Alert curiosity propels me farther into the trees, following the sounds of crashing waves until I reach a metal gate with a piece of yellow police tape flapping in the salted breeze.

The jagged end of the large rock is obvious from this distance, even in the fog. It looms majestically, promising a beautiful view but a horrific death, and I can't bring myself to try and get around the fencing.

I step back, the gray mist clinging to the roots at my feet, obscuring the forest floor.

A flash of movement brings my gaze up.

It's a foot, disappearing under a flap of fabric as whatever—whoever—it is, runs back into the forest.

A tightness fills my chest, and the rising nausea tastes a lot like fear.

I'm alone, in the woods, near the cliff where Piper died. Daylight doesn't change that.

"Nope. Not doing this," I mutter, and wheel around to march back to campus.

I power-walk so fast, the tops of Briarcliff's pointed roofs come into view within minutes, but not much else.

A flicker of movement brings me to a stop.

"Hey!" I call into the closest canopy of trees. "I see you!"

Nothing but the faded chirps of birds respond. Gritting my

teeth, I dare myself to say, "How about you go back to your boiling cauldron and leave me the hell—"

A figure steps out from behind the thick oaks, clad in a dark cloak, the hood so large, it obscures this person's face.

The fabric falls back from the figure's arm as they lift a finger to their shadowed profile, then whisper, "*Shhh...*"

My brows slam down, but before I can retort, the figure melts back into the fog, and I'm left with the birds.

A low-key buzz emits from my phone in my bag. I dig for it as I continue my trek to the main building. Lifting it, I read:

Unknown Number: WATCH YOUR BACK.
Unknown Number: <calliedidit.gif>

The GIF loads automatically and shows one scene where I'm pushing Piper to the dining hall's floor, in full-on *Carrie* mode with my face and hair soaked with pasta sauce. Then, it switches to a scene of me elbowing Piper in the nose, smiling as blood drips from between her fingers when she clutches her face. Same cafeteria background. Different day.

Importantly, the day she died, and showing evidence that I was angry enough to retaliate.

Three dancing dots appear, then are replaced by a video. The freeze screen shows me enough, but I press play, cringing before Piper's accusations sound out.

"*...so, you think hurling insults at me was nothing? Refusing to do your half of our history essay? Vowing to ruin my GPA and my life? What about vandalizing my bedroom? Smearing my lipstick all over our bathroom mirror? You're fucking nuts, Callie! Fucking certified!*"

I lower the phone, scanning my surroundings for a glimpse of that hooded man, but my mind's severed between the figure and what was sent to my phone.

Someone filmed proof of my possible motive to kill Piper hours before she toppled off Lover's Leap. Enough to reopen the case.

My phone buzzes again.

Unknown Number: STAY QUIET.

32

I'm being threatened.

Or blackmailed. How do they know what I've found? What I've read in Piper's diary? Is this about the existence of Mr. S?

This video ... it could go to Haskins with a simple 'send,' and whoever gave me this wants me to know they have the power.

I can't walk the rest of the way back to campus alone without fear of the Cloak coming back, despite the relative safety of the school nearby, so I do the next best thing.

I phone Ahmar. He's familiar. Safe.

He picks up after one ring. "Hey, kiddo."

"Hey. Am I interrupting you?"

"Nah ... well, sorta. I'm at a crime scene, but I could take five."

The lightness of his tone lets me know that the scene is more violent than he's letting on. Even in a different state, he tries to protect me from the worst—despite me already *seeing* the worst humanity has to offer.

"What's up?" he asks.

"I kinda ... have news."

"Oh, yeah?"

My pressing need to call Ahmar dissipates. I have to tell him about Piper. It's the type of billionairess death to go national, and Marron already put out a release to the parents and guardians.

Ahmar wouldn't receive that kind of head's-up, and I have no idea if my dad would care to fill him in. I haven't heard from Dad or Lynda since the tragedy happened.

I aim to get it over with in one fell swoop. "So, my roommate died."

"*What?*"

"She—she fell off a cliff. The police are saying it was an accident."

"Jesus Christ, Calla. Are you okay?"

"Fine. I mean, shaken up, but I'm doing all right."

"Should I come visit?"

"No, I'm handling myself. But I can't help but think there's something I'm missing."

Ahmar predicts where I'm going. "Hun..."

"What if there's suspicious evidence being overlooked, Ahmar?

"Sweetheart, the last time you thought this—"

I dismiss his argument before it starts. "This is completely different. Piper's death doesn't make sense. Kids don't go to this cliff alone in the dark to meditate. They go to hook up, or do drugs, or whatever they can while teachers pretend nothing's going on. There was a party that night. Why did she stay there when everyone else left?"

"If the police are saying it was an accident..."

"Sure, her fall might've been, but what is the reason she *stayed*?" I ask before I chicken out, "Can you look into it? Maybe find out her blood alcohol level and see if she was so drunk that she..."

"Calla," Ahmar asks. "Is this about your roommate or your mother?"

"It's about something fishy in this school," I say, in as calm a manner as I can. "This isn't some sort of crutch about my mom. If you could just call the precinct—his name is Haskins. You're a cop. He's a cop. Maybe he'll be candid with you."

"Hun, it sounds like the case is closed."

"Please?"

Ahmar sighs. "I'll talk to this Haskins guy. I'm not gonna promise anything. He's in a different jurisdiction. He doesn't owe me anything."

"I know," I say. "But I'd like to understand why he called it an accident."

"Okay. But please, Calla, try to focus on your studies and making friends. Getting involved in all this ... it's not healthy for you. Briarcliff was meant to be your escape."

"Now that you're on it, I'll back off, Ahmar. I swear."

Ahmar knows me well enough not to be convinced. But I know that he's at an active crime scene and doesn't have time to lecture me. "I love you, kiddo. I gotta go."

"Thanks, Ahmar," I say, and click off as I'm approaching Briarcliff's buildings.

That last message told me to be quiet. I'll do as they warn, but that doesn't mean I can't coax others to be louder.

And that begins with Piper's diary.

Ivy's sitting on the steps to the main building, absently scrolling through her phone when I arrive.

"Sorry I'm late," I say, breathless as I plop down beside her.

"No worries." Ivy gives me a second look. "Did you run here?"

"Not exactly," I say after a huff of breath. "Did you call a car?"

Ivy pats my shoulder affectionately. "Don't have to. Remember? Briarcliff Academy has a chauffeur service going into town and back."

I raise my brows. "Oh, right."

A town car pulls up the circular driveway, and Ivy and I stand. "See? All I had to do was request it on the app."

"The app," I repeat. "Just when I thought I was an expert on the Briarcliff handbook..."

Ivy laughs as I slide into the backseat. I nod hello to Yael, the driver, when he glances at us in the rearview mirror.

We chat about light topics like course loads and what it was like to rely on a subway in the city and not a car on the way to Briarcliff Village. My phone burns a hole in my pocket, and in the back of my mind I'm desperate to solve the riddle of who could've sent those texts.

Someone who filmed both instances, obviously.

But the second time Piper and I faced off, the dining hall was almost deserted. I didn't notice anyone holding up their phone, but then again, I wasn't too focused on my periphery. A determined filmmaker could've hidden behind the heavy drapery on each of the dining hall's floor-to-ceiling windows, or crouched in a corner, and I would've been none the wiser.

Especially if they donned a cloak.

"Hey, I have a question," I say to Ivy. The car slows with its arrival into the village.

"Shoot," Ivy says. She props her purse on her lap as Yael parallel parks on Main Street.

"How many students know about the Nobles?"

Ivy hisses, then latches onto my wrist once we stop and all but drags me out. I stutter out a thank you to Yael, and he salutes in response, unperturbed by whatever he happens to hear in the backseat.

"I told you not to talk about that!" Ivy says as I stumble to a stand on the sidewalk.

"Correction, you told me not to talk about it to *Chase*."

An annoyed growl comes from Ivy's throat. "Leave it to you to find a loophole."

"I'm sorry, but I need your help," I say, then take a deep breath. "You're the one person I can trust."

"When we talked yesterday, I thought we came to an agreement. Stay away from them—*that's* the warning I needed you to walk away with."

"Ivy, I ... I think they're watching me."

Ivy takes a moment to search my face before she lets out an exasperated puff of air.

"God," Ivy says, massaging the creases in her forehead. "I need espresso for this. Come on."

Ivy latches onto my wrist again and pulls me in the direction of the lobster shack I noticed during my drive through Briarcliff Village ... with Piper.

"I'm known to walk all by myself, you know," I say as I trail behind her.

"And right off a damn cliff," I swear I hear her say, but a passing car's large motor drowns out her words.

Armed with our lattes and lobster omelets, Ivy and I find a secluded seat near the back wall of the shack, which Ivy chose in hopes of nobody eavesdropping.

"Ironically, chatting about this in public is safer than on Briarcliff campus," she says as we sit down. She cups her hands around her mug. "So. Tell me what's been going on."

"Can you start first? And explain how this group works?"

Ivy stares at me, unblinking. I can't shake the unease as she and I silently war to be the winner of this information duel.

But Ivy was my friend and confidant during my first weeks at Briarcliff. It was *her* who brought the name to my attention. She has answers, even if she doesn't think she does. More than I could ever figure out on my own.

So, I give in.

"Okay," I say, and hunch over my coffee so she can hear my low words better. I confess about the roses, the first one black, the second one white. I hold back on my possession of Piper's diary, but I show her the text messages I received this morning.

"Shit," Ivy says as she holds my phone. She drops it facedown on the table. "I'm an idiot, Callie. I'm sorry. This whole time I thought you were stupidly curious about something no normal person should concern themselves over. But now ... jeez, now you're being gag-ordered. For what, though?" Her eyes turn to slits. "What have you been up to that's caused this kind of message?"

"I've been doing some digging on Piper," I admit. "Her death may not have been an accident."

Ivy's expression freezes.

"...And someone thinks they have the clout to frame me for Piper's murder if I don't leave it alone. This video is enough to cast suspicion on me," I say, then lick my lips. "There's one other thing."

Ivy leans back after a long swig of her coffee. "I'm a little afraid of what you're going to say next."

"I'm researching Rose Briar and her jump from Lover's Leap."

Ivy's forehead relaxes. "Okay. That sounds fine."

"It ties into Piper's death. Kind of. Chase and I both think—"

"Wait, *Chase?*"

"Yes," I confess, somewhat chagrined. "Piper's death is too similar to Rose's to be ignored, even if the police want to dismiss it."

"I ... what am I supposed to say to that?"

"We think there's more to it than what the police have concluded. Piper died on the same night Rose did, Ivy. September tenth."

"So now you and Chase are a *we*."

I'm quick to defend myself. "It's a lonely place, you know, when you're one of two people who think Piper's death is related to a scandal the academy doesn't want revealed."

"Hang on, now you think *Briarcliff's* involved? Like, Headmaster Marron? Come on, Callie."

"I don't have specific proof, but Piper was convinced she had evidence..." I trail off at how this must sound, now that I'm giving voice to it.

"Isn't your uncle a cop? Trust the investigation."

I give a nod, but switch tactics. "Doesn't this school stink of something sinister to you? Like there's something being protected behind the scenes, or hidden under the floorboards, or..."

"Callie." Ivy reaches for my hands. "You've had it tough. Piper zeroed in on you the *day* you arrived here. Then you got Chase's attention. And through them, the rumor mill. Aside from being a drama-magnet, you're going through a lot. For most of us, Briarcliff Academy is just that. An elite school that drives us into the Ivy Leagues, if we're lucky. Have you ever thought that maybe Piper's death is an outlet for you to release all this angst and frustration at being an unfair target?"

I shake my head. "It's not all in my head, Ivy. I got a text telling me to shut up and a Cloak's been haunting me ever since I started looking into Piper's death."

A flutter of confusion crosses Ivy's face. "A Cloak?"

"It's what I call this dude who I keep running into, for lack of being allowed to associate him with the Nobles, lest lightning strike me where I sit."

"Like I said, drama-magnet," Ivy jokes, totally unconcerned over my confession of the obvious stranger-danger on campus.

Now I'm positive she knows more than she's saying. I fold my arms onto the table. "I told you mine, Ivy. Your turn."

Ivy nibbles on her lower lip. "Do you need a refill?"

"Ivy."

"Fine. Okay." Ivy finds a spot on her shirt to pick at. "So, pretty much the whole country wants to send their kids to Briarcliff. You're practically guaranteed a spot at a top university. What's difficult is getting *in*to Briarcliff."

I reach for patience.

"Thousands apply for a scholarship here," she continues. "But if you're a legacy, you basically have instant access to these halls."

"Legacy?"

"You know, if your parents or grandparents are alumni. The academy will give you preference, but you still have to prove your worthiness in grades, or sports, or some extra-curricular."

"Okay…" I say, staring harder at my untouched coffee. "But I've seen no mention of the Nobles anywhere on campus. No clues, either. So, how do you know about them?"

"Well, that's what I'm telling you. The Nobles are the legacies." Ivy smiles, but it seems forced and untrue. "I … I haven't been upfront with you, but now that you're being singled out … I can tell you what I know. Which isn't much."

I urge her to continue with a nod.

"It's a kind of preferential treatment that no one talks about. The Nobles are guaranteed a spot in the Ivy Leagues, for example. Through not-so-obvious means, if you get what I'm saying."

I smell bullshit. "Go on."

"No one talks about it because a lot of what they do to get their kids on the elite track is illegal. If it ever came out…"

I think of the journal, and all of Piper's coded secrets. It's all that remains of Piper's working mind, and I'm keeping it from Ivy *and* Chase. I should tell Ivy, but I'm held back by something. Instinct. Caution.

She's lying.

Ahmar's warning sounds in my head. *Getting involved in all this … it's not healthy for you…*

I ask, "Who's a part of it? Chase?"

Ivy makes a see-saw motion with her hand. Noncommittal.

I let it go, since I'm prepared to find the source and ask Chase straight out.

"Whether he's a part of these Nobles or not, Chase is adamant about keeping it quiet." I pick at my lower lip as I parse through Ivy's explanation. My foremost thought being, *is any of this in the missing pages of Piper's diary?*

"Because the Nobles are to be feared, Callie. Don't let the name fool you. There's nothing noble about them."

My attention drifts to my bag, and the diary that rests in it.

"Anyway." Ivy says in an attempt to move the conversation along. "Why do you keep bringing up Chase? You interested in him or something?"

"Ugh," I say, but even as I make the noise, I'm conscious how overdramatic it is. "He's not my type."

"Chase isn't any girl's type, which is why they all chase after him."

"Not me," I say, and tell myself to *mean* it. "That goes to my point, though. If Piper became exclusive with him again, she'd let the entire student body know he's hers, right? There wouldn't be a dust mite in this building that wouldn't have heard."

Ivy frowns, thinking. "No, Piper wouldn't say anything this time around, because of their parents."

I perk up, sensing a clue. "Oh, yeah?"

"Yup." Ivy huffs out a laugh. "It was the scandal of tenth grade. Chase's dad and Piper's mom met on one of our Family Days. Don't ask. It's the lamest event on the planet, and it involves potato sack races. Anyway—they both left their spouses, and, when was it ... this summer, I think, they announced their engagement. So, to wrap that all up in a neat bow..." Ivy mimes tying a knot, "Chase and Piper were destined to be brother and sister. Their parents forbade them from getting back together, since it would be quite the scandal in Charleston society if they hooked up as step-siblings."

My mind whirs with the implications Ivy's brought forward, but she doesn't recognize any of it as she eats.

I think I've just found out Mr. S's ... *Chase's* ... secret.

Yet, Piper's last words to me won't stop screaming in my head.

How she shouted in the dining hall that I was stealing her boyfriend, basically telling everyone within her vicinity that Chase was hers. Was keeping their affair on the down-low becoming too much for her once she sensed my interest in him?

Ivy wouldn't have those answers, so I change the subject. "How can my researching Rose Briar make these Nobles angry enough to send me a blackmail text?" I ask her instead.

"If it was them." Ivy plays with her empty cup by spinning it in a circle. "Piper managed to turn the whole school against you, and even in death, she's still accomplishing it. That text could be from any of her followers who want justice."

"But I didn't kill her! Can't you see how much of an elaborate game this is?" I blurt out, and even to my ears, it's too loud. But hell, I'm shocked and perturbed by *all* of this.

Ivy shushes me, but it's too late. A couple of patrons look our way. One in particular catches my eye.

"Hey," I say to Ivy, unable to move my gaze away. "Isn't that what's-his-name? Addisyn's boyfriend?"

Jack must notice my deeper scrutiny, because he unfreezes and goes back to wiping down a front table, his apron stained with a morning's worth of boiling lobster.

"That's about as far away from elite Briarcliff stock as Addisyn can get," I observe.

"Yeah, I guess. Listen, whatever you're doing to gain attention, I'm better off not figuring it out. And you should put this to rest, too." Ivy rises, and I stand with her, handing over her purse. Before we exit, Ivy presses her hand into my shoulder. "And if you're thinking about Chase offering you any sort of protection while you keep at it—"

Damn her for reading into my thoughts.

"—don't. He's the one with the defenses, Callie. And I have no doubt he'll toss you aside the minute you lose your usefulness. Keep it in your control—ditch him. That's my final advice." She searches my eyes again. "Okay?"

I'm reading between Ivy's lines. She no longer wants to discuss the Nobles, and if I continue to press, if I'm determined to keep trying to decipher Piper's journal ... Ivy won't be any further help, and I can't blame her.

Yet, that inner doggedness of mine rears its ugly snout, and I know with certainty that I won't be able to let this go.

Not until I uncover the truth about Piper, lying within the hidden artifacts of an elite high school.

33

Ivy shows me the local marketplace, and I toss some apples, granola, chocolate bars, and potato chips into my basket for midnight snacking. I also buy manila envelopes and stamps. We don't mention the Nobles or Piper for the rest of our morning. I respect Ivy's need for distance, so I keep our topics inconsequential and innocent as we finish up, poke around a furniture store for some basic items, then wait for our chauffeur service on the sidewalk outside the lobster shack. As the cars pass, and I idle beside Ivy, I notice the post office on the corner.

"You know what?" I say, pretending spontaneity. "You go back. I'd like to explore Main Street."

"Really?"

"I like it down here. It feels ... real."

Ivy doesn't argue. "I'd stay with you if I didn't have to study for chem. Kinda jealous. It *is* nice in this town."

"Next time." I smile and start walking. "Send me the info on the car app. I'll see you at lunch."

"Okay ... um, Callie?"

I turn. "Yeah?"

"You're just exploring, right?"

"You and I made a deal," I say. "I'm not going to involve you."

"My fear is you'll turn to Chase instead."

"All I'm doing is getting some errands done. You don't have to worry."

"What is it about Piper, Callie? I'm trying to understand, but I just *don't*. Can't you leave this to the detectives?"

I deflect the question with a subject I'm coming to learn she's passionate about. "Now you're starting to sound like Chase."

"Well, that proves he has at least one thinking brain cell in his head. But you didn't answer my question."

"Would you mind dropping my food off by my front door?" I deflect. "I'll owe you one."

"Why can't you leave Piper's death alone?"

"Because it's not just my bully's death." I pause for a moment, staring out into the street before I turn back to Ivy. "It's her murder."

"But—"

I'm saved from further discussion when the Briarcliff car pulls up and Ivy gives up. She gets in, but not before sending me an assessing stare above the car's hood.

"Give me your stuff," she mumbles.

"Thank you," I say, and hand over my groceries.

As she pulls the door shut, I wave and promise I'll see her at lunch.

The post office is a block away, and I get to the entrance just as a man is stepping out. He holds the door so I can slip in.

"Thanks," I say, then walk into—

A library?

A row of stacks and the musty smell of well-worn books and much older carpet hits my nostrils. I pause at the turnstile for entry, convinced I walked into the wrong building.

"Can I help you?" a woman asks from the front desk.

She's wearing '50s-style glasses and curled her hair in a

vintage bob. She sets down the paperback she was reading—*The Duke's Hidden Duchess.*

"I'm sorry, I thought this was the post office."

"It is," she chirps. "We merged quite some time ago. You'll notice the mailboxes behind me. We're a small town with limited municipal resources."

I nod, then pull out my textbooks until I find the manila envelope I'd stuffed the diary in when Ivy wasn't looking. A quick search on my phone told me the police precinct's location, and I set the envelope on the receptionist's desk and scrawl the address, tilting it so the receptionist can't see. I'm hoping Briarcliff isn't that miniscule of a town that the librarian/post office clerk will make any connection to me and a newly discovered diary of a dead girl.

I don't have to worry, though, because she's cocking her head at my textbook I tossed out of the way. "Are you searching for something in biographies, hun?"

"Excuse me?"

"Your sticky note there. That's our library's reference code."

She's looking at the note I'd stuck to the front of my Calc text, hoping to ask Ivy about it but never getting the chance. I'd forgotten it was there. "It is?"

I stare at the numbers I wrote down: **01.08.05.Ha**

"Sure, honey." She points to the first number. "Number one means first floor, and eight is the number we give to our biography section. Five is the shelf-level. Then we end with the first two letters of the author's name."

"Well, I'll be," I drawl. I peel off the note and shove it in my pocket before depositing the textbook back in my bag. "So, my mail just goes in there?" I point behind her, fisting the manila envelope.

She chuckles, likely amused by Gen Z kids trying to relate to snail mail. "Yes, dear."

In an attempt to distract, I say, "How old is this library?"

"Oh, ancient in your eyes, dear. Maybe sixty years? Not as old as Briarcliff Academy's, however. Sad, how we lost it."

"I thought Briarcliff's library smelled a little too much like fresh paint," I say. "It's newly built, isn't it?"

"As it happens, it just reopened." The receptionist pushes up her rhinestone glasses and leans forward in her seat. I catch her nameplate: DARLA. "Quite the scandal. The old library burned down."

"It did?" I put extra *oomph* in my gasp, though a lot of it is real. Darla's interest has clearly bypassed what I'm mailing and is on to juicier gossip.

"And the new building was gifted by the victim's family. Can you believe it?"

"Wait..." Didn't Chase say his dad financed the library?

"*Such* a tragedy. If you have the time—" her phone rings, and she glances toward it. "Darn. Anyway, take a look around. Most of the original documents exclusive to this town were destroyed along with it. But this library has the rest."

My heart beats faster. I'm ready to track down the source of Piper's reference code. "Are there papers on the founders here?"

"Another intrepid student, I see. Briarcliff pupils don't think to come to this library for local research. I suppose they don't care, now that the web exists. The last girl here asking for founders documents was ... well, she's a tragedy, too."

The phone keeps ringing.

Piper. She was here and it hits me in a wave, confirming that the jumble of letters and numbers in her last entry point to this place. Piper said she found documents at the library. I assumed she meant Briarcliff's, but she totally meant *this* one.

"You should get that," I say, keeping my voice level. "Um, so, that section you mentioned...?"

Darla lifts the phone, covers the receiver and gestures forward. "Biographies are in aisle eight, dear."

I nod my thanks, then peruse the aisles until I come to 8. I don't run into anyone else as I explore, the library comforting and quiet, save for Darla's murmuring voice. Running my fingers along the dust-covered spines on the fifth shelf, I notice old texts on Briarcliff, most written by someone named Margaret Harris. I spend twenty minutes skimming through a handful and come to the resigned conclusion that I'm not going to find anything but dry material on the school's construction and the town's burgeoning economy. Maybe Piper scribbled the reference code down for no other reason than to come back to this section for additional, drab research.

Or to send me here.

It forces me to think. If Piper's death really is related to what she discovered, wouldn't she try to hide it? I focus harder on Piper and who she was. Vain, self-centered, and uncaring about the lives she ruined.

On a whim, I unfurl from my seated position and keep looking through the "Ha" section. After perusing the row, I find nothing, and I'm about to rationalize that I should be focusing on my *other* running theory, Mr. S, when I backtrack and come across a book by Allan Harrington about his life on the high seas. I have nothing else to go on except for Piper's vanity in choosing an author with her last name, but I pull it out, then let it fall into a random section when I open it.

A sheaf of paper, stuffed between the pages, flutters to the ground.

A surge of adrenaline jolts through me—part of Piper's missing pages?—but after unfolding the single page, it's too aged to be Piper's. But it's a handwritten letter, in feminine cursive.

...he thinks I'm unaware of the Society, but I know. I know, and I demand my part in it.

. . .

Much of the writing is illegible with scorch marks. My fingers tighten on the fragile paper as my brain moves fast, making the connection. When I skim to the bottom and find the signature, my beliefs are solidified.

Rose Eloise Briar

YAS!

I glance up, noting Darla's continued distraction on the phone. In a stealthy maneuver worthy of outsmarting any above cameras, I take one of my textbooks from my bag and nestle the letter within it.

Darla's back is to me by the time I get to the front, and without her noticing, scoot out the doors.

My heart leaves lighter, too. I picture the texts and the incriminating video on my phone, but whoever's responsible isn't watching me close enough to know what I've done. How I can curveball the investigation, too.

I've mailed the diary to the police and thus, pointed the finger at Mr. S.

I'm sorry, Chase.

I squelch the unwanted regret. It's a no-brainer that if it came down to him or me, it should *definitely* be him. If the detectives aren't going to focus elsewhere, then it's left to me to redirect the narrative, and if it buys me the time I need to uncover Briarcliff's deepest, most scandalous secrets, then I will.

After being dropped off on campus, I make it through the rest of the day studying for quarter-terms before enjoying the privacy of my room and smoothing down Rose's letter. In the low lamplight at my desk, I read.

They think they have control. They do not. I am the one they should fear, and I must maintain ground by carving my place within. I do not love him. Indeed, I despise him, and he can no longer stand the sight of me. Not after losing his fifth child. Thorne would kill me if he could get away with it. I must act before he does, create a section within this educational system for my protection. My quick thinking will either save me, or doom me to—

Indecipherable, charred jumble. Cursing, I move on.

He believes creating a Gentlemen's Society through a boys only school will provide the ample opportunity he requires. It will not. He cannot possibly imagine how far I have come. I must employ my plans now, before it is too late. I aim for balance, and in doing so, summoning a society in secret to operate under the auspices of Briarcliff Boys Academy. An elite group of souls who may protect my name and watch over these children. It is with this letter I deem you to be the wiser, my love. Keep my confession safe, for I am creating the V—

Damn it! Burned edges and holes obscure the rest, but I've been given enough.

A Gentlemen's Society involving Thorne Briar. Rose's discovery of it.

My hand curls into a fist over the page as I ponder Piper's reasoning for hiding this letter. To whom Rose was writing to remains a mystery, but there's a secret written within these pages, one Piper figured out.

For it can only be Piper who's seen these pages, too, and put them in the public library before she died.

After a final read, I switch to my laptop.

There's a way I can communicate my theory, write it out and make sense of it. It's because of them, these Nobles, that I can't think. Can't study like I used to. Can't sleep.

If I'm wrong, then all I'll get is Dr. Luke's brief admiration for delving so deep into Briarcliff lore. He's open to new theories. Piper said he loved out-of-the-box thinking.

And if I'm right, maybe I can flush my cloaked admirer out, and force that person to provide some answers.

After all, *two* girls can't die on campus without garnering a whole bunch of attention.

Right?

While placing my fingers above the keyboard, I tell myself to be brave. I tell myself to write about the *real* founding of Briarcliff Academy.

With Rose's hidden involvement. I open with:

While Thorne Briar and his two brothers, Richard and Theodore Briar, founded the Briarcliff Boys Academy, Thorne's wife, Rose Briar, created a clandestine internal organization as a form of protection against her husband's similar plan within these school halls.

What if, instead of literal skeletons, Briarcliff Academy hides two skulls of secret society members underneath their coveted grounds? One belonging to Thorne, and the other borne in retaliation from Rose.

It begs two questions: Why did these students need hidden protection, and which society was their true protector?

Soon, the words start flowing.

34

*I*t's been one week, and I've heard nothing about Piper's diary.

No news from Detective Haskins, Ahmar, or even my friendly Cloak. I'm walking on needles every day, thinking at any moment, someone will come around the corner and point the finger at me.

Detective Haskins asking, *Why didn't you give me the diary in person, Callie? What are you trying to hide?*

Ahmar, questioning, *I told you to stay away from this, kiddo. You're making it worse for yourself.*

Chase, accusing, *What have you done to me, you bitch?*

Nothing comes, save for quiet murmurings that Piper's case might have new evidence. That tidbit, I heard from Dr. Luke when he was conversing with Professor Dawson outside his classroom. He caught me listening, then went so quiet, I couldn't catch what else he was saying.

Immersing myself with the line of students wandering up the stairs, I don't register bodies getting closer to me until two forms practically step on my head.

The person brushing up against me on my left—James—grabs my elbow.

"What the—?" But I'm cut off by Tempest on my left. His jade green eyes link with mine.

"You're coming with us," he says.

"What are you, the campus police?" I say, attempting to struggle out of James's hold. Students mill around us, heedless of my wrestling.

"No," James says with a tug.

"Worse," Tempest adds, and holds a hand against my lower back, pushing me forward.

Struggling with these two is like trying to kick a tank, and I'm swept up in their grip and through Briarcliff's doors before I can let out an outraged gasp.

Riordan stands at the base of the steps to the Wolf's Den, leaning against the single wall and waiting for us with hooded eyes. When he catches sight of the three of us, he turns on his heel and walks up the stairs.

"This is—you can't get away with this bullshit!" I say, wiry and spry with useless maneuvers. I search around the lobby for any kind of friendly face—or teacher—but see none as these boys manhandle me up the stairs and onto a couch.

"Sit," Tempest says with a firm hand on my shoulder. "Stay."

I glare up at him. "The only dogs I see in this room are you jackasses."

James rounds the couch until he's standing behind me. "So, are we canines or donkeys? You can't have both."

I whip around to give him a piece of my mind, but I'm stopped by a form stepping from the shadows and taking a seat across from me.

Chase splays his legs and rests his elbows on the armchair, his chin dipped low in deep regard.

If it weren't for the Briarcliff crest on his blazer, I would've taken him for a mafia drug lord. His dark blond hair is slicked back from the curves of his face, his aristocratic brows lowered, a thoughtful line forming between. The one spark of light in his gloomy, shadowed form is his eyes, the color of icy scotch. Though, what that stare holds is anyone's guess. His outward purity is a natural disguise for the unmentionable sins harboring within that mind of his.

"Don't make a sound," he says to me. His direct stare communicates the danger I'll put myself in if I refuse his orders.

Perhaps, picturing Chase running an illegal empire isn't too far-fetched.

Up here, the lull of students heading to dinner below is hushed, a low thrum of voices and footsteps dissipating with time.

Chase glances left, toward the balcony overhang, the movement confirming that the lobby's emptied out.

"You can go, boys. Callie, stay here."

Tempest, James, and Riordan—whose position I hadn't clocked until now, near the coffee cart, move toward the stairs.

"Want me to save you some pork marsala?" James asks Chase as he passes.

"I'll take some, too," I pipe up, aware of what his response will be.

"You can have whatever scraps are left," James says before descending. "It's what you're used to, anyway."

I click my tongue, then slide my gaze back to Chase's. "Your friends are so charming."

Chase's expression remains impassive.

"Say, when you order them to harass me like the good little henchmen they are, can you ask them to say *pretty please*? Or, even better, can you have them stay the fuck away from me?"

"I wouldn't want to be you right now."

Oh, how fun. Chase is being cryptic again. I sigh and slouch against the couch. "And why's that?"

"I've just finished being re-interrogated by the police." Chase angles his head, his stare precise. "Did you have something to do with it?"

The diary. Haskins has it. "For the last time—*no*," I hiss at the exact moment my heart turns into an anchor and plummets. "I was as surprised as anyone else when I heard Piper's case might be reopened."

"You don't act like it."

"What's that supposed to mean?"

"You didn't shed a tear when your roommate died. I could easily label you a cold bitch for that. Or ... a cold-blooded murderer."

"What is it you want? For me to buckle to my knees the moment she's mentioned? Sob into my blazer? It's horrible what happened, but I refuse to do what everyone is asking just because I was her roommate for a week."

"You called me Mr. S."

Chase says it mildly, like he's semi-interested by the answer, but I sense the warning.

"Well, your surname *is* Stone," I retort. I cover up my tremors with a snarl.

"Funny, it's the obvious name the police used for me, too," Chase says, and it's so menacing, I wince. "So obvious, in fact, that I'd never use it if I were trying to hide my dastardly deeds."

"Was Piper one of your dirty secrets?" my voice rises with the question, and I let it. "Did you have something to do—"

"Are you a narc?"

Shaking, I reply, "No. Haskins hasn't said a word to me, and I haven't gone to him."

"Do you picture it?" Chase asks. "How Piper must've felt when she went off the cliff? The wind deafening in her ears, the air too fast for her to breathe, her heart beating out of her chest with fear. I do." His eyes glitter with the sharp amber of spite.

"I don't need to," I retort. "Since my nightmares are taken up by my mother sprawled on the floor in a pool of her own blood."

My breath snaps at the end, an audible whiplash that Chase has no right to hear.

Trembling, clenching my hands, I give him my profile, so he doesn't see the sudden tears.

Chase keeps silent, as if basking in the grief.

"My injustice may not come from the same section of my heart as yours," I say. "But we've both experienced the violence of a sudden death. Your girlfriend—"

"Again, with the girlfriend."

"Again, with the denial," I say.

Chase cocks his head, his cold stare tempered with assessment. "Why are you so convinced Piper and I were together? Do you have to sit on my lap to prove we weren't?"

His gaze dips to his spread legs, where I suppose he wants me to look, too. I don't because I can't. I *cannot* keep reacting to him like this.

"Your parents are getting married," I say. "Piper's mom and your dad. You two were about to be brother and sister. That must've horrified you."

Chase's temperament doesn't turn to outraged fire. Nor does he twitch at the mention of his and Piper's future. "Done some digging, have you? Do you find me that interesting?"

"I find Piper's secrets of particular importance, considering she's not breathing anymore."

Chase concedes my point. "That wasn't something we kept under wraps. Only an outsider would find that kind of thing interesting."

"But you would've kept sleeping together a secret."

Chase smiles, but it's not his perfect, half-moon crescent of a weapon, deployed on the female population. "No. We wouldn't have. And I'm sorry to disappoint, sweet possum, but I gave the detective an air-tight alibi. I was with my boys all night. We were at the party together, we left together. Riordan's my roommate, and James crashed on the floor next to my bed. It's been verified, and as such..." He makes an exaggerated sad face. "I'm not their Mr. S. Or yours."

Chase's answer makes me falter with a second's hesitation, but I'm not about to fall for it. James, Riordan, Tempest—they'd all lie for him.

Chase pounces. "If Piper and I were fucking again, we'd do it in front of our parents if we could. I can't stand my father, and Piper despises her mom. Getting back together would've been ideal for both of us, but unfortunately..." Chase trails off into deliberate silence, where only our heartbeats matter. "Save for a few weak moments, my proclivities moved on."

My cheeks warm, but I bite the inside to turn that heat into pain. It's so screwed up of him to be so devilishly hot with me, but Chase excels at it.

Against my better judgment, my gaze drops to his thighs. I kick my attention back up, but Chase catches my perusal with sexual, knowing derision.

I pretend deep interest in our surroundings. "You know, for a place set aside for seniors, you and your Nobles reserve it a lot."

Chase goes rigid. "What have I told you—"

"About the name? Yeah, I get that it's forbidden, but that only makes me want to keep tasting it on my tongue."

I toss a closed mouth smile his way, but my tantalization isn't as effective as his.

"And," I continue, "I think there's some sort of cover-up going on with Piper's fall."

The shadowed skin around his eyes tapers into a glare. "If, after all your digging, that's where you've ended up, you better get a shovel, sweetheart."

"What, you don't think a group of legacy bad boys could be responsible for it?"

Chase snickers, but on him, it's a darting snake bite. "That's what you think they are?"

They. I latch onto the meaning behind his use of the word. *Not we*.

I force a shrug, though my shoulders are heavy with wariness. "If you have a superior theory, let's hear it."

"Nineteenth century bones can't give you answers six feet under. Visit Rose Briar's grave all you like, blame Piper's death on this secret boy band you've concocted, and I'll do the rest." Chase dips his chin. "I figured you for an ally, Callie. I don't like to be wrong."

"The Nobles have something to do with it." I push to my feet. "And the fact that you're so dismissive of my theory proves it. I don't need your gratitude or permission to keep going. When I find the person responsible, you can thank me then."

Chase *tsks*. "You're so positive. Yet, your track record doesn't give me a ton of hope."

I freeze. "Don't you dare..."

"What?" Chase rises, then steps, with his shadow looming over me. "While your mom's rotting in the dirt, her killer is—"

He predicts the slap before it meets its mark. My wrist *thrums* under his grip, my pulse spiking to adrenaline levels that would make a racehorse shy away.

Chase waits for my flickering focus to steady on his. "If you're going to be so mean," he says, his gaze tracing the curves of my face, "at least let me get under you first."

It hurts to breathe. Not from pain, but from the amount of space my heart's taking up in my chest, crushing my lungs. Chase has never been so blatant before. Our encounters flirt with sex, but never have they felt so explicit, so *real*.

The animalistic urge to grab him by his school shirt, until my fingers dig into his flesh is insurmountable. The idea of bringing him close, of slamming my lips against his and putting his dark promises to the test kills any remaining rationale.

"Let me go," I grit out. My clenched jaw does nothing to settle the urge for him.

One corner of his mouth lifts, and he steps even closer. "Say please."

His thighs push into mine, but those streamlined muscles of his, refined to cut through the gloss of a lake, are nothing compared to the hard length I'm feeling in the middle.

My panties go damp. My unrefined, sedentary thighs tremble around his confident swell. I'm telling myself not to part my legs for him, even if he comes with the god-like gift of the best orgasm of my life.

"Is something the matter, Callie?" he asks kindly. Too languidly.

A trap.

In one swift arc, I grip his dick through his pants, the shaft encompassing my entire palm.

Chase's eyes flare at the sudden touch, but he doesn't flinch, or waver, or do any of the things I hoped he would when I called his bluff.

Instead, he drops his arms, my free wrist falling listlessly to my side. He lets his arms hang, no longer touching any part of me, but pushes his groin deeper into my grip.

Chase's upper lip curls as he gazes down at me through his lashes. "You ever channeled your anger through sex, sweet possum?" The tip of his tongue darts out when I don't move my hand away. I *can't*. He's too delectable in my grip, but I'll never admit it. Chase is under my control. I'm feeding off it like a succubus.

"Answer me," he says.

My eyes don't leave his, but I have what he wants. My palm rubs against the fabric, against *him*, and he twitches under the friction.

"Mm. Undo my pants."

My self-control is far from reach. The temptation to do as he pleases and act the way he expects is too strong.

But I want him. I've been dreaming of him. Chase Stone, who is under my heel.

I do as he asks. I accept the dare he's put forth and his cunning desire to see how far I'll take this.

"Stick your hand in." Chase smiles, the corners weighted with desire. "I promise I don't bite."

My fingers trace the light trail of hair under his belly button, then spread across the deep V. When I find the hot length of him, I come closer, my nose brushing his, my lips a velvet touch away.

Chase grunts when I tighten my grip, but it's a sexy sound, one that makes me stroke him faster. He growls, his tongue darting for control against my lower lip, but I stay a hairsbreadth back, wanting to witness his every twitch, each minuscule reaction, as I bring Chase Stone to the edge.

Unable to let him have all the pleasure to himself, I use my free hand on myself, lifting my skirt and finding the lining of my underwear.

Chase follows the movement. His hands clench. When he doesn't move to assist me, I realize he's wagering for dominance, too.

I smile, this inner vixen of mine lifting her sexy, deprived head, and she grabs Chase's wrist and trails his fingers across the lace of my underwear.

Chase wets his bottom lip. His fingers curl against my delicate skin. The breath I've been harboring stutters out. I didn't expect to get so wet at his wisp of a touch. I'm not myself. This isn't right. It's dangerous ... and I'm starving for it.

In retaliation, I drop his hand, choosing to finger myself than allow Chase to win any ground.

With both hands working, I bring us up, up, up and under, our eyes locked, our breaths as short and hot as my strokes.

I nuzzle his throat, licking the spot where his pulse patters beneath his skin.

When Chase's lips part, when his chin tips to the roof, I speak.

"Who's in control now?" I whisper near his ear.

"*Fuck*—" he rasps, and I know I have him.

Snick.

We both freeze at the foreign sound.

Chase moves, twisting as my hand goes slack, and I hurriedly smooth down my skirt. But Chase is flying across the floorboards and leaps across the stair's railing before I've registered Riordan's head popping up through the rafters, his phone's lens facing us.

"You motherfucker!" Chase roars, and I back up at the sound, even though he's nowhere near me.

I race to the balcony overhang in time to witness Chase grabbing Riordan by the back of his blazer's lapel and tossing him onto the ground with the ease of throwing a wet noodle at a kitchen wall.

Riordan's head makes a sickening crack against the marble, but he's conscious. "What the fuck, man? We agreed to record—"

Chase bends low, but leers above Riordan with the languidness of a viper assessing its paralyzed prey before swallowing it. Chase says something I don't catch, but I do see him grab the phone from Rio, tap the screen a few times, then toss the phone against Riordan's chest.

As he backs away, Chase looks up to my level. I cover my surprise at being caught under his scope by forming my lips into a tight, grim line.

I expect Chase to say something along the lines of, "Don't worry, sweet possum, it's deleted," but I receive nothing but an enduring glare as he twists on his heel and stalks to the front door, throwing them wide with one push.

Releasing a long, needed exhale, I back away from the railing, and, in need of a cool down, twist my hair at the nape of my neck. The air is a welcome balm, but I can't relax.

The heat in my cheeks ... and down there ... doesn't fade.

Sitting in the chair Chase vacated, still warm from his body, my palm still tingling from jerking him off, I'm left wondering what the hell I've done.

35

Unsurprisingly, I don't make it to dinner service.

I'm proud of my foresight to buy groceries, so I'm not left hungry when I step into my dorm room.

I'm leaning against the counter and gnawing on a delicious piece of sea salt dark chocolate when it hits me like a sack of potatoes.

I pleasured Chase Stone.

Power has never seemed so wanton before, but I had it in my hand—literally—unexpected and wonderful. The bottomless hole of greed even had me pleasuring Chase by independently pleasuring *myself*, a piece of delicious mastery I refused to give to him for free.

The chocolate melts into cloying sugar on my tongue, and its sweetness burns my throat. I swallow it much like the building orgasm I never got to receive, starting off so sweet and seductive, then ending with the sharp bite of reality.

I am such an idiot.

Never trust Chase. Cornering me in private with his daring grin and come-fuck-me eyes shouldn't have lured me the way it did.

If he's not a Noble, some of his friends are—they have to be—and I just gave them another picture or video to use against me.

Chase's back was to the camera, but I wasn't. I could hope that Chase's actions after turning his friend into a skid mark were meant to delete said video, but why would he?

Fuck. A stubborn piece of chocolate lodges in my throat. I'm dreading tomorrow and what could happen. Will they all see it? Will they all know I almost bent my knees to Chase?

No. I am *not* like that.

Tossing the chocolate wrapper aside, I storm into my room and grab my laptop, prepared to spend the night learning about Briarcliff *and* the Stones. *And* the Harringtons.

The laptop sits on my bed, screen at maximum brightness, and I prop myself cross-legged in front of it while reaching for my phone.

I'm prepared to cross-reference anything I find in Piper's journal with the Harrington and Stone ancestors at Briarcliff, and I'll stay up all night to do it.

I start at the beginning: Rose Briar. It's the one avenue police aren't pursuing, and my one Hail Mary should they start pursuing me.

Planning out a course of action is a million times better than stressing over what Chase could do with Riordan's video. Chase never managed to get to that point before I pulled his dick out and resisted the longing to taste the most intimate, sexual part of him.

To be so intimate and turned on with a guy, without any loving act of kissing....

I'd once told Piper she was dark and twisty, and I'm starting to think that pocket of sin lives in me, too.

My underwear pulls tight against the sudden swell. Dampness coats the fabric as each second with Chase tickertapes across the back of my eyelids, falling through my mind the way explosions of paper rocket into the sky during street parades.

I rub my eyes free from the image and focus on Piper's last words instead, putting Mr. S aside and searching for details of her innermost thoughts, such as any mention, however tiny, of Rose's rival society, starting with a "V," or the Nobles, and whether the Stones or Harringtons were a part of them.

I refuse to give any credence to that gnawing sound in the back of my head, teething its pattern of *denial* all over my brain.

Someone's in my room.

I jerk awake, my sheets tangling with my bare legs when I bring them up to my chest. The wild motion causes my hair to fly into my face, and I scrape it back, keeping my hand on my head as I survey my room, too obscured by night to make out much. The meager moonlight from my single window doesn't help illuminate what I swear is rustling in the corner.

Without saying a word, I fumble for the switch on my nightstand lamp, yanking the chain and flooding both the room and my feeble, sleepy eyesight. Squinting, eyes watering, I scan my room again while maintaining my position in bed, then decide I've made myself too vulnerable and crawl out of it.

Nothing's out of place. No footsteps stain the floorboards, no blood is splattered against the walls—

I gasp, blinking away the interposing nightmare, tugging my nightshirt over my underwear, feeling my clothes and skin, ensuring I'm in reality and not a night terror.

You're not there. Mom's not at your feet. You're okay.

Hefting my binder full of notes in one hand, I fly into the center room, ready to pummel whoever's decided to trespass and terrify me.

I glance left, where Piper's couch and entertainment system used to be. Nothing but the filtered moonlight from the large bay window glides across the hardwood floor.

The kitchenette stands silent, until the mini fridge lets out a gurgle and my skeleton nearly separates from my skin.

The urge to call out is a damn strong one, but I'm no damsel willing to point out where I'm standing for slaughter, despite my room's light illuminating my backside.

Someone was here. I was torn awake by a sound that wasn't supposed to be in my room.

Piper's shut door looms in front of me, proof that I'm not simply shaking off a nightmare. It was ajar before I turned out all the lights and went to sleep.

Same goes with my bathroom.

Gulping, I'm uncertain where to begin. Do I burst through Piper's room, or the bathroom?

And what do I do if I confront a hidden intruder?

I've taken multiple self-defense classes, even excelled in archery that one summer I went to sleep-away camp Upstate, but ... I've seen death. Its bleakness has poisoned me twice in two years, and I lack the confidence in my ability to cheat it the way I did before Mom. Before Piper.

I'm so busy staring down Piper's door that I hear the click before I sense where it came from—the front door.

The bathroom door's open now.

A whimper escapes my lips, and I buckle against my doorframe, the Briarcliff binder clutched tight to my chest.

Whoever it was, is gone, and I have the entrusting notion that the person managed to escape through the shadows because of a black cloak.

Damn my petrified state. Instead of flipping on all the lights like I should've, I gave him plenty of blind corners to escape into before finding the door.

And if you brought him into the light, how do you think that would've gone for you? An inner voice, sounding suspiciously like my mom, whispers.

She's right. The binder slips from my hands, and I race to the bathroom, banging the door against the wall and switching on the light.

The bathroom is as pristine as I left it, meaning there are bottles stacked along the bathtub's rim, and my make-up scattered across the sink's counter with my flat iron's wire tangled inside the sink's rim...

With one thing tucked under it that doesn't belong.

Swallowing, I move closer and lift the foreign object, inspecting it closer to the mirror.

A single white rose petal, softened and bruised from too much handling, is all that remains of my unwelcome visitor, left to rot in my sink.

36

The sun is slow to rise on Sunday morning, unlike me.

Sleep didn't come after my baleful attempt at catching a shadowed figure in my empty dorm room. The rest of the early hours were spent with me sitting cross-legged in bed, holding my lamp as a better weapon, should anyone—even poor Ivy—decide to visit me while the moon was still out. I disregard reporting last night to Headmaster Marron, or even Haskins. What would I say? Someone's harassing me by leaving roses? My room's being broken into, but nothing is taken or moved around?

My breakfast consists of a handful of dry granola and a large thermos of coffee before I pull on a plaid button-up over my white tank and zip up my comfy, ripped jeans—Callie Ryan B.B. (Before Briarcliff).

Having the lonely beats of my heart for company last night, even during someone's scare attempt, I'm eager to surround myself with people, even if they wear Briarcliff gear, and even if they are mostly mean. I decide to do some Sunday study in the library.

It's better than waiting in a room with no security for the Cloak's next move.

I take the stairs instead of the elevator today, choosing the safety of using my feet over becoming easy prey in an enclosed space.

My night wasn't entirely ruined, however. When the lights were on and my brain in peak study mode, I learned a lot about the Stone and Harrington contributions to Briarcliff, and consequently, the small town named after it.

The Stones' donations to Briarcliff were substantial—incredibly so. The very library I'm heading to is even named after Daniel Stone's wife (read: divorcée), Marilee Barclay, called the M.B.S. Library of Studies.

A huge amount of dough is required to donate a building, even from a top defense attorney, and I circled that discrepancy, but never returned to it. Daniel Stone's serious money donations might not have anything to do with Piper, other than him potentially inheriting partial ownership to Moriarty Oil—a company bequeathed to Paul Harrington's *wife*, Sabine Moriarty, when he marries her. Ivy didn't have the whole story—the Harringtons owned the multi-million dollar company, Comfy-At-Home, but she missed the part about them having some serious old family oil money.

All these names twisted in my mind. It's hella difficult to keep rich people's fortunes straight, especially when they intermingle. Yet, arming myself with this information was empowering. I felt less like a goldfish swimming in open waters and more like a baby shark.

In heading to the library, I take the public path. It's a longer trek, but farther away from the forest and in flat plains. If any Cloak wants to introduce himself, he'll have to do it in view of the entire campus.

No one greets me as I enter the pavilion. Students are peppered throughout. It's getting colder, and many are choosing the Briarcliff winter uniform of sweaters and cardigans over their regular clothing today.

The library is behind Briarcliff's primary building, and I detour around the side, still in plain sight, until I reach the modern glass doors of the two-story library.

A light, warm breeze hits me from above as the automatic doors swish open. As I swipe my keycard and step through one of two turnstiles by the librarian's desk, I keep my expression impassive, despite the awe I experience whenever I enter.

It's an open concept, with wide, scarred wooden desks placed in rows in the middle, scores of books rimming all four corners and stacking to the ceiling. A balcony stretches across, midway through the rows upon rows of books, to access the ones shelved higher. Rolling, metal ladders lean against the walls, ready to be used by the librarian upon request. I love the hushed, papered atmosphere of this place, despite the majority of our work being on our computers and online.

I find the closest table, despite most being available. Wanting to be near the exit in case of an emergency—or a wayward bully—is a difficult habit to break.

A low laugh grabs my attention, and I scan the cluster of students who have decided to make their Sunday morning a study session, too.

There. In the far corner, near the stacks with the least amount of sunlight, sit Chase and his posse.

When Chase catches my eye, a half-cocked smirk dancing across his face, I look down, intent on spreading out my textbooks for our English and Calculus quarter-terms coming up this week. My stomach reacts, butterfly wings unfurling at my core.

Echoing whispers and hitches of breath—disguised laughter—emit from Chase's corner of the room.

I curl my hands over a textbook, the words blurring into smudges. Mom's words whisper through my ears.

Falling is a mistake. But staying down? Staying down is a choice, Calla.

My textbook shuts with a smack. I stand, and with hands fisted to my side, stalk over to Chase's table.

Riordan sees me coming and ducks his head, pretending deep interest in his calc text. James catches Riordan's movements, but unlike his buddy, lays his direct gaze against mine, watching me approach as he sticks a pen between his teeth and leans back against his chair. Tempest spins his stylus in a graceful, distracted maneuver, then taps it against his bottom lip as he reads his iPad. The watercolor green of his eyes, however, shine in my direction.

Chase doesn't change his stance, studying his laptop, then writing something down on a spiral-bound notebook.

He's left-handed, I think, which is a ridiculous observation to make when I'm about to ask him if he made a sex tape of us.

James drops his gaze when I reach their table. Nobody speaks.

Hissing, slithering whispers catch my attention at my periphery, and I notice Piper's old friends nearby. Falyn, Willow, and Violet.

My vision turns to slits when I see them, all hunched over their phones.

God, don't let it be what I think it is.

I turn back to the boys, crossing my arms and clearing my throat.

None react.

"What are you going to do with it?" I ask in a low voice, uncaring of who responds. James and Tempest are well aware of what their boys got up to yesterday evening.

James speaks. He feigns confusion and asks, "With what?"

"You know what." I'm hoping my tone cuts through their infuriating ease but know I'm about to be sorely disappointed.

"Chase?" I ask.

One carved, bronze eyebrow rises, but he doesn't stray from his computer.

"Don't you think our attention—no, scratch that—the *school's* focus should be on Piper, not what we—" I catch myself, not even able to say what we did out loud. "I thought Piper was the one deserving the spotlight. Why the hell did you do that to me?"

Chase slow blinks at me. Riordan laughs under his breath, so I shove at his shoulder, turning his laughter into startled chokes.

"And why the hell did you film it, you second-hand creep? Do you get off on seeing your leader's junk?"

Riordan sobers. "Hey, now. That's mean."

"You should've seen my video," James pipes in, smiling with the pen in his teeth. "Hottest Rated for a while there. Maybe yours woulda been, too, had you shown some—"

The table cracks with Chase's fist. The only human who doesn't jump in the whole damned room is Tempest.

A velvet-calm voice floats up to my ears. "You can relax, Callie."

I stare down at Chase. He was speaking to me, but is back to focusing on the screen in front of him.

"See this?" Riordan redirects my attention by pointing to the reddened, swollen skin around his eye. "It's deleted. Believe me on that."

I stop the habit of chewing on my lower lip nervously. "You're sure?"

Riordan lifts his phone. "There's nothing on here. Technically, that show you and Chase put on wasn't supposed to happen, ergo, shouldn't've been filmed…"

"What were you supposed to be filming, little Spielberg?" I ask. "In fact, what else have you filmed? You get off on girl fights, too?"

"Rio," Tempest says, sitting on Chase's left. "Time for you to shut up."

"What's wrong, Tempi?" James asks, letting his head fall to one shoulder. "Is this sort of chit-chat too human-like for you? Should we go back to our lizard forms like yourself?"

"Call me that again." Tempest's stare snaps to James's.

I inwardly flinch at the cool murder in Tempest's expression. It's a miracle I got away with calling him *Pest*.

Chase shuts his laptop. Hard. "All of you, fuck off over to the girls. They look in need of quiet entertainment. James, show them your vintage porn video and get back some of your previous popularity."

"I'm not going anywhere," I say. "Until you explain."

"Not you," Chase clips out. "You can sit."

"Again, with the *be a good girl* talk." But as the boys stand and drift over to Falyn's table, I take Riordan's seat across from Chase. "I don't believe you. You don't put a camera on something like that and just delete it before being able to use it for some gain. I know you at this point, Chase."

"No." Chase laughs. "You don't."

"Then what?" I fold my arms over the table, keeping my voice as low as his. Somehow, the entire exchange with Chase and his boys happened in soft, snappish voices that were overlooked by the librarian. It's undetermined how long this free pass will continue. "What else have you recorded? Piper and me fighting? Did you *send* that crap to me?"

"I wish I knew what you were talking about, sweet possum."

I lean closer. Now that his computer's shut, it's much easier to look into his scotch-brown eyes, as clear and placid as the manmade lake he trains his muscles on. "What you did was an insane violation of my privacy."

"That may be, but with the grave you're digging for yourself, if you go second, I don't want anyone pointing to me as a suspect. Again," he adds drolly.

Ignoring the tarantula-sized creepy crawlies in my gut, I retort, "You were all for my looking into Piper's death. And now you're against it?"

"Not quite. What I don't appreciate is you constantly referencing me as a Noble."

I swallow a scornful laugh. "Are you trying to tell me they

have nothing to do with Piper? Because the harder I 'dig,' the faster they tell me to fuck off."

Chase squints at me. "They're communicating with you?"

The dirty white rose petal I found in the bathroom sink takes a spot in my mind's eye. "In a sense. Do they wear cloaks?"

Chase takes his time studying me, the type of survey that leaves invisible goosebumps on my skin. "Callie. At what point are you going to understand they may be warning you away from something and not toward it?"

"Once they start being direct. Like a letter. A *word,* even, instead of skulking around with roses."

"Roses?" Chase sits back and crosses his arms. "You're playing with the devil."

"I am. I even had his dick in my hand, if you recall."

Chase stiffens. But he breaks character with the barest lift to his lips. "How can such a shy, quiet, nerd-girl have such a mouth on her?"

"Who said I was shy?"

Chase stares at me like I should have the answer. Then he answers for me. "You have no friends."

"Correction," I say, despite the sudden lump in my chest. "I have few friends at Briarcliff. That doesn't mean I'm friendless."

Matt and Sylvie come to mind, back in NYC and together, living their new Insta lives without their third wheel wobbling them off track.

"Really?" Chase shuts his laptop, then leans his elbows on the table. His scent drifts into my vicinity, and I pull back on instinct. Now isn't the time to be drawn in by his lure. "Your pathetic month here tells me I'm right."

"Stop changing the subject. The devil isn't a member of the Nobles. It's you, if my earlier opinion didn't point that out. All my problems come from *you* and your salivating followers. So, as long as you can prove there's no video by letting me look through your phone, you can stand down, and I'll leave me alone."

Chase effortlessly tosses his phone, so it lands in front of me. "What if it all comes down to your protection? What if I'm causing you shit in order to distract you and prevent you from taking the path Piper did?"

I hold up his phone for inspection, my grip tight. "Because there's nothing that tells me you have my best interests at heart."

"Oh, no? Was yesterday not enough?"

My cheeks warm. It's one thing to think about it in silence, but when Chase brings it up, in that earthy, dirty voice of his, all the secret, pleasurable areas on my body tingle under his summons.

"If you know something about Piper, you should go to the police, not dangle it in front of me like a rotten carrot," I say.

Chase's phone flashes with a message from James, but I ignore it and swipe to his lock screen. He plucks it from my fingers, types in his code, then drops his phone back into my palm. "I have nothing to say to them. Those Dudley Do-Goods will never get to the bottom of it, and neither will you, sweet possum. Stop while you're still receiving bouquets."

I frown at him, but my focus is on his photo library, scanning the tiles for anything dated yesterday that he could've sent himself from Riordan's phone. No way would Chase leave it as Riordan's sole responsibility. I also look for the day Piper died and any possible fight scenes. But Chase does not record his life in photos. All I see, as I scroll higher, are photos of him training on the water and a few with his arm slung around Piper's shoulder—those caused a tug in my chest— and some random group shots in the dining hall, until my thumb stamps on the screen, stopping at a photo of me. *Me.* In Briarcliff's foyer, staring up.

"That's..." I spin the phone's screen to him. "Is this my first day? Did you take a *picture* of me?"

Chase angles his head, his beatific angles in stark relief. "I took it without thinking."

I study the picture harder. He caught me at a flattering angle, my chin raised, my eyes wide with anxiety and curiosity. Chase had zoomed in, Piper and Headmaster Marron standing somewhere outside the frame.

I appear vulnerable in my mom's old college shirt and jeans. Too innocent for what was to come, despite the shadows of grief harboring in the hollows of my cheeks and the crescents under my eyes. Definitely too war-torn to be filed away as Chase's pixelated prisoner.

I find the Trash icon and send it in.

"I deleted it." I fling his phone, so it lands on his laptop with a tinned thump. "I'm not yours to save."

Chase's brow angles up again. "In more ways than one, I assume."

A commotion splits my attention, and I see Eden picking up textbooks from the floor. Willow's walking away, covering her mouth as she laughs, her auburn ponytail dancing.

I push to my feet with a disgusted scowl, but say to Chase, "We're done here, so long as whatever you caught with your wingman's lens never sees the light of day. If it does, I'll have the NYPD come down on your ass so hard, not even your lengthy appendage will be able to cushion it."

"I'm glad my cock made such an impression on you," he responds, and my cheeks flame. I hate it when I speak before I think. Chase continues, "Take a minute to consider I might not want that video spread around, either. I don't punch my friends in the face on the daily. What happened yesterday ... it wasn't expected. By any of us, I don't think."

Chase waits for my reply, but I turn around instead, ashamed of my traitorous cheeks and the heat at the base of my throat.

No, it wasn't expected.

And, *damn it*, it better not ever be reenacted, regardless of the determined, sexual promise in his hooded eyes as I walk away.

37

I tell myself I'm rushing to help Eden and not trying to outrun the angelic devil staring at my back.

"Here," I say once I reach her, bending to lift a textbook. "The filthy rich are clumsy fuckers, aren't they?"

Eden releases a mirthless laugh, but she covers her crestfallen expression by allowing a hank of dark hair to fall against her profile.

"Eden," I say, falling into stride with her and directing her to my table. "You're crying."

"Not about that," Eden says, dropping her books near mine. "That bitch has had it in for me for years."

"Then ... can I help?" I sit beside Eden, in front of my stuff, and spin my legs to face hers. I keep my voice low, since we're closer to the librarian's monitoring scowl.

"No. Not if you're becoming one of them." Eden focuses on positioning her books and laptop.

I jolt. "Who? Like Willow? Hell-to-the-no, Eden."

Eden shakes her head. "With Chase. Nobody will say it to your face, but it hasn't gone unnoticed that you're trying to be Piper two-point-oh."

"I'm *what*?!"

A loud *SHUSH* sounds out, and a quick check shows the librarian zoning in on me, a finger to her lips as her eyes grow small. I nod an apology but get back to Eden.

"Eden, come on. Rumors swirl around here. I'm trying to figure out what happened to Piper, not take her place."

"Yeah, there's that rumor, too. Our own Harriet the Spy."

"I thought I was more of a Lara Croft."

It works. Eden's cheek—the part of it I can see—twitches with a smile.

"Eden." I risk a hand on her shoulder. She doesn't shove me away, and I take that as encouragement. "I will never be like them. I don't enjoy being bullied, but I'd *never* become the bully as a result. I'm not hanging out with the Witches of Briarcliff, and I'm talking to Chase because Piper died, and I'd like to know what happened. If you're wondering why I'm involving myself in a bully's death," I say as Eden stiffens, "It's in my bones. I can't leave her death alone, not when I'm seeing what everyone else doesn't."

Eden doesn't argue or cut in. Her chin tilts ever so slightly in my direction. I continue. "Doesn't this school seem like there's poison in the wood that built it? In the forest? The water? I think Piper's fall was orchestrated, not an accident, and not a crime of passion."

There. I said what I couldn't even form into sentences for Chase. *Briarcliff Academy's responsible.*

Eden tucks her hair behind her ear, exposing her profile. She doesn't look in my direction, maintaining her tunnel vision on her pile of texts.

"Eden, I don't know what it is, but my instinct is to trust you."

"Why?" Eden bites out the question.

"Because everyone here wears a mask, but in the time I've known you, you've never put one on."

Eden's lips part. "Have you told anyone else this theory?"

I shake my head. Eden's warming up to the conversation. If I bring up Ivy, I'm positive it will shut her down. "I'm only realizing it myself."

"Good. Don't." Eden turns, the force of her sage brown eyes as powerful as Mother Nature herself. "This place hides its iniquity, and it starts with your research paper on Rose Briar."

I gasp. "Wait. I'm right about Rose?"

"The alumni, the rich, the privileged, the tenured, nobody gives a damn, so long as they get a diploma or a hefty paycheck."

I bend closer, our heads touching with this conspiracy. "What do you know?"

"You have all the pieces, Callie. Put them together."

"Not when each person I encounter speaks to me in tongues!" I whisper through my teeth.

"There's a reason I notice certain things but stay quiet," Eden says in a hushed voice. "I don't belong here, and neither do you. So, you either become part of the crowd, or you stand out and get banished."

"By who, the Nobles?"

Eden's expression goes blank, but she keeps her eyes on mine. "You've figured out their name."

"The creepy guys who lurk around campus in cloaks? Yeah, you can say I've seen them."

Eden's face falls. "You mean, they've seen you."

"Don't you get all prophetic on me, Eden. Someone needs to give it to me straight, and I'm betting it's you."

"I'm the one who sent you the video."

I stare at her. A ball of saliva lodges in my throat. I cough, and out of pity, she hands me her water thermos. I chug, then, as if my actions weren't obvious, say, "What?"

She repeats, "The video of you and Piper fighting. I sent it."

"Eden—why would you threaten me?"

Eden rolls her eyes. "Please. If I wanted to intimidate you, I'd've tied you up, blindfolded you, and stuck you in one of the hidden tombs under the school."

I choke again, then pretend I didn't.

"I'm protecting you," she says simply.

"By sending me a recording that could get me in big trouble with the police?"

"No, dummy. By sending you something *someone else* has. I'm telling you to be careful."

"I don't understand."

"I stole that video from someone else's phone. I'm quiet, remember. Unnoticed."

"Who?" My face goes numb as all the blood rushes to my chest. "*Ivy?*"

Eden's gaze flits to something over my shoulder, then back to mine. A freakish wave of anger crosses her face. She says in a wet whisper, "You're so fucking clueless."

My back turns rigid. "Hey—"

She adds, much louder, "If you're so positive the ghost of Briarcliff Academy killed Piper, shut your mouth, you crazy slut."

I jerk back. "Eden, what?"

"Take my advice. Stop earning the name Asylum Possum."

I balk. "That's a thing?"

Eden stands, but bends her head close. "Piper wasn't a Noble," she whispers as she puts her elbows into hefting up the books. "She was a Virtue."

"Wh—?"

I'm stopped from finishing the question when I follow Eden's path. Falyn leans over the librarian's desk, so obviously inattentive to what the librarian's saying, it's a wonder the woman keeps talking.

Falyn's assessing stare follows Eden as she exits the library. Eden darts a single look at Falyn, then glances once more at me before walking through the doors, as if communicating the reason for her sudden outburst.

Falyn was watching us.

I pretend to have an itchy cheek, then spin in my seat until I'm facing my computer and my back is to Falyn, but my fingers hover over the keys.

Piper. A Virtue? WTF, Eden?

As if that's not enough, Eden blows my mind further by letting me know she's the one who sent me the incriminating video in the same tone she uses to answer basic questions in class.

Like it's nothing.

But she stole those videos from someone else...

It all starts with your research paper on Rose Briar. And Rose created a society with a V ... the Virtues.

I fall back against the chair.

Everyone else is researching the founders, too. This can't be the first time someone chose Rose. Why did I get stuck with Piper's theories about a secretive woman concocting plans to go against her husband's secret gentlemen's club?

Ugh. My head hurts.

I whip my attention over my shoulder in an effort to mentally will Eden back here but meet Falyn's acute stare instead.

Grimacing and slamming back against my seat, I figure I have another long night of reading between the lines ahead of me.

38

Who, in all the hells, am I supposed to trust around here?

It's safe to say that studying at M.B.S. Library of Studies is a no-go, not with Falyn lurking curiously behind my back and Chase hovering dangerously in my horizon.

Before Briarcliff, I was a straight-A, determined student, and I'm not willing to give that up. Briarcliff and all its hidden passages isn't my future. College is.

My cavernous, two-person dorm room with one resident (me) is the best place to get my shit done, but it's also the loneliest. Even Piper's cold, superficial heart was better company than the invisible spirit that's taken her place.

You have no friends.

Chase is wrong. I may be able to count the people at Briarcliff I've endeared myself to on one finger, but she's worth it, because Ivy greets me with a toothy smile the instant I step through Thorne House's doors.

"Hey!" she says, rounding the check-in desk. My worries that she was who Eden got the video from lessen in her presence. She *can't* be the one who filmed it. She was at a crew meeting that evening. "I was looking for you this morning."

"All you missed was my sad attempt to get some studying done at the library," I say.

"M.B.S. Library, also known as the G.P.S. for the latest gossip."

I raise my brows. "And here I thought the single juicy tidbit I had revolved around its name."

"Briarcliff named it after the Stone family, yeah. They're deep in Briarcliff's pockets, tracing back to the founding," Ivy says, propping her hip against the desk as I come to stop in front of her. "In fact, it was through some of their ancestors' trusts they gifted the library, not Chase's parents alone."

"There's my missing piece!" I hold up my index finger. "I was wondering how they got so much money to construct a new library."

Ivy nods, and I'm assaulted with guilt. What did I say to Eden? That she's the one who doesn't wear a mask around here. But Ivy's never been anything but kind to me, welcoming my presence when the majority didn't, not to mention, eagerly providing me with information.

Why then, do I hold my heart back? Is it because of the one moment we've had where she stood back and watched me get attacked by Piper? I gotta admit, that one hurt.

Ivy adds, "Because the old one burned down. It's a crazy story."

I smile wryly, remembering Darla's, the public librarian's, words. "Don't tell me. Briarcliff has another sinister secret to tell?"

Ivy smiles back. "In due time. Where rich people go, scandals follow, and there's many that would make you cringe."

"Now you have me intrigued. Hey..." I hesitate. "Wanna come up and pretend to have a study sesh with me while you tell me all about it?"

Ivy makes a pained sound. "Can't. I have fifteen minutes left on my shift, then some mat work."

"Mat work?"

"Gotta keep this body bangin'," Ivy jokes. "Crew may be off-season, but we still train just as hard in the gym."

I nod in understanding, even though the boathouse resembles a Resort & Spa Lounge, not a high school fitness center. "No problem. I'll see you around."

"Wait." Ivy glances around, as if her boss is about to materialize from a corner at any second. "I can knock off for fifteen. I'll grab one of your snacks and tell you about the burning, then head out."

I snort, but then smile as Ivy pulls out an OUT TO BREAK bronze placard and places it on the desk. "You make it sound like a witch hunt."

"It kinda was." Ivy wrinkles her nose. "Involving the most popular girl in school."

My eyes go wide. "Piper?"

"No, Piper didn't become cool until ninth grade when she started hanging out with Chase. She was invisible before then, but once they started dating, it's like she changed the narrative of the school's social order and crowned them both Prince and Princess of Briarcliff."

"How come we haven't talked about this before?"

Ivy presses the elevator call button. "Why are you interested? Because it could relate to your insane obsession with Piper's fall?"

"Well ... yeah." We step into the elevator.

"I dunno. Maybe because you've been so focused on the days leading up to Piper's death, and not two years before."

I make a noncommittal sound, despite the obvious opening to tell Ivy about Piper's diary. It never seems like the time.

We step out onto my floor, and I'm staring at my shoes as we walk. I wish I could enjoy my time at Briarcliff and stop with the questions and suspicion. I could get to know Ivy better, as well as her friends who sit with us during meals. I could talk to Eden like I want to get to know her, instead of pressing her for information she's reluctant to give. I could be a senior and make senior memories before scoring a diploma at an elite private school, getting into college, and leaving the East Coast *far* behind.

And never solve shit, the meaner part of my mind hisses. *Just like your mom's murder.*

"Earth to Callie, we're at your door. Unless you're thinking of busting through the emergency exit straight ahead." Ivy nudges me lightly.

"Sorry," I say. I dig out my keycard and *blip* us in, our footsteps seeming to echo once we leave the carpeted hallway and enter my furniture-less main room.

"When did they say the couch would be delivered?" Ivy asks, reading my thoughts. "Or the TV?"

"Tomorrow, thankfully," I say, dropping my backpack by the kitchenette counter. "Make yourself comfy on my bed, the only piece of furniture I own at the moment that can fit two people. I'll be in there with some guac and chips in a sec."

"'Kay." Ivy wanders over to my room, which, out of habit, I still keep shut.

She pushes it open, and screams.

39

The glass bowl of guac I was keeping fresh in the fridge crashes to the floor, and I slip in the green goop as I hurry into my room.

"Ivy!" I cry. "What? What is it—?"

I slide to a stop in front of her, then hang on to her arm for dear life.

Ivy's gasping beside me, her face bone white. Her free hand goes to her mouth, and her skin is cold beneath mine.

As chilled as the blood that stops coursing through my body when I see what's scattered across my bedding.

Photos. A ton of pictures printed on A4 paper, blanketing my bed to the point where no one would know the color of my lavender sheets.

They're spread across my sheets, taped on my wall above the headboard, and plastered over every flat surface I have.

My desk harbors shot after shot, print after print, stuck and spread and scattered.

"What ... what..." Nothing else can pass Ivy's lips.

My hands might be clinging to her, but my feet want to walk. To bring me closer to the horror.

One word breaks through my throat, one syllable made into a shattered prism of sound. "*Mom...*"

She's not looking at the camera lens in the photo. She can't. I remember how she stared vacantly, blood pooled around her head and her hands curled in a final round of defense. Her irises were milky and clouded with death.

But here, in this putrid reminder vomited all over my room, a large, yellow, smiley emoji takes the place of her face, its inky grin obscuring the violence of her dying expression but made no less obscene.

I fall to my knees, grabbing the closest picture. "Mom," I cry brokenly.

"Oh my God, Callie." Ivy breaks out of her frozen stance and comes up behind me, holding my upper arms and trying to lift me back to a stand. "We need to get out of here. Report this."

Swirls of yellow smiley-faces mock me. No matter where I turn, there's a picture of my murdered mother with an emoji head, the blood obvious around the perfect circle of a grin, until they blur into a nauseating watercolor, because my eyes can't focus, and my stomach promises to produce a similar result.

"You need to get out of here," Ivy mumbles desperately. "Callie, come on!"

"I-I-" My eyes won't close. They'll dry up and blur my vision, but they won't shut.

"This is so *fucked*," Ivy says, then all but drags me out with her athlete's arms.

"You cursed," I say in a daze. "You never swear."

"I'll fucking swear up a fucking goddamned storm after that fucked-up scene, Jesus Christ!" Ivy takes a breath. "Are you okay?"

I stare blankly at the walls, still clutching a picture until Ivy rips it from my hands, tosses it back in my room and slams the door. She pulls out her phone. "I'm calling campus police."

"I..." Gulping, I stand on wobbly knees, and that's when the dam breaks.

Tears pour down my cheeks, my hands start shaking, and my lip trembles on a barely contained scream.

"Callie, sit back down. You're white as—shit, you're gonna pass out. Sit, babe. C'mon..."

I sit, but my gaze drifts to the door. And once I see it...

"*No!*" I cry.

Ivy startles. "What?"

In a burst of energy, I fly to my backpack. The flap is unbuckled, and it wasn't five seconds ago. I dig through it like a groundhog, textbooks flying, laptop sliding across the hardwood, until I hit nothing but fabric at its bottom.

"Fuck," I say. Then scream, "*FUCK!*"

"*What?*" Ivy shouts again, holding the phone away from her ear, color yet to return to her cheeks. "Is there something else in there?"

I tear through my pile of texts, opening Calculus and a flash of relief zaps through me when I find Rose's letter still nestled in the middle.

But as for the rest...

They took my phone! Piper's diary pages are on there!

Someone used Ivy's and my distraction to take it from my bag and sneak out. Or was it while I was in the library talking to Chase?

Piper's bullying, I could handle. She was a basic playground bitch, utilizing tactics better served in a teen rom-com flick, but I managed it.

This, though ... this isn't a simple message of dislike or diversion. This is *hate*, and it's directed at me. Another Cloak warning? He's never been this violently obvious before. Why start now? Why *hurt* me like this?

I lean forward, clutching my temples and moaning. I can't think. I can't *think* with Mom's blood behind my eyes, made fresh by these goddamn pictures somebody printed off like they were nothing but pages for a school report.

Is this related to Piper? Or does it have to do with my continued presence at Briarcliff despite the multiple requests by Piper's friends that I GTFO of this school?

Piper's friends.

They were at the library with me when I got there. But other than Falyn, I lost track of them when I started talking to Chase, every one of my senses attuned to *him* while my background faded to gray.

My nails claw at the hardwood as I form into a leap and fly out the front door.

"Callie!" Ivy cries, but I'm already busting through the emergency exit.

✻

What was it Ivy said?

Mat work.

Boathouse.

My heels tear into the dirt and grass of Briarcliff's perfect landscape before I hit the trail and storm down the hill.

I don't slow until I see the three ponytails ahead of me, bobbing in time as they navigate the terrain in single file, chatting snidely and laughing.

The middle one—Willow—doesn't see me coming. Her ponytail goes flying when I crash into her, the fire in my eyes redder than her hair.

Tackling her to the ground is easy. Pinning her arms on either side of her head as I scream in her face is concerning.

"Omigod!" the quiet one—Violet—cries behind me.

"Get off her, you crazy slut!"

I don't need to tell you who that one is.

"*How could you?*" I scream. Willow twists and writhes underneath me, her starched white Briarcliff fitness shirt dirtied up and wrinkled under my grip. Her maroon sports skort rides up on her thighs when she tries to knee me in the back, but I rear back on a snarl and slap her across the cheek.

She wails. "What the *fuck*?"

Arms grip my shoulders, but I elbow them back. I'm hot all over, my tears cascading lava from the volcano erupting behind my eyes.

I bend close to Willow's face, her head-twists slowing the closer my teeth come to her delicate skin. My throat doesn't emit the sounds I'm used to. They're keening, unhinged wails, its notes hitched with trembling breaths. I manage to speak, broken words that hold the entire meaning of my world.

"*That was my mother!*"

Willow breathes hard, but she gasps out, "What the hell are you talking about?"

"My-my room," I stutter. "What you did."

"I don't—"

"You hate me. You've made that obvious." I glance over my shoulder at Falyn, who's nursing the bicep I elbowed into, and Violet, filming the whole thing on her phone.

These goddamned rich kids and their forest cell service...

I push to my feet and round on her. Violet squeaks and stumbles back into the trees but doesn't lower her phone.

"Stop recording!" I yell. With a trembling hand, Violet keeps the phone on my face. "Why do you all want to catch my weakest moments? Why can't you leave me *alone*? If Piper was a Virtue, who the *fuck* are you guys? *Give me back my phone!*"

At least ... I think that's what I said. Thick tears blur my vision, and it's unclear whose voice I'm using, but it certainly isn't my own. I don't sound like this. I don't talk like this.

I definitely don't want to punch a person tinier than me in the face, but I won't regret it when I smash Violet's—

Strong arms envelop me and shove me to the side, but they won't let go. They're bare, muscular, masculine...

"The fuck?" Chase snarls into my ear, but his warm breath is forced to leave my neck when we stumble over tree roots and rocks, and he uses his balance over mine. "You're spouting off the name Virtue now? Do you have no sense of survival?"

"*Let me go!*" I scream.

"No way in hell, sweet possum," he grits out, then holds me to his torso with a tighter grip. "Not until you tell me what the fuck's going on."

"She attacked me!" Willow screeches, brushing decaying leaves and twigs from her clothes.

"A fucking psycho is what she is," Falyn spits, then flanks her friend.

Violet tiptoes from the foliage, phone still on.

"Turn it off," Chase hisses. "*Now.*"

Violet clicks the phone off and shoves it into her gym bag. My face momentarily goes slack, because of course she listens to Chase's commands the minute his lips move.

"Take it back out and delete that shit, Vi," he says.

I'm somewhat thrown off by the familiar use of her nickname, but it also sends a harsh reminder. These people know each other. They grew up together, always, and have garnered the type of loyalty only decades of familiarity can gift. I can't trust any of them, and most of that distrust has to go to their leader. Their prince.

"I said let me go, Chase." I struggle within his forced embrace, but his elbows don't even tick up with movement.

"Not with your teeth and claws out." His chin digs into my hair. "What the fuck, Callie?"

"They ... they..." I growl in frustration and grief. I can't get the meaning out.

"I told you, Chase," Willow says, her bruised wrists going to her hips. "She attacked me out of nowhere, for no reason. And

Violet's going to keep the evidence, because my next stop is Dad's office, and this bitch is gonna be expelled. You hear that, rat-face? You're *done*."

I spit and snarl with such sudden intensity, Chase has difficulty keeping me in place.

"Not once I show him what you did!" I say. "The pictures, all over my room. That's crossing the line, even for you bitches!"

"Looks like it worked," Falyn says dryly, and that earns her another escape attempt by me.

"Jesus—stay still," Chase says, his voice strained. I'm trying to kick my way out, and my shoes come concerningly close to his groin. "What pictures?"

"My *mother*," I say, my vocal cords tearing as the memory rips through my throat. "Pictures of her crime scene. Deranged smiley emojis where her face should-should—"

My knees buckle. Chase catches my sudden dead weight and holds me still, his grip becoming less imprisoning as I pull the images forth, pages of my mother's death fanning into my mind's view.

The three of them—Violet, Falyn, and Willow, wobble into my present, but Falyn's catty smile remains clear, and Willow's obvious derision is in the twist of her lips.

Even while messed-up, wrinkled, and pale with shock, they resemble princesses-in-training, looking down at their latest prisoner, asking their knight to ready her for a beheading.

Violet is the disconcerted leftover, pulling her lips in and working her jaw nervously, her reluctance at being a part of this shit-show made clear.

Chase's hold lightens, and he shifts so it's only his body I see. Only him. He lowers his head so his dazzling, angelic face takes their place, and I'm able to blink again. Chase's normally arched brows smooth and his lips turn supple with understanding.

He waits until my eyes are steady on his.

"Leave it to me," he says, then waits a beat to ensure my

permission before he turns. "Is what Callie's saying true? Did you three put her mother's murder on blast?"

Chase's voice is so low, it's demonically dark. His cadence slows so the threat is evident in each syllable he utters.

His broad back, covered by his thin unisuit, shades my view, each tensed muscle popping against the maroon and black fabric. I don't need to be a witness to know that the three witches have gone white under their bi-weekly spray tans.

Falyn's voice comes through. "She's a lunatic, Chase, like Piper always said."

"We may not be responsible," Willow adds, "But whoever it was deserves kudos from us. You should be proud, too, Chase, since you and Piper—"

"I never participated in Piper's juvenile cruelty," Chase bites out.

"But you watched it." Willow's voice turns playful. "And you silently loved it as much as Tempest. Laughed like James. Observed with your hand sneaking into your pants, like Rio—"

"Fuck your theories, Willow," Chase snaps. "I'm not a part of your run-down traveling circus as you collect your freaks. Whatever you're hoping to win now that Piper's gone, it ends now."

"And what'll you do about it if we don't?" Falyn trills. "Push us off a—"

Chase rears so fast and hard, his sneakers kick dirt up my shins as he flies in front of Falyn, his fingers twitching with his effort at restraint, but his mouth holding no such reservations.

"Mention her death and my name in a sentence again, you'll see what it's like to bend under my will, and you know better than anybody that I don't use force. I like my games." Chase tilts his head, his face bitingly close to Falyn, who stands her ground, but shakes at the effort. "I love my silent cruelty. I'll inflict every skill I have until you go to sleep screaming. You'll wake up with a voice so raw, you'll have blood instead of a tongue." Chase leans in. "And it will all be from your own doing. My hands'll be clean."

Fuck.

Even I gulp at his words, and I'm the one with a clear view of his perfect ass in tight shorts, the complete opposite of the Satanic lip service Falyn's receiving.

The corners of my mouth tic at the thought. *I'm coming back.* The scarlet vision recedes, and my fingers and toes tingle, like they've been asleep all this time and at last are returning to life.

I breathe.

"Go clean up the shit you've tossed into Callie's room," Chase continues. "I'll explain to Coach you're skipping practice because you didn't want to miss your manicure appointment."

"You know what Coach'll do if she hears we missed training!" Willow sputters, her face blotchy and red.

Chase angles to include Willow. "And you know what *I'll* do if you follow me to the boathouse."

"You're a fucking asshole," Falyn spits, now that his hell-spawned eyes are directed elsewhere.

"There's no need," comes a small voice.

I think it's Violet, but when I look at her, she's clutching her gym bag to her chest and pretending not to exist under Chase's ire.

"Marron's in your room now, Callie," the voice continues, and I recognize its tone.

Ivy steps out from the trees and onto the path. Her eyes are red-rimmed, like she's been rubbing them. Her nails are bleeding from picking at her cuticles too hard.

"He is?" I'm surprised at the rough, off-key tune of my voice, but it sounds more familiar than it did a few minutes ago.

Ivy nods. "The campus police, too. Once they heard what was in there, they, um, they also called ... Haskins is on his way."

Chase asks, "The detective?"

"Yeah," Ivy says, wringing her hands in front of her. "Callie, I think they want you to meet them in Marron's office."

We climb the trail to the school together, Ivy taking my hand at some point and squeezing. Reality continues its shaking camera view as I walk, but I'm happy to leave Chase and Piper's friends in my rearview lens.

They would've had to hack into someone's computer to gain possession of my mom's crime scene photos and used connections they were born with to get it. A password wouldn't be required—all it would take was a simple phone call, an underhanded favor exchanged, or blackmail enforced.

Chase's dad is a criminal defense attorney.

If I looked at that fact on its face, it'd be hard to believe. Chase defended me on the trail to the boathouse. Yet, I can't discount that Daniel Stone had the easiest way to gain access to those photos.

Did Chase do it? Will he defend me one minute, then plow my face into the dirt the next?

He's conniving. I've seen his two faces, one running hot and the other ice cold.

Ivy puts her hand between my shoulders, nudging me into Headmaster Marron's office. Somehow, we'd navigated the Briarcliff lawns and hallways without me noticing.

Haskins sits in one chair across from Marron's desk, where Marron reposes, his elbows propped against the wood and index fingers pressed to his lips. The second visitor's chair is vacant —for me.

Dr. Luke steps out stage left, his arms crossed and mouth grim as he nods his hello, and it's with a quick hug from Ivy that I step into the office and shut the door behind me.

40

Two grueling hours later, I leave Marron's office shakier than when I'd entered.

Stepping into the hallway reminds me that Sunday at Briarcliff continues the exact way it would had I not had my waking nightmares reinvigorated. Students filter through the school, and the Wolf's Den above is loud with footsteps and laughter as seniors drink their caffeine of choice and study, enjoying the time and privilege away from their younger counterparts.

I don't bother to look up as I pass under, but I file away the craving to sleep there tonight, instead of the place where I've been so wholly violated.

Piper, and now my mother, share their final moments with me in that dorm room. I may not have Piper's missing pages, but her feelings stay with me, the fear she must've felt, the betrayal and helpless rage ... the precise feelings I know my mom felt when she'd realized her life was over.

I close my eyes tight once I take the stairs down and hit the pavement outside, intent on keeping the tears in, on forcing my screams silent. The last people who deserve my anguish are those who amble around me, unaware and unconcerned with how their school is run.

My mom's photos being unearthed also meant Haskins's renewed attention on me. I fielded questions from him, with Dr. Luke at my elbow and my stepdad and Lynda on Skype, full of their own questions. Soon, it became Dad and Lynda attempting to understand the situation more than it was any sort of interrogation of me. They didn't know my roommate had died under suspicious circumstances. Had no clue I was being bullied by her, too. Yet, when it came to questioning my motives, Lynda reared up and threatened legal action the minute Haskins's voice bordered on suspicion. She also threatened to pull both me and her family's substantial donation if this line of questioning continued.

I respected her for that.

When she voiced her preference for both Ahmar and her family's lawyer being present if I'm "brought in" again, I appreciated her shrewdness.

Maybe she isn't that bad, after all.

I swipe the dampness from under my eyes, then reach to pull out my phone to call Ahmar, until I remember it's been stolen. During the rare moments Dad spoke, he said he'd overnight me a new one. We've always been strained, he and I, but we're on an entirely different level now that Briarcliff has shown its teeth.

During the questioning in Marron's office, who, in his defense, voiced his deep concern over the "violation" to my person and property and vowed to find the person responsible (yeah, right), I remained silent unless asked a direct question. Even then, I mumbled short answers. My eyes stayed downcast, my hands demure.

What no one caught on to or suspected, is that I. Am. *Pissed*.

Damn if anyone is going to scare me away, cloak or no cloak, Noble or Virtue, past or present.

Somebody doesn't want me to find out the truth about Piper or about this school.

Too bad for them.

I spring from the elevator and into my dorm's hallway with a burst of vengeful energy, but trip on my own feet when I notice who lingers at my door.

Chase unfurls himself from the floor, clad in a pair of Briarcliff sweats and a plain white tee, tight against his pecs. His tawny blond hair is ruffled and askew, like he's been running his fingers through it or just finished an epic work-out, the color to his cheeks mirroring the same energy-sparking habits.

"Can I help you?" I ask, my voice still ragged from my earlier rage session.

Chase licks his lips, something a six-figure, in-demand male model would do once the photographer trained the lens on him. It's endearing and sexy, with the perfect amount of feigned contrition to make a girl want to melt.

"I wanted to see if you were okay," he says.

"How so?" I keep my question innocent. "Because my mom's real, violent murder was plastered all over my walls?"

"Well, yeah."

"Mm." I move deliberately close, and the maneuver is so surprising, Chase steps back, and I'm able to elbow my way to my door. "Sucks for whoever did it, considering I walked in on the real thing. Pictures don't have the same impact, unfortunately."

Chase's heavy breath hits the nape of my neck, and I stiffen at the shiver. I expect a *shit, Callie, I'm so sorry*, at my blunt statement. Instead, I get this:

"Jesus, I wouldn't have wanted to see you then, 'cause today you were a fucking banshee whose tits were just bit off by a werewolf."

I whirl. "What is the *matter* with you? *All* of you? It's like you get turned on by pain! You're all fucking masochists with pretty faces."

Chase's hands cup my face. He ducks low, his brown eyes glittering like he kidnapped the stars to light the way for his inner beast. "Aw, sweet possum, do you think I'm pretty?"

"Stop calling me that."

"You want sympathy? You won't get it from me."

"Then why the hell are you here?" I raise my chin. "To enjoy the aftermath?"

"This may come as a surprise, but I didn't like what I saw today. Blood and murder? Not what I enjoy jerking off to." He bends closer, and I smell the mint on his breath. "Think about it. Piper was your enemy. Stands to reason my motives for finding her killer are a helluva lot stronger than yours. She was my—"

"Girlfriend."

"*Friend.*"

"Sister."

Chase cedes my point, then says, "Not anymore."

"So, what? You want us to work together? You have a fucked-up sense of team spirit, you know that?"

"I'm excellent at leading my crew, sweet possum, and even better at turning their spirit into discipline. Don't think I can't do that to you."

"Ah. So, you're here to threaten me."

Chase chuckles, low and slow. "Not in the way you're expecting."

I force steel into my voice. "What if I told you I'm here to pack up my stuff and leave?"

"You tried that once." He trails a finger down my cheek, and I stifle the sigh that wants to coat my throat like honey.

"This has gone too far," I say.

"I agree. It has." His thumb traces my bottom lip, flanging it out, then letting it snap back into place as he continues to map my features.

"You can't possibly think to seduce me, not after everything."

Chase nails me with a boyish, innocent look through his

lashes, as if I can't see the monster as his puppeteer. "Is it working?"

My back is flat against the door. I'm pressing into it so hard, I'm wishing for the superpower to just fall through. But the pieces of me without the bone structure to withstand the pressure surges and piques with need.

I choke out, "Did you use your father to gain access to those pictures?"

Chase doesn't flinch at the change in topic. His hand keeps traveling, keeps *finding*, his fingers playing around my breasts, but not touching them.

Please touch them.

"No," he says. "And to answer your follow-up question, I have no idea who did."

"But you can find out."

"Maybe." Chase's lips take the place of his finger, starting at my ear, the wisps of his breath like curls of smoke, drawing my chin up and my mouth to his jaw, lured by the flickering flames beneath.

My lips brush against his stubble when I ask, "Are you striking a deal with me, Chase?"

"You mean, help me find out about Piper, and I'll help you find your harasser?" Chase nuzzles where my neck meets my jaw, and I suppress a whimper. "What if they're one and the same?"

This is crazy. There are four rooms on this floor. A neighbor could walk through those elevators or the side stairs at any moment—neighbors I've never met, girls who've predominantly ignored my presence.

If they walked in and saw me now, however, I bet my presence would be squealed all over campus.

"What if," I manage to croak out, "they're a Noble? Or a Virtue?"

Chase stills with his lips on my nape, his teeth so close to my jugular.

"You know the meaning of those titles, Chase."

Chase's hands grip my waist, so hard, his fingers create dents in my skin.

"Chase. Tell me—"

My demand loses meaning when Chase rears up and crashes his lips against mine, sealing his secrets with a searing, wrath-fueled kiss.

41

My heart slams its warning against my ribs, my pulse points following their leader's commands, but my hands won't heed.

They rise up, my fingers tangling in his hair, and he tastes like the alcohol I'm too young to crave.

Mint and liquor duel for their time on my tongue as Chase yanks my hair until I'm at an angle he can devour, his mouth as devious and hellbent as his brain.

I'm not supposed to want this, but my body presses against his, the hard length of him spearing against the softness of my belly.

It's twisted and unusual to desire the boy who scares me and wants me to bend to his will any chance he gets, yet here I am, parting my lips so he can possess me deeper, spreading my legs so he can access me longer.

While our lips spar, Chase cups my ass and lifts until my legs wrap around him. He steals the keycard from my fingers and swipes us into my room without the need for sight, and with inhuman, graceful strides, he has us in my room with seconds to spare.

Chase throws me onto the bed, and my eyes pop wide, the mist of seduction waning. I glance around with terrified awareness.

"There's nothing here," Chase assures. "It's all been tossed."

He stands at the end of my bed, devouring me with such intent that my sudden fear must be fueling him.

He's wrong for you. He's too dark, too much a part of the underworld. He'll drag you under—

I stop my inner angel from speaking further.

What if, for once, I want to appeal to my demons?

My lips curl on a hungry snarl, one that takes Chase by surprise, but he doesn't flinch when I rise up to my knees and pull at his sweats, wanting him naked. Vulnerable. Mine.

He catches me by the wrist and pushes me back until my butt bounces against my bed. I push up on my elbows, my expression nothing but a question mark.

"You first, sweet possum."

If I were in a better, less screwed-up mindset, maybe I would've considered Chase's reluctance to come undone before I do, but as he yanks my jeans down, I tug my shirt off, my chest braless and bare, a sight that triggers a rumble in his chest.

Chase climbs on top, pushing me flat, and reaches down to flick the side strap of my G-string. I flinch at the sharp pain and moan.

"Does that turn you on?" Chase whispers against my lips, his hair falling into his eyes the way a turned angel's wings must sag and wither once they descend into wickedness.

He does it again.

Then again.

I cry out, writhing with need, a base desire to have him fill me so instant, I'm choking with want.

Chase hooks the strap, and it snaps apart in his grip, leaving me exposed. His fingers move, dancing across my skin, stroking the soft hairs there, until he finds my folds and spreads them.

Chase rises and sits back on his heels. Once I've sobered and can figure out what he's doing, I move to clench my legs shut, but he keeps them spread with a firm grip on my inner thighs.

The crescents of his lashes are the darkest part of his fair form, and they're all he'll allow me to see when he murmurs, "Just as I thought. Sweet possum."

I *knew* it. When he utters that cursed nickname, sexual promise follows, so much so that he has to be meaning something other than *possum*. And here I am, proving him right.

So, so, bad ... so wickedly against my norm ... I shouldn't ... I can't ... I ... I...

He curls a finger through my folds, and my back arches in the same choreographed movement.

"I'm going to taste that sweetness," he says, then his dark gaze flicks up to mine. "This isn't a request."

"I'm not about to beg," I say hoarsely.

He slow grins in response. I allow my head to fall back into the pillows as his lowers into my personal sin.

Chase thrusts two fingers in before he allows his tongue to play, too. My hips grind with his movements, in no way delicate, and harsher than I've ever experienced.

I'm no sex kitten, having done it one time. Matt was gentle and clumsy, mumbling sorry after every feeble pound, until four seconds later, he was done. My back ached from being crushed against the bodega's cupboards behind the cash register. I'd cranked my hip from him leaning his palm hard into my inner thigh, spreading it unnaturally. My clothes stayed on, with one breast exposed when he pushed my shirt halfway up for a quick grope.

In short, my entire sexual encounter with Matt, Chase could sum up with one finger joint, and he was using a helluva lot more than that.

He's sucking on my clit in a way that makes me throw up my hips and squirm, the ambrosia too much, too sudden and unrelenting. It spurs him on, flicking my clit with his tongue and pushing a third finger in, pounding and thrusting so hard it burns.

But oh, the burn.

It's bliss through fire, a hint of pain with the promise of desire, and I ache for more, *more*.

His fingers aren't enough to fill my craving. His tongue is hot and eager to taste, but not what I want. A mere pittance to what I *need* after the hell his friends have put me through, what *he* might've instigated...

My warnings turn to ashes when my orgasm releases its rays of sunshine, my voice screaming its blinding brightness. I melt in Chase's hands, the thrill so shattering, I can't draw breath as I come down.

Chase lifts his head, his lips dampened by my release, but not his smile.

I glower at him—or hope I do. My muscles are too satiated to care.

"I see my reputation precedes me," he says, then reaches for his sweatpants puddled on the ground and pulls out a condom.

This time, my frown comes easy. "You came here with *that* in your pocket?"

Chase shrugs. "I always like to be prepared."

"I see. So, if a chick crossed your path on your way to my room, you would've fucked her, instead?"

"You have it wrong, sweet possum." Chase stands naked with that reputed cock of his standing at full attention. "I was waiting for you."

My mouth becomes too dry to swallow. "I'm so going to regret this."

"Maybe," he says as he rips the condom packet with his teeth. He does it without his eyes straying from mine, dilated with lust and famine. "But you'll enjoy the fall from grace. I promise."

Chapter 41 | 279

I never saw you coming, I think, but the scent of sex in the air prevents me from whispering it out loud.

Chase starts to slide the condom on, but I hold his wrist to stop him. He arches a brow, questioning, but I take the condom and slide it on myself, keeping him tight in my grip. He's a Siren's call, and I'm the stupid sailor who can't fight the song, but you know what? Fuck it. I want some release, goddammit, and if it's going to be physical, the person I've wanted to do it with—Chase—is naked and willing in front of me.

I'm not going to look this gift horse in the mouth; I'm going to swallow it whole.

I pump him a few times to keep him rigid and wanting, bemoaning the fact that I've already covered him in bitter latex, because taking him in my mouth would've given me the utmost sense of possession. And to make him come from my choice. My doing...

Chase grips my shoulders and presses me against the bed. He positions his elbows on either side and looks me in the eyes for what seems like a hundred heartbeats before I reach down, wrap my fingers around his base, and line him up to my entrance.

"You scared?" I whisper.

He searches my face, a rare moment of hesitation. "You sure?"

"It's a little late for that, isn't it?"

The skin around Chase's eyes crinkles, yet his pulse is pounding against his neck. "I like to be a gentleman before I fuck you into oblivion."

"Then stop dicking around and *do* it."

Chase takes me for my word. He buries himself in me in one all-consuming motion, then pulls out entirely. He does it again. And again.

I'll be bruised by the time he's done, but I tell him not to stop. His brows crash down with craving.

I use my fingers and find my clit, massaging circles in time to his brutal thrusts, and he looks down in surprise.

"You don't get all of me," I murmur into his hair, and he lifts his head and presses his lips against mine, shutting me up.

My circles become faster, ardent with pressure, the harder he pounds. It becomes so vigorous that my hand starts to ache, and he bares his teeth against my mouth, expelling his roar onto my tongue. The stimulation is so much, and I'm so filled in ways I've never been before, but I push past the ache and meet Chase thrust for thrust, until we're both sweating and gritting our teeth, our rough, animalistic grunts taking over our human forms and bringing us carnal satisfaction.

I hate being the first to come, but I can't hold on. I tangle my free hand into his hair and bring his head down to my neck as I cry out, my thighs clamping around his hips as he furiously grinds, gaining momentum for his own release.

Chase spears up onto his hands, pushing in and out in quick bursts. I'm so tender from the high of my orgasm that it's a wonder I can contain him. The moment he comes, his dick pulses and twitches inside of me, and I take that moment of weakness by curling my legs around him and palming his ass, driving him deeper.

Chase collapses beside me with a heavy exhale, the sheer length of his body far surpassing mine.

I dare rolling over.

I risk curling my arm against his heaving chest.

I chance kissing the salted skin of his shoulder, shocked that I just had sex with the dark prince of Briarcliff.

And liked it.

"What was it like? Finding your mom."

I'd been dozing, but snap awake at Chase's voice.

He's still here?

If Chase had grabbed his things and waltzed out of my room

the instant my eyes fluttered shut, I wouldn't have been surprised. Or insulted. It's how these things go, right, when you find yourself in bed with the most popular guy in school?

I am not the girl meant to change his ways. I understood that as soon as his lips crushed mine, slick and demanding. I was in it for the ecstatic release, like him, since the burden of Briarcliff was getting to us both. In different ways, maybe, but the frustrating, unsolvable load is the same.

"Hmm?" I ask, buying time.

I've pulled the sheets around my delicate parts, a lot like Venus rising from the clam, my long hair just as wild and free. But if I were to compare Chase to a stunning piece of art, he was David, full-frontal and confident, spread atop my sheets like the famous sculpture cast in gold.

"Your mom," Chase says again. "You said you walked in and discovered her body."

He says it so coolly, like he's the host of an investigative crime show, but surprisingly, I don't resent him for it. Most people are afraid to broach the subject, and when they do, it's all soft lilts and prying gazes.

Death is everyone's greatest fear. But murder? That's their worst nightmare.

"It was ... like you'd expect," I say, gnawing on my lower lip. "It was a Wednesday. I was late coming home from school because I'd missed my bus. I remember turning my keys in the lock to our door and crashing in—making plenty of noise, because I felt bad. Usually Mom and I went to our favorite Italian place on Wednesdays. I called out her name, but she didn't answer. Not surprising, since she was on call a lot and was probably asked to join an investigation..." I trail off, deciding it's easier to fix the sheets around my body than look at Chase.

He comes up on his elbow, staring down at me. "Go on."

"I don't—I don't like talking about it."

Silky, sand-colored strands obscure his eyes, but not his

assessment. I may be covered by bed sheets, but I've never felt so exposed.

I whisper, "She was in her bedroom."

Chase pushes my hair back from my face, tracing my eyebrow, then my cheek.

"On the floor," I continue. "Behind the bed. I didn't see her, but I smelled ... I smelled the tang of blood. Like that sharp, metal smell that you just *know* is coming from an open wound. I climbed over the bed and—and there she was, on her back, one arm flung out like this..."

I find myself in the exact position I found my mom, one hand thrown over my head, the other curled over my stomach. I grimace as she did in her final moments. What she didn't do was clench her fists. What she *couldn't* do was scrunch her eyes shut when her killer pulled the knife out of her chest. And sliced again.

"Is this what you wanted, Chase? To feed off my lows after pushing me to my high? To test my limits?"

"No," he says, and leaves it at that. Or so I think. "My sister used to go here."

Chase's calm tone brings me back to reality. I tilt my head, catching him in my view again. He's eyes are still on me, but the thoughts behind them, they're not soft. Not hard, either.

"Emma Loughery," he adds. "Heard of her?"

I furrow my brows. The name sounds familiar.

"She took our mom's name after the divorce."

"The ... when your parents separated two years ago?"

"No. That was Dad's second escape attempt. His first was with our mother, who he kept around for twelve years, give or take. Dad's a cold fuck, and my twin sister understood that before I did. I idolized our father for a long time. Too long. Emma saw things in him that clouded her happiness, and she thought leaving Dad behind and going with Mom would give her a fresh start."

"I see." I don't see. Chase has a *twin*?

"Ems ran around with Piper's crew when she was here," Chase explains, and I nod, making the connection, except for why Chase is bringing up his sister.

Then, it clicks. "Why isn't she here? Was she...?"

"Killed? No." Chase falls onto his back, causing the sweet, billowing scent of our sex to float into the air before it settles down again. "She was attacked, though. And was trapped in the library's fire, before a fireman pulled her own."

My fingers knot in my sheets. "Here?"

Chase nods in my periphery as we both stare at the ceiling. "In the library. The one before the slab of concrete that was built from my family's pockets."

It's my turn to push onto my elbow and stare down at Chase. His cheek muscles pulse, the curvature of his jaw becoming sharp as a knife. "The old library? The one that burned down?"

He nods. "Who my sister used to be will always be in the soil under the name of his second wife, who lasted what, two-and-a-half years?"

My lips fall open.

Chase slides his gaze to mine. "Told you he was a fucker."

"What happened to your sister? To Emma?"

"She was assaulted in the old library and left for dead. According to the investigative fucktards, no one will ever know who did it. A random event, a stranger break-in, Marron says. No student could've done that kind of atrocity."

I place my hand on Chase's arm. I squeeze, but it's like trying to crush granite between my fingers. "I'm so sorry." I add, "This is why you're so invested in Piper. Why you don't want her forgotten the way your sister was."

Chase blinks slowly but keeps our connection. "We all have our motivations. Emma was fun, happy, and wanted a future. Now, she's one hundred pounds overweight, afraid to leave the house, and refuses to get the help she needs. My father wants to erase her with money. Cast her off to his estate's basement to rot."

I risk laying my head on his chest and listening to his heartbeat. Chase doesn't push me away, but he doesn't wrap his arms around me either. It's simply not what he does.

Ivy had said the fire involved the most popular girl in school. Chase's *sister*.

It's Emma's story that's tied to the burning of the old library, and Chase's father is tethered to it, too.

"Briarcliff has so many sharp edges," I murmur against his skin.

"Both times, with Emma, then Piper, I stood by, because I didn't know." He combs through my hair, lifting and curling it between his fingers. "It's not going to happen again."

I close my eyes at the lull his massage brings and sigh beneath his hand. "Then tell me about the Nobles or why Piper was a Virtue."

His fingers stall in their movements.

"They're a part of this," I push, keeping my eyes closed. It may be because I'm afraid to watch his sated features realign into his iced-over composure. "And now I'm a part of it, too."

"I'm keeping you away from it."

My eyes open. "You don't have a say in what I do."

"Were you not listening to anything I said? I will not let another girl be destroyed."

"That's all well and good, Prince Not-So-Charming, but I can handle my own." I sit up, collecting my hair and clearing it from my shoulders. "You're late to the party, anyway. Someone's been breaking into my room, and I swear it's a Cloak."

Chase's expression smooths. "What did you just call them?"

"I knew it." I point at him, reposed in bed, but his limbs primed to leap. "The Cloaks *are* them. The Nobles." I gather the courage to say what's been nibbling at the back of my mind since I received the initial rose. *No*. Since I saw that mysterious envelope on Piper's desk. "They're a secret society, aren't they?"

Chase snatches my wrist and slams my palm onto his chest.

His heart pounds beneath skin, as hard as the bones that cage it. "Feel that? Isn't that what your heart did when you found your mother? Is it a sickening adrenaline you swore never to have to feel again?"

I suck in a breath, because he's much too accurate. That type of pounding, the seasick strain of my heart desperately trying to beat for two ... that memory is a terrible mark on my soul I'd pay Satan to remove.

"Because *I* endure it every damn day I'm stuck in these school walls, which is why I'm here to remind you, *don't get involved*. Your mom's death was a fucked-up twist of fate and not your fault. Seeking out these Cloaks of yours and testing their boundaries? If you do, the smudge her murder left on your heart will be nothing but a cute butterfly tattoo compared to the mutilation they'll inflict."

"And yet they have nothing to do with Piper or Emma," I say dryly.

Chase catches my jaw, holding it as he rises to sit and look me full in the face. "I'll say it for the last time. No."

He releases his grip, and I gasp in a breath, unaware I'd stopped breathing under his hold. Chase stands and pulls on his sweatpants, his back to me.

"Distract me all you want," I say. "I won't stop. I'm not adding a second unsolved crime to my list of life's achievements."

Chase tosses his tee over his shoulder, his bare back rippling with muscle as he prowls to my door without a look back.

"Like you said, Chase, we all have our motivations!" I call.

His answer, predictably, is to slam the front door.

42

Over the next three days, I expected Chase to tell the entire school that I slept with him, ensuring my humiliation by saying he nailed me so hard, I was possum roadkill by now.

It's with that thick, expectant armor that I leave Thorne House and head to the dining hall. But I eat breakfast, then head to calculus without issue. Ivy speaks to me without underlying horror. I make it through the entire day—and the entire day's *meals*—without anyone bothering me, a first since stepping onto Briarcliff soil.

The second day goes similarly, where no one pays much attention, save for the professors when they call my name in class. It is a weirdly lightheaded experience, and it lowers my barriers enough to where I don't have to look over my shoulder every two seconds.

On the third morning, I become suspicious.

Chase is either absent or deliberately obtuse, never seeking me out in the classes we share. His friends, however, do, and within minutes of crossing Riordan's path, I know he knows, and wishes he'd filmed it.

Tempest doesn't have the same eagerness behind his indolent stare, but he watches closely, flicking that spot where a lip ring should be with his tongue as I pass his desk.

The sexual duel between my internal devil and angel has to be put on pause, however, because I have crucial avenues to pursue, like where my phone went, and if the person who stole it is as disappointed as me when they realized all they got for their efforts was Piper's endless drone of unicorn poop. I never possessed the full diary, and now, neither do they.

Which ... they're now looking for, too. When Chase left that night, I'd checked the cloud on my laptop, in hopes my copy would be there, but it was deleted, and suddenly, my midnight intruder made a lot more sense. The only item I have at this point is Rose's letter, hidden between my calculus pages.

I shiver under my Briarcliff cardigan on my way to history, unable to shake the compulsion to do as Chase says—stop getting involved.

Mom wouldn't let this lie. *All victims are the same once they come to me, Callie. They are people who deserve justice, regardless of how they lived their lives. Somebody took that choice away from them.*

Since I'm so distracted and in my own head, history zooms by, and so do the rest of my classes. I cancel dinner with Ivy because I'm so behind on my calculus studies. A certain something happened on Sunday to prevent me from catching up, but I'm not about to confess my turbulent, naked afternoon to my sole friend.

I see Eden a handful of times, but she keeps her gaze away from mine, holding her textbooks tight to her chest, even though she has a rolling backpack she drags around.

I'm desperate to ask her where she stole those incriminating videos of me, and if she had the forethought to delete the original, but she's as evasive as all the other secrets Briarcliff stifles within its walls.

When Falyn kicks the wheels into Eden's path, I stick my foot in front of Falyn while she's busy admiring her handiwork, then smile when she trips over my shoe and mutters an expletive at me.

Eden doesn't thank me. She glowers, then storms in the opposite direction, her damaged, off-kilter wheels bouncing in tune with her steps.

"Miss Ryan," Dr. Luke warns as I pass his classroom door, where he stands and observes the students as we disperse in the hallway.

"Sorry," I say.

"Uh-huh. With more contrition next time, maybe I'll buy it."

I smile with sarcastic contrition, then exit the main building, intent on getting my studies done.

But, as it turns out, Chase has other plans.

※

For the second time, Chase makes me come.

I'm stripped bare on my bed, lying face-down and ass-up, and what should be a humiliating pose becomes the best oral of my entire, formerly innocent life.

My fingers curl into the sheets, my nails biting into the mattress below as I moan through gritted teeth, wanting to be quiet not for my neighbors, but for my own self-respect.

I push my butt back, my sensitive area too exposed for his tongue to be doing such things. But I can't ... I can't ...

"Shit—Chase! Chase, I ... I..."

He groans into me, the vibrations of his voice snapping the last strands of sanity I have left.

Chase pulls away, and I land on my bed in a heap, pieces of hair fluttering as I blow out meager breaths through my lips.

"You're welcome," Chase says. He stands with a grin, wiping his lips with the back of his hand. He's clothed in Briarcliff gear, while I'm naked and vibrating in front of him.

How did I myself get into this position, you ask?

I'd had every intention to crack open my calculus text when I took the elevator to my floor, my legs too rubbery and sore from my adventures over the weekend to take the three flights of stairs.

The hallway was deserted. It was only when I keyed into my dorm room that I noticed an intruder reclining against a sable-colored, suede piece of furniture.

"Your couch is here," Chase says, head angled as I step in.

"Why is this dorm room such a free-for-all?" I toss my book-heavy bag at him, which he catches.

"The delivery guys were here when I arrived," he explains, letting my bag fall to his feet. "I thought I'd sign for it, then show them where to put the couch."

"How chivalrous of you. I'm so glad my apartment complex has no security measures whatsoever."

Chase tsks. "That's highly insulting to the many college grads who come here and sleep at the reception desk. Or is it Ivy you're pissing all over? She's pretty scrappy security if I do say so."

I cross my arms. "What's your problem, Chase?"

"And your sentiment continues."

"I don't possess the patience for your hot bullshit in addition to your cold shits. Why are you here after ignoring me for days? What do you want?"

"Mm." Chase licks his lips as if deep in thought. My toes curl while watching his tongue run along the pink, sensitive skin. "Solid question. I'm here because I'd rather eat your pussy than whatever the dining hall has to offer for dinner tonight."

"W-what?"

Jesus, I sound like a centuries-old Victorian woman whose consort just threw the word pussy at her. But really, it's that surprising.

"Do you disagree?" he asks. Chase rests an ankle on his opposite knee as he does so, allowing me full view of the strain happening between his pantlegs.

"I can't. I have stuff to do."

Chase rises. He's at a safe distance, but I back up nonetheless. "Are you sure about that?"

"Y-yes."

"Nope. You're not. Take your sweater off, Callie."

Damn it, I love it when he uses my name, how it flows out of his mouth with such familiarity.

"Nope, I will not," I say.

"Mm. You will." Chase slides his blazer off, then tosses it ... somewhere. He loosens his tie, then slips that over his head, too.

My butt hits the wall, and as his body covers me, his delicious scent is the first to seduce.

"I know what you're doing," I manage to gasp when his tongue finds the pulse in my throat. "You're trying to distract me. Prevent me from ... drawing ... drawing—shit, what was I saying? Drawing attention! You don't want me to be involved in Pip—"

"Callie?" he murmurs against my lips. "Shut up."

Thus, here I am, splayed naked in my bed like the feast Chase vowed I'd be.

Watching him round my bed in full uniform, then take a seat on my single chair and cross his ankles on my desk, I have the added incentive to reclaim the unsuspecting part of me that he took.

I roll over on my stomach and prop my head in my hands. "Chase, tell me something."

Chase pulls out a—is that a *joint*?—from his pocket, followed by a lighter. He sticks the joint between his teeth and responds while flicking his lighter against the tip. "Your ass looks great in this light."

I ignore his half-assed attempt at distraction. "Are you supposed to be doing that? I mean—obviously you shouldn't be doing it in my room, asshole, but your sports career. Your rowing."

Half his face crinkles with a smile as he puffs. "Is that what you want me to tell you? Whether or not I'm a good boy to Coach?"

"No. The opposite." I sit up, taking the sheets with me. I've yet to come to terms with being completely naked with a boy in the room when he's not on top of me. "Have you ever been known as Mr. S?"

Chase holds in a waft of smoke, then puffs it out slow. "This again?"

"Is it true? Tell me that much." I hitch the sheets higher. "Did Piper ever call you that?"

"Why is it so important to you? You've never told me where you heard that name."

"It's just something I heard ... around."

"Uh-huh."

"Well, is it a thing?" I grapple for a better stronghold. "Is it the name your girlie fan club calls your dick?"

Chase snorts, flicking ash on my desk, then placing the joint back between his lips. I growl at him.

"You're cute when you try to be rabid."

"It's a simple question."

"Fine." Chase's shoes *clomp* against the floor when he swings his legs down. "No. Piper never called me Mr. S, and my cock sure as hell doesn't have that name. It doesn't have to." He gives me one of his panty-dropping grins. "It speaks for itself."

"Dang," I mumble, then look to the side. Unfortunately, I believe him.

"What's the big deal? Why are you and the cops so revved up about it?" His gaze narrows. "What do you know that I don't?"

"I don't have to tell you." I collect the top sheet, wrapping it around my body and sliding off the bed. "You keep shit to yourself. So can I."

It's tough to discuss a personal item of Piper's that I never deserved access to, sent the original to the police, then lost my copy. Chase would be full of questions and demands. I wouldn't be able to answer them to his satisfaction, earning his wrath. Frankly, these past few days of quiet were like sunbeams on my soul, and I don't want to ruin it when I can't even offer up the missing pages as proof of my efforts.

Chase stubs out the joint and stands, but I catch him when his hand cups my doorknob.

"Chase, um, would you mind staying a bit?"

Chase cocks a brow. "Really?"

He has reason to be confused. The guy truly infuriates me, we whisper veiled threats at each other more than truths, and we don't trust one another. But the thought of being in this room, alone and available for the next unwelcome intruder...

"I need help with calculus. I'm just not getting it," I fib.

Chase's head falls back as he stares at the ceiling in thought. "What if I told you I've been fucking Professor Lacey to get an A in that class and have no idea how to find the derivative?"

"I'd say that's a steaming helping of your hot bullshit."

"Fine. But I can't promise I won't want to fuck you in between."

I go all tingly and wet at the thought. "I—we can come to a deal on that."

"Oh, can we?"

I squeak when I land back on the bed, with him shadowing my body until his hands land on the mattress on either side of me. "I'm calling in that favor, sweet possum."

43

Chase and I come to a ceasefire. Of sorts.

In public, we don't acknowledge each other, except to add any additional information we find about Piper, which so far, isn't much.

I discreetly asked the college receptionists at Thorne House if there was any camera access to the night my mom's pictures were strewn around my room (I left out the part of someone using that distraction to steal my phone), but was told Marron took the footage and handed it over to the police.

That's a positive step. Evidence of my harasser went to the police. Piper's fall was in the hands of the police. The police were in charge of Emma's case, too. I should leave it up to them. Mom would want me to. Ahmar would encourage it. I could lose myself in Chase the way he loses himself in me, carry on at Briarcliff in the relative safety of his protection, then graduate out of these suffocating, deceptive hallways.

Except ... the roses still exist. The Nobles and my hunch they're not a separate danger keeps popping up, despite Chase's lame attempts to convince me otherwise.

The cops are doing shit-all about those doozies. Marron, even worse.

Is Briarcliff just one giant cover-up for a litany of crimes committed under its purview?

It all starts with your paper on Rose Briar.

Eden's voice won't go away. I'll have to scratch that itch after my history and calc quarter-terms today, then sneak away to the public library to see if I can find anything more on Rose. If any old texts exist, it would have to be—

I spear up in bed on a gasp.

"The hell, Callie?" Chase mumbles into the pillow, then searches for my hand and presses it against his groin. Smiling in the waning moonlight, he adds, "Are you waking me up early for a good-luck rub before quarter-terms?"

"What if the library didn't burn down because of Emma?" I say breathlessly. "What if it was the Cloaks trying to hide something?"

"Christ, really?" Chase rolls so he's on his back and peering at me with slitted eyes. "That's reaching, don't you think?"

"I can't find anything on Rose Briar, yet I keep being reminded that in order to solve Piper's death, Rose's mystery has to be looked into, too. The original documents about the Briarcliff founding would've been in the old school library, right?"

Chase rubs his eyes. "I suppose."

"Then that means anything else original to Rose Briar was destroyed."

"Anything *else*?"

Shit. *Shit.* Chase doesn't know about the portion of Rose's letter I found in the public library.

I ignore the slip-up in hopes Chase deems it unworthy enough to ignore, too. "This all dates back to the beginning of Briarcliff, but how?"

"Cal."

"I'm just like the cops. I've got nothing."

"I'm surprised you're not backing the police up. Wasn't your mom a cop?"

"No." I frown at him.

Chase sits up with a grunt. "Seriously? This whole time, I thought she was one. Partnered with your uncle or whatever."

"She was a crime scene photographer," I say distractedly.

"Huh."

"You and Piper's research into me didn't go far, then, if you didn't know what my mom did for a living."

Chase's jaw works, the muscles in his cheeks tensing and releasing, but he says nothing.

I continue. "The library could've been burned down for another reason. We have to cross that possibility off our list."

"No. We don't."

"I see we're back to one syllable demands."

"Just get off that line of thinking, okay? Here. I'll help." He lays my hand back on his junk, rigid and firm under his pants. "I take exams better when my spank bank's empty."

"Gross. And no." I pull my hand back. "This is important, Chase."

"It isn't."

"It *is*. I thought you wanted this. You keep saying you have better reasons than me to solve Piper's death, yet here you are, wanting to have sex instead of talk it through—"

"My sister lit the fire, all right?" Chase's voice crackles in the air. "So, can you please be over it now?"

"She ... she did?"

"Yes. Our dad paid people to keep that detail away from the press and prevent Briarcliff from pressing charges. She burned the place to ashes a few weeks after her attack. Became trapped in a fire of her own making. And I can't fucking blame her when nobody would bring her the guy who hurt her. And before you ask, *no*, she did not burn it down to prevent your research of some chick jumping off a cliff almost two hundred years ago."

I can't think of anything to say.

Chase's dark eyes shine in the gloom. "Don't say a word of that to anyone. You understand?"

I nod.

"Good." Chase throws the covers off and leaps out of bed, searching the floor for his pants. "Now that I'm up, I'm leaving."

"Chase, wait."

For the past week, Chase has been sneaking into Thorne House and staying with me, leaving before dawn, but not like this.

"Can't." He scrapes his hair back. "I'll see you in class."

"Chase, I'm—"

"Don't say it. There's nothing to be sorry for. You're doing what I want, and that's asking the type of questions the cops aren't. So, keep at it. Just ... leave Emma out of it. She's for me to figure out."

I nod with a noncommittal bob. If Emma and Piper's situations are related, then it's critical I prove that, too, despite the meager access I have to either of them.

Chase pauses at my bedroom door, smacking the frame in thought. "Good luck today."

"Sure," I say, distant. "You, too."

Chase leaves without another word.

※

I fall back asleep with Cloaks and roses clouding my thoughts, and Chase's confession about his sister ringing in my ears.

A blaring sound wakes me, and I smack my hand across my brand-new phone on the nightstand and drag it toward me to turn the stupid thing off.

It's exam time, and I feel better prepared for them than I do the rest of my problems, which is to say, *not much*.

I shower, dress, then exit the dorms with the rest of the Briarcliff girls, clustered in groups and chatting about possible exam topics. I follow behind, content not to be involved—or noticed—by any of them.

I scan the heads for Ivy or Eden, but I'm disappointed when I don't see them. Maybe they're at the main building or at the library doing last minute preparations. A quick text would let me know, but I've left my phone in my room, as we're all required to do.

History with Dr. Luke is my morning class, and mercifully, it doesn't come in the form of an 8 AM exam. Our papers were our quarter-terms, and Dr. Luke is handing them back today, containing my first grade at Briarcliff Academy.

It's funny, worrying about my GPA when it *should* be my top concern. Instead, bodies fill my head, damaged and dead ones vying for attention.

I'm envious of the girls walking the path ahead of and behind me. They have no idea what Briarcliff truly is, what it hides. Secret societies don't take up their headspace. The founders didn't linger in their minds longer than writing a paper about them. Chase doesn't sneak into their rooms at night, promising ecstasy and escape one minute, then vengeance and truth-telling the next.

Their roommate wasn't here one day, then dead the next.

As if summoned, Chase merges onto the path with the rest of his crew, Tempest and James flanking him, Riordan trailing behind with his nose in a textbook as they prowl.

A group of girls stare at Chase, whispering something to their friends, then glance back at me. None possess the bravery to blurt out what they're thinking loud enough for Chase to catch. He'd rather stare straight ahead and pretend to listen to what James has to say than acknowledge I'm close behind.

We all filter into the school, then spread into various hallways, trudging to class. Dr. Luke is in the classroom when I walk in, sorting through the pile of essays.

"Morning, Miss Ryan," he says without looking up.

"Morning," I reply, and take my seat as the rest of the class funnels through the door. He greets each by name.

"All right, class!" Dr. Luke claps for attention once we're seated. "I have good news and bad news. Good news: three people got an A on these papers. Bad news, the rest of you scraped by with a B minus or lower. To say I'm disappointed is an understatement. These are the people who built the walls you study in and cinched your education for entry into prestigious universities." Dr. Luke strides through the rows, plopping papers onto each desk he passes. "A little more resourcefulness, next time, okay?"

My paper plops in front of me, and Dr. Luke says in a voice meant for me alone, "I expected better from you, Miss Ryan."

Brows furrowed, I glance down at my essay and gasp. **C-minus.** *What?*

"Dr. Luke, I—"

"Anyone who has a problem with their grade," Dr. Luke says as he continues to meander the rows, leaving nothing but his masculine cologne behind, "can speak to me after class."

Students gasp in response. The few who got an A are obvious. Falyn smiles, then shows her paper to Willow sitting behind her with a bright, sharpie-red A. Chase leans back and crosses his arms on a grin, a cock in charge of his roost. Shockingly, James is the third, and he waves his paper like a beauty queen greeting the crowd until Dr. Luke tells him to sit his ass down.

I clear my throat instead of grunting any jealousy, and frantically flip through my paper, scanning Dr. Luke's comments.

My section about the possibility of Rose being part of a secret society is crossed out in red as thick as Falyn's A.

Dr. Luke scrawled in the margins: **While this is intriguing, you have no facts or references to back Rose's involvement in any sort of underground society. This is history class, not creative writing. I need real, historical facts, Miss Ryan.**

So much for appreciating those who think out of the box. I tried to be different and talk about a skeleton that's *actually* interesting, and Dr. Luke crossed it all out.

I sag into my seat, my stomach lurching with failure as Dr. Luke finishes handing out the essays.

"What a fucking douche," the guy behind me mutters. William, I think. "You think with his family inheritance, he'd be more forgiving, you know?"

"No shit," his friend agrees, sitting in the desk beside him. "I thought he took this job for kicks, not because he actually wanted to do it."

"*Mold our futures,*" William mocks in a clogged voice. "*Nurture our minds offline, blah-blah-barf.*"

"He's the black sheep of the Stevensons," the friend adds. "His brothers are happily living off their trust funds and parties and tits. Why would you give that up for this?"

I whip around in my seat, startling William. "Did you say Stevenson?"

"Oh, hi, possum," he says.

I ignore his mocking tone. "What do you mean by that name?"

"Uh, it's his last name. Ever heard of Stevenson Banking Co.? I guess he doesn't want to be associated with it since he calls himself lame-ass Doctor Luke, but we all know it, anyway. Except for you, but what else is new."

"Stevenson," I mutter, my eyes downcast. "*Stevenson.*"

"Can you turn around now? You're creeping me out."

I blurt, "Does anyone call him Mr. S?"

"Uh ... do you call him that when you're going down on his dick? Be gone, possum."

I bare my teeth and hiss at him, which causes William to startle again like the little jack-off he is. I twist in my seat, mentally answering his rhetorical question. *I don't. But maybe Piper did.*

My stomach, feeling sick before, creates a tidal wave of nausea.

Dr. Luke stops in the front of the room, turning around with his hands interlocked behind him.

"It's quarter-term day, but do any of you think you deserve the rest of this period free to study?"

Students groan and rustle papers. Dr. Luke's gaze drops to mine, rests there for a few seconds too long, then moves on.

I swallow, an internal fire building in my cheeks.

This can't be the answer. I have to be so, so wrong, just like my essay on Rose Briar. Just like all other avenues of thought I've dead-ended since enrolling at Briarcliff. Piper's death is about the secret society. She *knew* something they didn't want revealed to the public, and Piper would've done that through our paper. The Cloaks didn't begin their stalking of me for no reason. Piper didn't hide Rose's letter for kicks. I have to be right! I HAVE TO.

My essay sags in my hand, answering my affirmations with palpable failure. Piper may have wanted to write an exposé, but Dr. Luke wouldn't have cared. He would've crossed her theories out as easily as he dismissed mine.

Unless he was fucking her as Mr. S, and he's the one who ripped out identifying pages in her diary.

No. *No*, I groan inwardly, lowering my head to my hands. I want it to be the society. It has to be Briarcliff's secrets, not something as obvious and conclusive as a teacher-student affair.

But, it makes a twisted sort of sense. Dr. Luke is the one who broke up the party at the cliff. What made him go there in the first place?

Piper.

She could've texted him. Oh my God—she could've *pretended* to go back to the dorms, when all the while she was hiding in wait for the party to end so she could see Dr. Luke!

"So, who wants to tell me about our guest of honor, Abraham Lincoln? You've all heard of him, yes?"

Dr. Luke uses his usual dry humor to keep the class's attention, his expression serene, kindness and pride in being a teacher exuding out of his pores.

As I raise my head, his wafting scent hits me like the front of a McLaren going at Mach speed, now that it has more context. I'd always associated his masculine, sandalwood scent with comfort, but I was confusing comfort with familiarity. I thought that scent belonged to Chase, but I've tasted the salt of him, and it never washes away no matter how clean he becomes.

No, I've smelled *Dr. Luke* on someone else before. A person I thought was carrying Chase's scent with her when she sat down to tell me about Rose Briar for the first time.

Piper.

Is it just me, or is there a fresh coldness behind Dr. Luke's eyes? So different from Chase's, yet similar in their sharing of ... of what? I can't grasp the word, but I know it's there.

Dr. Luke calls on Falyn, who happily gives him the answer he was looking for: "Abe Lincoln is, like, a president..."

As Dr. Luke gives off every indication of listening intently to Falyn, I slip through his cracks. I study the nuances.

And I catch the word.

Guilt.

Guilt is the darkness lying dormant behind his eyes.

44

My attempts to corner Chase after history are thwarted. He leaves Dr. Luke's class with Falyn and Willow skipping behind him like he's the be-all of their existence.

Maybe he is, now that Piper's not there to redirect them.

Eden isn't in this class—heck, I never know where she is on normal occasions—so I can't corner her, and Ivy, as is her habit, has only surface-level Briarcliff gossip to impart.

Not that I don't appreciate it, but as I ask Ivy under my breath before Professor Lacey hands out the calc tests whether she knows anything about Luke Stevenson, she meets me with a blank stare.

"Who?" she asks, her legs angled toward me as we talk across the aisle.

"Dr. Luke," I say. "The history prof."

"*Oh*. The hottest teacher in our school." She mimes hitting her forehead. "Duh. What about him?"

"Does he, I dunno..." I pretend I don't care at all about what I'm about to ask, "flirt with girls in his class at all?"

"Jaysus, I wish." She guffaws. "I can guarantee every girl in the senior class has fantasized about him, but I have no idea whether any of them have done it with Dr. Luke. Why?" She leans forward. "What rumor are you trying to spread, and do you want my help?"

I laugh, but it sounds forced even to my ears. "It's nothing, but—"

"Ladies! Eyes straight ahead, please."

Ivy and I straighten at our desks as Professor Lacey reads the rules before we're allowed to open our exams.

I try my best to stay focused and answer the blur of numbers before me, but instead of equations, I see Piper's handwriting, confessing her encounters with Mr. S and how he insisted the affair be kept quiet. I'd had heavy focus on Chase or his father, but now I believe I didn't spread the net wide enough, too distracted by my gut reaction to Chase and his relationship with Piper.

Could it be true?

Dr. Luke never came off creepy or touchy-feely, and I've been alone with him. He was the teacher I turned to when questioning got rough and fingers pointed to *me* as Piper's killer. Dr. Luke exuded calm and good-naturedness, with an innate motivation to groom and be kind to his students.

I can't put him on blast by reporting my suspicions to the school. Piper's code name, Mr. S, isn't proof.

You know that's not the case. Think back to your fight with Piper.

My mouth falls into an O as I stare at my exam. During that final confrontation, Piper accused me of stealing her boyfriend. I assumed that boyfriend was Chase, but Piper never said it was. At no point did she say his name, and I was so confused at the timeline. My last encounter with Chase happened over a week before Piper screamed at me in the dining hall.

Because it was Dr. Luke. I've been alone with the teacher. I'd fallen into his arms in the hallway when I tripped on a rat. Is *that* what Piper was referring to when she accused me? My accidental trip over a corpse and into Dr. Luke?

It's possible. Piper's diary is lined with more jealousy and hate than goodwill.

I need to talk to Chase. Now.

The clocktower clangs the end of the period, and I blink back into existence, my fingers tightening against my pen when I realized I missed the final ten questions. Professor Lacey's hand comes into my vision, then retracts with my exam before I can do anything about it. I'm left with a blank desk and a cluttered mind.

"Wanna eat lunch together?" Ivy asks behind me. The dull noise of the rest of the class packing up reaches my ears. "It's mac 'n' cheese day."

"I'll meet you there."

"No worries. Come find me."

Ivy trots away, none the wiser to my paranoid convictions. I swear, every day that I dwell on Briarcliff's secrets means losing another chance at true friendship.

I beeline into the halls, taking shortcuts I'm now familiar with, catching Chase as he's about to take the stairs to the Wolf's Den.

"Chase!"

His head turns at my call, and it's with an implacable expression he mutters something to James, who bounds up the stairs ahead of him.

"What have I told you about addressing me in public?" he asks once I come to a stop in front of him.

"Sorry. Your Highness. Your Lordship. Your Majestic Prick."

Chase's eyes narrow into slits. "While I like the last one, I gave you the protection you wanted by getting people off your back during the day, but it has limits. If the girls around here heard I was banging you, the rats in your locker will look like pieces of cotton candy fluff."

"Glad to see your over-inflated ego remains intact, despite

lowering yourself to *banging* me." I wave his cutting retort away. "I'll worry about headless Barbie dolls stuffed in my locker tomorrow. What I have to say is important."

I grab him by the elbow until we're under the stairs and out of view to the students headed to lunch.

"What's so important that it couldn't wait until tonight? I had plans for you after crew." The shadows under the staircase assist in shading his eyes with desire.

Ignoring the inevitable pull my nipples seem to feel toward him, I say in a low voice, "I think I've figured out who Mr. S is."

His chest concaves with an exasperated sigh.

"I think it's Dr. Luke."

Chase waits a beat. "And?"

"And?" I give him a smack. He doesn't flinch or move at the contact. "I think he was having an affair with Piper!"

I manage to get a startled eye-blink out of him. "What?"

"Yes! Piper used a codename for the guy she was having an affair with, and it's been driving me crazy because it has to be important, and the police never brought up anything about Piper having a secret boyfriend—"

"Hold. Hold up." Chase raises a hand, and I shut my mouth, but not because he asked me to. Because he never stutters. "I never did ask you where you heard that name. And I thought the police were keeping it under wraps after they questioned me. Motive evidence, they called it. And why ... why am I only hearing about the affair shit now?"

"Because..." I squeeze the back of my neck, needing something to do. "I ... read her diary."

I'm met with silence, but I'm afraid to raise my eyes.

Chase's question is tight with restraint. "What. Diary."

"There was one hidden in her mattress. Nobody saw it, not even her family when they cleaned out her room, and—"

"Show it to me."

"I can't."

A second beat of silence. The school orchestra could be marching by in full practice mode, and I wouldn't hear it, so tunneled are my ears to Chase's every twitch. "Why not?"

"I ... gave it to the police."

Chase's silence contains the pressure to move the tectonic plates beneath our feet. It's deadly, powerful, and I'm at his mercy. He asks, "And you didn't make a copy?"

"I did, on my phone. But it was stolen from me the day ... well, my mom. Whoever it was also broke into my room and deleted it off the cloud on my laptop."

Nothing but breath escapes between us, but I'm hit with an utter need to fill our space. I step into his comfort zone, clutching his hands, though they remain stiff at his side. I search his face for any emotion other than a cruel blankness. Anything.

I say, "I'm sorry I kept it from you, but it can't come as a surprise. You and I, we share what we want to, when it conveniences us. That's how it's been these past weeks, and I promise, I'm growing to trust you. I know you didn't hurt Piper, but..."

Chase's unblinking gaze centers on me. "You don't trust me."

"That's not—"

"I trusted you enough to tell you about my sister."

"Chase, I told you about finding my mother. But this was never a quid pro quo—"

Chase cocks his head and breathes cold fire onto my lips. "Wasn't it? What stopped you from telling me about your friend who OD'd? Or the shit that went down with your dad?"

I stare at him.

"I read all about it, Callie ... how you and this chick went to a party and her coke was laced with Fentanyl and she almost died. Her parents blamed you, but it was a freak miracle that you didn't snort the same shit she did and end up just like her."

I swallow. Excuses won't come, because my mind's too busy flashing back to a lifeless Sylvie who only had me to give her drunken, shrieking CPR until someone thought to call 9-1-1.

"That's not what interested me most about you, though," Chase continues, rounding his sentence in soft tones, but the words are hard. "You accused your stepdad of your mom's murder."

I wince. "You're angry I didn't tell you about Piper's diary. Fine. But don't throw my past at me like it's your weapon to wield."

He ignores me. "You must've been so convincing, with those big, honeyed eyes of yours. The police believed you for a long time, didn't they? You had that detective on your side..."

"Ahmar," I rasp.

"Yes!" Chase snaps his fingers with enunciated conviction. "You raked your dad over some hot fucking coals pretty good. Ruined his rep. Had him arrested for a time, and when he came out, he had to deal with your involvement in an overdose. And all because of what, Callie?"

His tone is mocking, unreal. I'm desperate to cover my ears. "Stop," I whisper again.

"All because of *you*. You almost ruined a man's life over a hunch. You two don't have the same relationship now, do you? It's why you're here and not with him."

"Chase, I mean it."

"You fly after theories you pull from the sky. You drive yourself insane with your unsupported convictions. Didn't your dad put you in a psychiatric hold once he proved his innocence and he untangled you from your friend's near-death? Because you'd lost it?"

Scalding, unshed tears blind my vision. Clog my throat. "That's not..."

"What is it you think you're doing now? Is making Piper's death into a mystery your next psychotic break? Quit while you're ahead, Callie." Chase widens his eyes theatrically. "Stop the madness."

"You're sick," I say through my trembling jaw. "How dare you cut me down like this, after we—"

"Fucked? Yeah. Maybe I've gotten all I wanted out of you."

I ignore the sting. "Is this another diversion tactic of yours? To push me away from the truth?" I search his eyes, praying he sees me. The *real* me. "Who are you protecting, Chase?"

He laughs cruelly. "There you go again."

My fingers clench on his slack ones. "You don't mean that."

"Oh, I do, sweet possum. Thanks for the fucks. It's been real." He pulls away.

"Chase, stop."

"I appreciate you deeming me important enough to hear your latest theory. I'll see what I can do."

I flinch. "Wait."

But he's stalking away, like he always does, and I wish I had the strength to grab him by his infuriating Briarcliff blazer and throw him across the ground like he did with Riordan.

But Chase has already done that. Twice.

Because now he's made a tire mark out of my heart.

※

Another gloppy, cheesy macaroni noodle falls from my fork.

"Dude, you need to eat that quick," Ivy says around a mouthful of her lunch. "Even fancy, overprivileged mac 'n' cheese goes gummy if left out for too long."

"Not hungry."

"Since when? On the rare occasions you're actually in the dining hall, you turn into a hiker lost in the wilderness for three days when food's in front of you."

I push my plate back, leaning against the chair with a sigh. I can't help but search the dining hall, despite being perfectly aware of what I'll find. Or what I *won't*.

No Chase. Anywhere.

"Then we need to improve upon the source of your energy," Ivy says. "Since biology is next period, and Professor Dawson is no joke."

I'm far away from the importance of exams. It's maddening, considering how hard I used to study, but not as gut-wrenching as facing Chase's accusations, like it's my fault I've kept Piper's diary from him.

It has *nothing* to do with my stepdad.

Nothing to do with Sylvie.

One may have been an accident and the other wrong, but I was right to suspect him. It was a given that I'd put my entire being into avenging my mother.

Chase keeps so much from me. He has secrets that could fill the entire library built by his devious sire, and I'm meant to feel guilty for shoving my possession of Piper's diary in the most private drawer I have? Chase knows everything about me—too much. He's exposed my mind the way he's worshipped my body. He's ... he's felt my heartbeat.

"Callie? You okay?"

"I ... I don't feel well. I'm gonna go lay down before class starts again."

"Don't be late. Dawson won't let you through the door if you're one second past the bell."

"I'll be there. Swear," I say to Ivy, then stumble through the aisles between tables, lightheaded and sore.

Extra energy balls up tight behind my chest. It's desperate to be expelled, but my body is too sluggish to let it. What is this? What's wrong with me?

Heartbreak. It's called heartbreak, sweetie.

I squeeze my temples and scrunch my eyes to rid my mom's voice from my head. It's not real. She's not here, so why must she become my inner voice? I don't want her echoes. I want my *mom*. She'd have the correct answers. She'd hold me as I cried over a boy.

I come close to breaking my nose as I storm around a blind corner. At the last second, I jolt back from the trophy case, leaving smeared fingerprints on the spotless glass.

I almost smashed into the case by Marron's office, and I glance around with an unbalanced waver to my steps, hoping no one witnessed my moment of weakness, or put it on their phone.

The hidden crest, its motto carved in iron, still rests behind a rowing trophy from 1921. The half-wing I can see, spread to the tip of the circle, has those words, the ones so familiar yet impossible to grasp, scored into its feathers.

altum volare in tenebris

My phone's at the dorm, so I can't translate it. Instead, I squint at the writing, hoping I've committed it to memory to decipher it later.

Thump.

Something heavy thuds against the wall behind the trophy case. I jump, but I don't run.

Bang.

A shatter follows from inside the office opposite Marron's, glass breaking.

Human grunts ripple into the air, the last one more laced with pain than the first.

I glance around with wide eyes, then sprint toward the sounds of struggle, and when I stop at the office where the noises come from, I read the nameplate.

"Shit!" I cry, then burst through the door.

45

"*Chase! Chase, stop!*"

My yells go unnoticed as two men—Dr. Luke and Chase—grapple for leverage in Dr. Luke's office.

Books have toppled from the shelves. Dr. Luke's desk lamp lies shattered and flickering with exposed electricity on the ground by their feet. Picture frames are crooked on the walls, and one even has blood spray next to it.

A frantic search of both their faces reveals Dr. Luke with a blood-soaked eye. A cut leaks from his eyebrow, and Chase … Chase is clean-shaven and flawless with his hands around Dr. Luke's neck.

"*Chase!*" I burst forward, gripping one of his arms, but it's like climbing an oak tree out back. Immobile and entrenched.

Dr. Luke's back arches over his desk as Chase bends him at an unnatural angle, teeth bared and saliva dripping, resembling the very wolf Briarcliff touts as its mascot.

"Listen to me. Chase, listen!" I say, my heart pounding in tandem to my words. I attempt to get into his view, but he's channeled his focus into Dr. Luke and is no longer programmed to look anywhere else.

"He can't talk if you strangle him to death!" I say, pulling at Chase's arm despite the uselessness of it. "Chase, look at what you're doing!"

I slip between him and Dr. Luke, between Chase's rigid, jointless arms, and push at his chest. Dr. Luke gurgles behind me, clutching at my shirt, pulling at my hair, begging for help.

"You're killing him!" I scream. "*You're killing him!*"

Chase blinks. His eyes become focused. He glances down at me, the brown of his irises clearing.

He releases Dr. Luke without warning, who sags behind me and nearly takes me down with him. Chase hooks my waist and pulls me into a safer zone, then stands in front of me as a shield.

Not that Dr. Luke appears to be able to do anything but gurgle at the moment.

"You fucked her," Chase spits. Literally. He lobs a loogie onto Dr. Luke's panting chest. "Then you killed her."

Dr. Luke stares at us, sweat and blood dripping from his brows, his button-down shirt torn and sprinkled with blood, both from his nose and forehead. "Mr. Stone, I did not—"

Chase kicks him in the gut. I screech at Chase, pulling him back. "Are you out of your *mind*? What are we supposed to do now, huh? You attacked a *teacher*, Chase. You—"

"What evidence do you have, buddy?" Dr. Luke regains the breath to spit blood, then smile a toothy grin rimmed in red. Chase doesn't respond. He glares at Dr. Luke with such unearthly promise, I have renewed terror over what he's capable of.

"Just as I thought," Dr. Luke rasps. "You have nothing."

"She wrote about you."

Dr. Luke's eyelids flutter. He licks the top row of his teeth, his only reaction to my voice. "Did she now?"

"Explicitly," I continue. "Down to your nightly meet-ups on school grounds. She had a diary."

Dr. Luke stares at me from his place on the ground.

"And I found it."

Chase keeps still beside me.

"You told her to wait for you after the party ended at Lover's Leap, didn't you?" I ask. "For her to act drunk and pretend to go back to the dorms, when really, she found a place to hide until you came along, broke up the party, then met up with her."

"What a silly detective you'd make, Miss Ryan."

Chase's mockery over my dad echoes in the shells of my ears, but I stand with conviction. "You're the cool teacher, the one kids respect the most. If you were the teacher to break up the party, Briarcliff students would listen, because you'd promise you'd keep their secret, so long as they cleaned up and made it look like they were never there in the first place."

"She's right," Chase drawls. "We listened, didn't we, Teach? But you didn't walk back with us."

Dr. Luke's eyes slide over to Chase's. "So, I'm a nice guy. I've been where you are, Mr. Stone. The power of popularity is electric, isn't it? But I got my ass reamed for allowing the gathering to disperse without punishment. You have it entirely wrong. I almost lost my position here, and it's not because I slept with a student. It's because she died while apparently under my off-duty supervision. And you two," Dr. Luke growls, then coughs, "are in so much goddamned trouble for this."

"What makes you think you're not under police watch?" I lie. "What if, the minute I found the diary, I took it to Detective Haskins?"

Which ... I kinda did.

Dr. Luke grunts. "Then you wouldn't've been brought in for questioning over your own involvement, Miss Ryan."

I smile. "You didn't let me finish. What if it was all a ruse? A way to get your guard down, to make you feel safe? Intelligent killers don't just *confess*. You have to give them a reason. Make them comfortable enough to make a mistake."

Dr. Luke glances between me and Chase. "You're full of shit."

I *am*, but he doesn't need to know that.

He points. "Whatever you two are concocting, it's on the wrong side of the law. You assaulted me, Mr. Stone, and you are aiding and abetting, Miss Ryan."

I fake a loud snort. "Who? Me and him?" I thumb over to Chase. "You think we're in cahoots? I hate him, Dr. Luke. You've seen how he's treated me. Like roadkill on his shoe since the day I walked in here. Piper's death didn't change that. Just this morning he made me well aware of the disgust he has toward me."

My voice cracks at the end, and Chase's gaze moves to me, his brief survey unreadable in my periphery, but I see his eyelids flicker, maybe, *maybe* with remorse.

"Plus, our methods are different." I exert all my efforts to stay cold, calculated, and unengaged with the boy I'm falling for. "I didn't want to come in here and beat the shit out of you, Dr. Luke. I just want the truth. I'm a lot like my mother that way."

"Punching him in the face is the quickest way to reach that goal," Chase murmurs, his survey moving to Dr. Luke. He raises his fist. "Shall I continue?"

"I broke up the party and let you assholes go, since any sort of delinquency report is shredded, or forgotten, or deleted," Dr. Luke snarls. "This is what I get for trying to do the right thing when I should've just left you all to drink and smoke yourselves off the damn cliff. I've never, in my entire career, had inappropriate relations with a *student*—"

Chase kicks Dr. Luke in the teeth.

"Chase—" I begin, but Chase throws up his hand to me and takes one step closer to Dr. Luke.

"Callie may be trying for diplomacy here, but you and I both know that's not going to work," he says to Dr. Luke, sputtering on the ground. "Not with men like you. Did you kill Piper Harrington?"

"No—!"

Crunch.

Chase steps down on Dr. Luke's knee, crushing it at such an

angle that I make silent gagging noises behind him. Dr. Luke squeals, becoming less and less human to me the further Chase's torture goes.

"I'll ask again ... did you kill Piper Harrington?"

"Christ, boy, how did your parents raise you—"

Pop.

Dr. Luke cries out as his knee's dislocated, and I step forward, unshed tears in my eyes. I'm all for catching Piper's killer, but not like this. Not through someone's physical breaking point...

"Fine! Jesus, fine! I met with her, okay? I saw her that night *to fucking dump her!*"

I freeze with my arm in midair, aiming for Chase's shoulder to pull him back.

Chase lowers his chin. "Continue."

I've never seen Chase this cold and unmoving. Like his sole purpose in life is to hurt and maim to get what he wants, and he's not about to lose any sleep over it.

It unnerves me. Forms a fissure in my heart.

"We had an affair, okay? Get off. Get off my leg. *Please.*"

Dr. Luke's begging now, his confession turning into sobs as Chase increases the pressure before he releases his foot, Dr. Luke curling into a fetal position on the ground as soon as he does.

In need for balance, comfort ... steadiness, I hold onto Chase's elbow, staring not at Dr. Luke whimpering on the ground, but at Chase.

"Chase," I whisper, unnamed fear curling at the base of my throat. The longer I watch him breathe, the more that fear gains meaning and takes advantage of that meaner, hidden part of me that's grown her fangs these past two years.

"Did you steal my phone?" I ask Dr. Luke, starting off soft.

"Why ... would I take ... a fucking teenager's phone?"

"Because it had sections of Piper's diary in it."

"Oh." Dr. Luke's head moves with a clogged chuckle, then he

winces. "Might've. You were looking good for Piper's death, too, Callie."

"Did you record my fight with Piper? Did you plant those pictures of my *mom*?" I put one foot forward, my voice as tumultuous and rough as my step.

"Record...?" Dr. Luke squints up at me with added strain to his expression. "What about your mom? This is about ... Piper, no? And finding her killer? She didn't jump, did she? She was pushed."

Shadows cross his eyes, unrelated to impending unconsciousness. I fixate harder. "Did you do it?"

"Do *what*?"

"Hit him again, Chase." I'm shocked—and terrifyingly satisfied—to say those words.

Chase isn't told twice. He slams Dr. Luke's head into his desk with an open palm, rattling Dr. Luke enough that he spits off obscenities.

"I'll ask again, did you spread pictures of my mother all over my room to stop me from figuring out it was you? Then stole my phone?"

"What? I used Piper for a lay. You got that? She acted all sweet, and cute, and desperate for my attention, and if you'd had the life I've had, you'd understand I couldn't help but fall for a girl like that. Then she tells me she wants to work it out with Mr. Punch-a-Thon over there. Piper wanted to continue fucking me *and* shack up with your psychopath of a boyfriend. What a sad sight you are, Callie. I had higher hopes for you."

I ignore the swipe. "You killed her for dumping your ass."

"I can't say she didn't get what was coming to her," Dr. Luke spits with a copious amount of venom. "She was a *slut*. Am I right, Mr. Stone? A fucking—"

Slam.

Well. I could've predicted that much.

Dr. Luke cowers, covering his jaw against another blow from Chase's heel.

But Dr. Luke won't stop. "How many guys did she fuck, eh buddy? We were two of many. She manipulated, used her beauty, and fed off my dick like a goddamned succubus. Men in this world are better off without a girl like that." Dr. Luke's lips peel back in a gaping, blood-soaked smile. "I was cutting my losses that night."

Chase punches him again.

"Chase, no!" I shout.

"What in God's name is—Luke? *Lucas?*"

Headmaster Marron bursts in, folding his body over Dr. Luke and placing a hand on his shoulder. Once he assesses the situation, he glares up at us.

"If you were aiming for expulsion, Mr. Stone, consider that the tip of the iceberg of penalty that's about to fall upon you. And you, Miss Ryan, I cannot believe the lengths you've gone to prove how much you do not belong here."

Chase doesn't blink. "Tell him, *Lucas*, what you told us."

Dr. Luke nurses his cheek, keeping his eyes closed as he moans.

"Marron's presence will *not* prevent a kick to the balls," Chase growls.

"Mister *Stone!*" Marron cries, aghast.

"I had an affair with her!" Dr. Luke gasps. "Just get that boy away from me. Get them away. Please. Please!"

"Lucas, what...?" Marron rips his attention away from us.

"With Piper Harrington!" Dr. Luke continues, "We had an affair."

"I..." Marron trails off. "Lucas, you're not of sound mind at the moment—"

"I did it! I met with her that night! I didn't 'catch' those kids doing anything. I knew they were there. At the cliff. She called me. Piper hid until everyone was gone, and I waited to see her.

But it was to break up. I wanted to end it." Dr. Luke sobs. "But I didn't ... just tell them to stop!"

"Well, howdy, people. How are we all doing?" Detective Haskins says as he gnaws on a toothpick, standing in the doorframe and taking in the scene.

"Detective, I ... this is a formal matter," Marron stutters, attempting to rise.

"Nope, it ain't. I heard it all. Thank you for the tip, Callie."

All eyes, even the bruised ones, turn to me. I nod at Haskins, but I have no idea what he means.

Haskins pulls at the handcuffs clipped to his waist, flicking them open. "*Doctor* Lucas Stevenson, you're under arrest for suspicion of sexual relations with a minor..."

Chase drifts closer to the door, and so do I, but Haskins pauses in his reading of Miranda rights to snap, "You two go nowhere. I have questions once back-up arrives." Haskins's gaze zeroes in on Chase. "A *lot* of goddamn questions."

※

Haskins's questioning over what occurred in Dr. Luke's office went on for hours. There was the matter of notifying, then getting, my stepdad and Lynda on FaceTime ... again. There was the problem of locating Chase's parents. We each needed a guardian present, and since my former ad hoc guardian was on his way to the hospital in handcuffs, Professor Dawson became my righthand man.

Luckily, the questions weren't as pressing as before, or as suspicious. Haskins, while heading to his meeting with Headmaster Marron, heard the end of the exchange between Dr. Luke and Marron, where Dr. Luke confessed to the affair. He didn't witness how Dr. Luke received so many bruises or a dislocated knee, and I was forced to speak to some of that. I asked if charges were going to be pressed against Chase. Haskins wouldn't expand on an answer.

I told him all I could, what I saw, and what I knew. Feeling terrible at having participated in such violence, I confessed to holding Piper's diary longer than I should have and was prepared for whatever punishment would follow. I couldn't keep the knowledge of Mr. S to myself, not once it led to Chase's impromptu beat-down of a teacher.

"Like an obstruction of justice charge?" Haskins asks, amused as we sit in Professor Dawson's office. My stepdad's silent and fuming face is on the computer monitor, also awaiting my response.

"I had every intention of turning it over to the police," I say lamely. "Which is why I went into town and—"

"Just got it this morning. What a coincidence. It's the reason I was on campus at lunch and meeting Marron."

Haskins's blunt statement brings my head up. "Sorry?"

"You sent the diary to the police station as soon as you found it. That's what your accompanying letter says anyway."

"I ... I see." My brows twist, and I glance to the side, the implications of Haskins's statement pounding against my temples.

"Uh-huh. You also insist you found it as-is and know nothing about the pages that are missing."

I'm caught between a truth and a lie, and I have the sense that the lie is what will save me.

I didn't give them anything this morning. I mailed the diary weeks ago...

I swallow. "Right. Yes."

"Gotta say, I appreciate the apology flowers. Unnecessary, but the letter explained how contrite you were to have found the journal yesterday and read it, but that you made the connection to this ... Mr. S ... right away. As it happens, we already recorded this alleged code name. One of our witnesses mentioned it to us a while ago. But I appreciate your shrewdness."

I try for a humble smile and not one that trembles so hard it'll fall off my face. "You don't have to explain any further, Detective. I know what I wrote."

I didn't write anything when I sealed the diary in the envelope. Someone must've intercepted it before it got to the precinct. Intercepted and ... used this time to doctor up a letter and a lie.

"Yes," Haskins says, his stare never leaving mine. "I'm sure you do."

"If I may ask, what sort of bouquet did the flower shop choose?" I fist a hand into my stomach as I lean forward, popping the acidic bubbles building in my gut. "I requested that it be whatever they thought best for an ... apology."

"Roses."

I keep my voice light. "How nice. What color?"

"White. Beautiful, I must say, in an office of mostly gray cubicles. Our receptionist certainly appreciates it."

"I'm so glad." I fold my hands, hiding the pounding pulse at my wrists. *The Cloaks intercepted my mail.* "I hope they got my request for an ebony ribbon around the vase."

"They did," Haskins says, then snaps his notebook shut. "I appreciate your candor, Miss Ryan, though, next time, just come in with the evidence and be honest. You're not gonna be arrested for handing it over." Haskins turns to the computer screen. "And you, Mr. Spencer, thanks for jumping on a call without notice."

"Happy to," my stepdad's canned voice responds. He cuts a look over to me. "We'll talk later, Callie."

"Yep," I say, eager to be out of here. It's difficult to look at Dad's expression so soon after Chase brought our unresolved conflict back to the surface.

"Detective?" I ask as Professor Dawson starts leading me to the door.

"Mm?"

"Did Dr. Luke do it? Did he kill Piper?"

"I can't talk to you about the specifics of the investigation, Callie."

"I know, but ... cop instinct. What's your gut telling you?"

Haskins raises his eyes, a knowing twinkle in them. "You know, I never got the chance to say it to you, but I'm sorry about your mother. It's terrible, what you went through as a result."

"Yes," I say, but I don't want to get into Sylvie or my dad. I turn for the door.

"As for your question," Haskins adds, and I pause. "Yeah. I think we nailed him. Sleep easier, will you?"

I respond with a closed-mouth smile, then leave Professor Dawson's office with his droll warning to try and stay out of trouble for at least twenty-four hours.

46

"Callie! Callie, wait up!"

I walk faster on the path outside the main building.

"Hey! Callie!"

My steps quicken, eager to escape the voice.

"*Possum!*"

That brings me to heel. I spin, showing my teeth. "Our fucked-up Bonnie and Clyde moment is over, Chase. Get away from me."

"Not a chance," Chase huffs out as he jogs the rest of the distance between us. His cheeks are pink from the chill in the air, his hair mussed and adorable, and every bit of it infuriates me.

No one should look this perfect after a beat-down *and* a police interrogation. Not even a princely Stone heir.

"You okay?" he asks.

"Dandy. I feel nothing but joy over the stunt you pulled." I stare hard at the clotted cuts on his knuckles, then turn to leave.

He hooks me by the elbow. "Wait."

"For what?" I snap. "For you to decide what to do with me now that we found your girlfriend's killer? After I've given you all that you wanted? That's what this was, wasn't it? I was just a vessel of possible evidence that you fucked to keep happy until I weakened enough to tell you what I knew."

"You're not mad about how I fucked you," he responds. "I've tasted how hard I make you come. You're pissed about what I said about your dad."

That earns him a smack in the gut, which is like fine bones meeting hard concrete.

"I was a goddamn *dare* to you, asshole!" I scream, then sweep my gaze over him. "You don't get to repeat my past like it's an advantage you have over me. You have no idea—*none*—of what it was like to see your mom murdered and think that your stepdad was the—was the—" My voice strains. I hitch in breaths. I have to get away from this.

"Okay. It was bad form." He spins me back around by the shoulder when I twist to stalk off. "Callie, come on."

"No! You know what I hate the most? That you're probably right." I trip over my words. "The Nobles, the Virtues, Rose Briar —it's not my secret to tell. They—*you*—made it clear when you stole Piper's diary from the town mailbox and trussed it up with roses and ribbons. Tell them I got the message."

Chase cocks a brow. "Come again?"

A strangled cry releases from my throat at his utter obtuseness. I push at his chest. "*They* sent it to the police. Your secret society. Not me. To show me who's in control and their power to make or break me. Isn't that how you termed it? You win. I won't meddle in their shit and I'll forget everything I know about them, so leave me alone."

"Callie." Chase's voice softens as mine spikes with hysteria. "I'm sorry."

I'm so outside of my usual self, I don't register the rare apology coming out of him. "What if I was *wrong*, huh? What if Dr. Luke wasn't Mr. S? What if the Nobles decided to protect him and not me? This is what's driving me crazy—I don't know if they're good or bad. They keep doing both. You would've beaten an innocent man—a teacher—and gotten kicked out of Briarcliff. Worse, you could've been arrested. And it would've been because of me. Again."

Chase frowns. "But you weren't. He was the guy."

I recoil. "How could you believe that? Based just on what I said?"

"Because you're you, Callie. You kept Piper's diary from me until you were convinced he hurt her. Killed her. And besides that, I wouldn't have been booted from Briarcliff." He scoffs. "My father simply wouldn't allow it."

"I ... I..." I raise my hand, palm forward. "I can't find the words for this. For *you*. Why won't you mention the Nobles at all? Is it because you won't? Or *can't*?"

Chase sets his jaw. A few seconds pass, silence I'm certain he won't fill, and my heart collapses.

I turn to leave.

"What I said under the stairs ... I've been trying to protect you," Chase says. "Your issues with your dad and your friend, it was wrong of me to throw them in your face. But you have to know, powerful people have access to it."

"Like your father?" I bite out.

Chase's implacable expression doesn't change even when he agrees with me. "He's one of them."

If I hadn't witnessed Chase's unleashing, his pure intent at defending Piper and tangentially, his sister, I'd think this apology was more of his crafted bullshit, wrapped up in a contrite, carefully placed, bow.

Except, I've seen what undulates behind his flawless bronze.

"I'm not *like* you," I say. "I can't beat a man to tears—even an awful one—then leave the scene with a bounce to my step. I can't make another person feel the way—the way you made me *feel*—and use the worst parts of them to satisfy a secret society agenda. I don't feed off people's emotions until they're nothing but husks of themselves." My voice breaks. "You made my position clear once I told you about Piper's diary. I was rat-shit to you after that. You squeezed my heart until it burst in your hands, then left without a second look."

Chase's expression grows dark. "Stop putting words in my mouth."

"Do I have it wrong, then? Were you not walking away from me for good?"

Chase's cheek muscle tics, his single response.

My heart drops to my feet, as useless an organ as it ever was when it comes to choosing the right guy. "That's what I thought."

"I walked away for different reasons," he says, "and if you'll let me talk for half a second, then maybe—"

"You don't deserve half a *milli*second, with the way you've—"

"Callie—"

"You've had your fun at my expense. Our mystery is solved. If you want to tell all your friends what I sorry lay I am, how a former psych patient has been in their midst this entire time, fine. Just take your Noble hounds *off* my scent. Tell them to stop fucking with me, and I'll stay quiet."

"Would you just—"

"Don't worry, I didn't breathe a word to anybody how much you lowered your standards. Your popularity status is intact. We never have to—"

I'm lifted off my feet. His fingers barrel into the soft skin of my upper arms. And he crushes his lips against mine.

"Have you ever thought," he growls after he pulls us apart, "that it isn't *me* who lowered my standards?"

"That's ... that's absurd," I stutter. "I'm not stupid. You used me to avenge Piper. I didn't think about the consequences of how we'd end, how it would affect me—"

His mouth molds with mine, his fire melting my iron with nothing but a match's flame.

That's the kind of hold Chase has over me, and it tilts my world until it's on his axis.

His lips move over my own, his tongue dipping out to taste, then retreating. "Is this cold to you?"

No. You're the danger of blue fire. "It's wrong." I breathe the words into his mouth. "It was stupid to ever let you into my bed."

Chase pulls back again, the merest of inches spaced between us. "Why couldn't you just assume I was pissed over the fact you kept her diary from me for so long and lashed out?" he says, gliding a finger down my cheek. "And that I wasn't doing anyone's bidding and leaving you for trash under the stairs?"

"Because that's not how you operate," I say. "You made that clear when we met. And every other time we slept together."

He smiles, his eyes like chocolate melting through his lashes. "That's a solid amount of times."

I feign an attempt to get out of his hold. Chase is weakening my defenses, and I rein in the yearning to punch him for it. "You're following someone's orders."

Chase grows serious. "There's no one but me and you. Some kind of shift in my reality happened when I met you. And I'm not talking about death and destruction following both of our lives. Or maybe I am. I see the darkness in you, Callie, and maybe I like it. I was beside you when that part of you took over with Dr. Luke. Perhaps, I enjoy it more than any of the other hollowed-out, happy girls who've skipped into my path, then walked away limping." He tucks a piece of hair behind my ear. "Your past with your dad, I haven't told a soul. There's a strength in you, like you can withstand the rusted and mangled pieces inside me."

"You're dangerous," I whisper, remembering how he looked when he beat up Dr. Luke. How he *felt* in my grip when he did it, cold and unyielding.

He may be content that Piper found her justice, but where will that energy go now? Where will Chase direct the curse of his endless anger that he keeps in a block of ice inside his soul? His sister's unsolved case? Or ... does he want to place it in me, for safekeeping, instead?

Chase responds without hesitation. "You're my compass, Callie. Redirect me."

"I'm no one's morality beacon."

"Didn't say you were. Now." His hands fall to my lower arms, squeezing. "Can we try for a truce? Or if you don't want that," he adds when I open my mouth, "can we fuck the angst out?"

"Chase..."

He brings my hand to his pants, and I feel the length there, the growing hardness that mirrors the throbbing at my core.

"Tell me that finding Piper's killer, that putting it to rest and beating the police to the punch, doesn't turn you on," he says, and my stomach lurches at the truth of it. "I'm so fucking glad he's caught. So *pumped* I got to lay him out, but it wasn't enough. I need to expend this ... this firebolt inside me, Callie. I need *you*."

It will never be enough, I try to say, but can't.

Maybe Chase has a point. I'm as dark as he says I am, and like recognizes like.

"We're in public," is the meager defense I can come up with.

"Then let's make it private."

Chase takes me by the hand and leads me the rest of the way to Thorne House. I won't say we're holding hands, because that's not what this is. His grip is too powerful, his physical intent too direct. We're not showing affection in public. Rather, he's demonstrating to the scattered students outside that I'm his. Those people will tell their friends, who will tell *their* friends, and on it will go, until it reaches the entire school's ears. Not even the scandal of Dr. Luke is sufficient to distract from Chase's claim of ownership.

Don't mess with Callie. She's Chase's now.

She's the Nobles' prize.

But, I can't be hasty. Chase's attention and the Nobles' protection, however surface-level, could provide me with the time to finish out the year.

And discover the truth behind the secret society.

I tell myself that's what I want as we race to my dorm room, our classes long over and dinner a passing afterthought. I focus on the unveiling of secrets instead of the hard certainty of my downfall planting its seed at the base of my skull.

⁕

The buzzing of my phone pulls my awareness to the surface, tugging with the type of urgency shaking me awake would.

"What time is it?" I mutter, the cold air of my room hitting my body as I sit up and scrub my eyes.

I'm shivering more than usual and realize I'm naked and just left the comfort of the warm, hard form beside mine.

Chase.

My phone goes silent. I figure it was Ivy blowing up my phone again with her shocked emojis and exclamations once news hit that Dr. Luke was arrested for Piper's murder.

But Chase is here. In my bed. We screwed our brains out and fell asleep. And he ... stayed.

He's never done that before. I don't cover my awe as I memorize the planes of his face, dewy with moonlight, his lashes casting long shadows under his closed eyes.

Chase is softer in slumber. His full lips are supple with dreams, his brows smoothed by the removal of reality.

The buzzing starts up again, and I snatch my phone off the nightstand, reluctant to wake him.

"Hello?" I whisper without checking the ID.

"Calla? Hey, sweetie. Did I wake you?"

"No. It's okay," I say to Ahmar while delicately sliding out of bed. I creep into the main room and shut my door with a soft click.

"I'm sorry to call you so late. There was a gang murder in the Bronx, and I was caught up in that, couldn't get to my messages until later. And, well ... you've had some criminal fun since we last spoke. You good?"

"Fine. Great." I can't help but glance at my closed door with the knowledge of who sleeps on the opposite side. "Piper's killer was caught."

"I know. I heard your voicemail. The fuckin' teacher, huh? What a turd."

"It's shocking." My gaze skirts away from my door, remembering how fury transformed Chase's face when I told him of Piper's affair. That she was having sex with someone else.

Quit it, Callie. It's never like you thought you could have his heart along with the sex.

But it still feels vacant inside my chest.

"Guess you don't need any digging from me, then. I'm sorry I didn't come up with much. It's been nothing but crime sprees over here."

"That's okay. Maybe if you could keep me updated on the process Dr. Luke's gonna go through," I say, perching delicately on my couch. I'm butt naked, after all. I pull a throw blanket over my legs as I talk. The shivering doesn't abate. "So, I can make sure he stays where he should. Did you find anything at all that points to him? There's his confession, but, I dunno, it could be argued it was made under duress..."

Ahmar chuckles. "Always your momma's daughter. Wanting the hard evidence, never the statements."

I'm ecstatic we figured out Piper's killer, but strangely disappointed that Dr. Luke's reasons had nothing to do with secret societies or Briarcliff history. Shouldn't I be relieved that Piper's killer was so obvious, once the connection was made?

But, the stealing of my phone, the interception of Piper's diary, using the distraction of horrendous photos ... it was all them, not Dr. Luke. It has to be, and I'm not crazy for thinking that.

Or is that my desperation coming through?

"I gotta say, Calla, I didn't find much." Ahmar sighs into the phone. "Though I tried, kiddo. Called all the connections I have over in Rhode Island. I did get to reading the coroner's report, though, before it's been made public."

"Oh?"

"It's sensitive information, but I know I can trust you and you got my back. Right?"

"Yeah, of course." Ahmar's like the dad I never had. He can trust me with anything.

"It'll come out once this Luke guy is finished with processing. The victim, your roommate, the girl…"

"Piper," I nudge.

"Yeah. This all goes toward the airtight motive of an affair and spurned love."

"What is it?" I ask.

"Well … Piper was pregnant. Once DNA comes in on the fetus, that'll be a strong case against your teacher…"

I don't hear anything else Ahmar says, though he rattles off sentences. The roaring dread in my ears won't let me.

I'm frozen, naked, and shivering, and I can't stop staring at my closed door.

Chase is there, sleeping soundly due to an exhilarating round of sex, where he showed me his skills, his prowess, and the utter addiction he's become in my bed.

And Piper was pregnant.

AFTERWORD

Thank you so much for reading RIVAL! I can't tell you how this story haunted my thoughts, day in and day out, for months. If you have the time, I'd love for you to leave a review on your preferred platform. Those golden little stars are what drive me to keep writing.

If you'd like to read more of my books, check out the next page.

xoxo, Ket.

ALSO BY KETLEY ALLISON

Players to Lovers
Trusting You

Daring You

Craving You

Playing You

Rockers to Lovers
Sing to Me

Strum Me

Sync with Me (Coming Soon)

Falling Paper Duet
Play the Man

Win the Game

Vows Duet
To Have and to Hold

From This Day Forward

Briarcliff Secret Society
Rival

Virtue (Coming November 12)

Fiend (Coming Soon)

ABOUT THE AUTHOR

Ketley Allison has always been a romantic at heart. That passion ignited when she realized she could put her dreams into words and her heart into characters. Ketley was born in Canada, moved to Australia, then to California, and finally to New York City to attend law school, but most of that time was spent in coffee shops thinking about her next book.

Her other passions include wine, coffee, Big Macs, her cat, and her husband, possibly in that order.

- facebook.com/ketleyallison
- instagram.com/ketleyallison
- bookbub.com/authors/ketleyallison
- amazon.com/author/ketleyallison
- goodreads.com/ketleyallison
- pinterest.com/ketleyallison

Made in the USA
Columbia, SC
20 January 2022